"Excellent. A wonderful book." —*The Rumpus*

"A propulsive literary thriller. Finn, who writes with a psychological acuity that rivals Patricia Highsmith's, switches between Europe and Africa in tense alternating chapters, rewarding close attention. The book is terrific... subtle and thrilling. Remarkably well-paced and well-written... Don't expect to be able to set this book down or forget its haunted characters." —*Kirkus Reviews*, starred review

"Finn's sure-footed prose, an intricate, clever plot, and the novel's powerful examination of cultural divides enrich this story, leading up to its shocking, brilliant conclusion as Pilgrim and the others search for salvation in an unforgiving land." —*Publishers Weekly*

"Intense, impressive... Told with force, and bracing directness... It's a book that smashes into you." —*The Guardian*

"A thought-provoking novel... deftly set in a world of mercenaries, philanthropists and witch doctors in polyester suits, the book asks how one atones for atrocity." —*Tatler*

"There's an eerie, existential quality about Melanie Finn's new novel... A paean to a magical continent of silent forests, slow, dark rivers, wild green mangroves; a world populated by child ghosts, haunted whites and AK-47-toting rebels. It is through this heart of darkness, a landscape rich in possibilities, that Pilgrim stumbles towards the light." —*New Zealand Herald*

"Full of empathy and intelligence... The ending is startlingly optimistic and very moving." —*Sydney Morning Herald*

"Compelling." —*The Australian*

"[*The Gloaming* is] intense, raw, a story less about moving on with ones' life than learning how to live aware of life's messy, connective tissues. And of course, it's a testament to the striking writing of its author, Melanie Finn." —*Weird Sister*

The Underneath

Melanie Finn

a novel

Two Dollar Radio
Books Too Loud To Ignore

Two Dollar Radio
Books too loud to Ignore

WHO WE ARE Two Dollar Radio is a family-run outfit dedicated to reaffirming the cultural and artistic spirit of the publishing industry. We aim to do this by presenting bold works of literary merit, each book, individually and collectively, providing a sonic progression that we believe to be too loud to ignore.

TWODOLLARRADIO.com	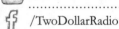 @TwoDollarRadio
Proudly based in **Columbus** **OHIO**	 @TwoDollarRadio
	/TwoDollarRadio

Love the PLANET? So do we.

Printed on Rolland Enviro, which contains 100% post-consumer fiber, is ECOLOGO, Processed Chlorine Free, Ancient Forest Friendly and FSC® certified and is manufactured using renewable biogas energy.

PERMANENT · 100% · BIO GAS ENERGY · PROCESSED CHLORINE FREE · Ancient Forest Friendly™

Printed in Canada

SOME RECOMMENDED LOCATIONS FOR READING *THE UNDERNEATH*: pretty much anywhere because books are portable and the perfect technology!

AUTHOR PHOTOGRAPH→ Libby March	ART→ *An Encyclopedia of Plants*, 1841	COVER IMAGES→ *Ladies' Home Journal*, 1889; *Atlas de poche des mammifères de France*, 1910

For Molly and Pearl
my bright star, my deep sea

The Underneath

Very quickly, the thick bush obscured the town, vanished it like a magic trick behind a curtain of green. Seldom is the disconnection so sudden. We were used to the slow fade: you can drive out of such African towns for several miles as bean plots and shabby huts fritter into wilderness. But fear kept Kitgum tightly contained, people cordoned inside the perimeter. They had abandoned their shambas *and their homes and their ancestral graves, and within one rainy season, Uganda's voracious herbage had taken repossession. It was very green and very quiet and you'd never guess how families had so recently toiled upon the land. There was no trace, not even a path.*

For 30 minutes, we just drove, hypnotized by the flat, straight road, the simmering green. The horizontal banality of the landscape became hypnotic, almost reassuring. It lulled us. And then: a government roadblock, so sudden, Marco slammed on the brakes. The soldiers demanded our passports, scrutinized Marco. In the photo he looked like Carlos the Jackal; you'd never want to let him into your country.

"This is you, Marco Morals."

I bit my lip to suppress an ill-timed snicker.

"Moral-es," Marco corrected.

A young soldier stepped in, examining the name for himself. "Why is the E not silent?"

"It's Spanish," Marco explained. "The '-es' in Spanish is pronounced. Frijol-es—beans. Not holes, *like English."*

The soldier nodded, "I see." Then flipped open my passport, "And you are Kay Norton."

I nodded.

"Kay is a name? I have never heard this name. It is a letter, yes? An initial? What is your real name?"

"Kay. That's it. K-A-Y."

"Perhaps your passport is false."

Marco brought forth a couple of packs of Rothmans to change the subject. "Would you lads like a smoke?" The soldiers began arguing about how to divvy up the smokes. So I handed them two six-packs of Coke. As there were five of them, an intense negotiation began. Was one Coke worth three cigarettes or two?

When you travel to such places, with such intentions as ours, you must be prepared. You will need not just water, food, insect repellent and extra fuel; but cigarettes, matches, sodas, snacks, money in small bills, phone vouchers. Mostly, you will need your wit. You will need to be funny and friendly because these boys in uniform teeter between boredom and fear, and they are heavily armed, and they want the comfort of your good humor.

At first, they refused to let us pass. They told us it was too dangerous, some other journalists had disappeared the week before. But we promised them more cigarettes on the way back, so they let us through. Marco's contact had told us to continue on to a village 15 miles past the roadblock, to wait there for an escort.

The village was, of course, ruined and deserted. All the metal roofing, furniture, and doors had been scavenged. I had

in mind the Beatrix Potter story, The Tale of Two Bad Mice.
*I imagined General Christmas's soldiers, like Tom Thumb
and Hunca Munca, carrying off the wooden benches from the
school and the plastic table cloths from the small café and
prying off the roof from the shacks. I had the impression of
mischief: children let loose to undo the adult world. Because
they were children, these merchants of horror, some as young
as nine. We journalists jokingly called them The Elves.*

*Marco and I wandered together as he took photographs.
I doubted he would ever use any of the images, but we were
fidgety, we had only our professional habits. It was hot, we
didn't know how long we'd be waiting for contact. An hour
passed. Marco finally stopped photographing and fiddled with
the settings on his Nikon. We sat in the shade of a charred
wall and sweated. Another hour, and another. The sun down-
shifted and time felt gappy—ill-fitting, itchy. I started not to
care anymore. What did we want with General Christmas
anyway? Whatever we printed simply fed his hunger for pub-
licity. He had no insight, he had no grand plan, no sense of
justice. He was just another asshole with a big gun.*

*I got up and walked off for a pee—not far, just the other
side of the wall, what must have been a pen for goats. The
fencing had been pilfered—probably for firewood, but the
holes for the posts remained. Sockets in the earth. The word*
socket *rolled around my head, one of those perfectly innocent
words. A hole once filled with something necessary. A dark
space, emptied out.*

*Beside one of the holes—the sockets—there was a pile of
rags in the dust. I splayed the rags open with my foot. It was
a woman's dress, ripped open from the neck down the back.
Possibly, she'd worn it over another dress or wrap, the way
very poor people layer clothes because they only have pieces*

and if they put the pieces together they can make something whole.

But, when I knelt down to examine the fabric, I could see the rusty patina, thick and dried and flaking. There was no other evidence of what had happened here: no smears of blood, no grooves of desperate fingernails in the dust. The crumbling walls were deaf to the screams or sobs of the woman who had died here, the sparrows had turned away and refused to witness. Why watch when you can't help, when you can't understand the human purpose of knives and guns, of inflicting pain just for the hell of it?

Deliberately, I put my hand on the fabric. I needed to be sure of its reality, the congregation of molecules. It was all that remained of a woman, maybe just a girl, who'd walked barefoot every day to collect water. Her bones, her body were buried or scattered, consecrated by jackals, hyenas and maggots and scarabs. Selfishly, I felt my own fear of obliteration. Like a climber losing a foothold, I felt the need to grab on, cling tight, but what to? The air, the dust, the still, indifferent afternoon.

General Christmas's contact never came, and as evening leaned in, Marco "Morals" and I drove back to Kitgum. We drank too much cheap Ugandan beer, we had obligatory sex in the bed that was too small, and when we were finished, he immediately fell asleep, and I could not stand the feel of his body, the smell of him, the shabby whiteness of his skin like the underbelly of a fish. But mostly, it was his gender. Somewhere inside his brain, I was sure, the place he dreamed or pocketed his masturbatory fantasies, lurked that enduring and atavistic hatred of women.

Ten years later Kay felt the weight of the hammer in her hand.

She imagined the heavy tow of gravity as she lifted it back and up, the beginning of the swing, then the arcing of her hand through the air. Up, up, above the back of his head. And she imagined the tipping point, where cause irrevocably becomes effect.

My husband, she thought. He's my husband.

Michael stepped forward, out of reach, and Kay dropped the hammer back down to her side. She was amazed to find how she'd committed to the swing, her hand all the way back and up, shoulder height.

She exhaled.

"Maybe this is where they hid the bodies," Michael joked. He was moving straight ahead of her, poking about in the dark with the flashlight. Something was banging in the far corner of the cellar. The wind started up last night and then this incessant, insistent *bang, bang-bang, bang, bang-bang.*

Waving the flashlight back and forth, Michael scanned for the light switch. There was one at the top of the stairs but when he'd flipped it, nothing had happened. At last, he saw the empty socket hanging from a naked wire.

"Jesus Christ," he mumbled, batting it out of the way. "The

wiring is from the '50s. I bet the whole house is like this. Behind the walls."

Wires tangled and twisted behind the walls, Kay imagined, the danger unseen. The wrong wires touch, the house burns down. Obviously, with such imminent danger, they should move out, right away; they should abandon their summer plans, run from this pretty white farmhouse, so lonely and serene and picturesque among the green hills.

But Michael kept going, and she followed. They were battle-hardened, after all.

The flashlight illuminated a neat and sparse sub terrain: white walls, a clean workbench, a stack of sturdy wooden cabinets and drawers labeled "Wrenches," "Screwdrivers," "Saws"; a tier of metal shelves stacked with two large grey plastic Walmart tubs, "Quilts" and "Union Bank 2009–2016." She noted that the floor, too, was white.

If we had a basement, Kay thought, it would contain heaps and piles, willy-nilly, what we don't really want anymore but can't quite throw away: Freya's baby clothes, Michael's early scripts, my journals, Tom's Thomas the Tank Engine collection. But we don't have a basement, no one does in London. We have a storage unit in Luton that we never visit.

Then she thought about the hammer. Already, she felt vaguely cartoonish—she hadn't meant it. But there was a residue on her tongue, a metallic taste.

"Look." Michael aimed the light into the darkness.

A doorway through the cement wall, utter blackness beyond and the distinct *bang*, *bang-bang*. There was a horror-movie feeling to this and Kay almost reached out to touch Michael and make a creepy noise. *Oooooo-oooooo.* Almost.

He was ahead of her, poking about with the flashlight. He was saying something something I-think-it's-alive something something but she was wondering: What if he'd turned and seen me wielding the hammer, and shouted, "Crazy bitch!" and caught my arm and held me at bay, his eyes on mine?

No one would believe him, not really. It would be a funny story he'd tell at parties, with other couples, oh, the time Kay got so mad she tried to hit me with a hammer, ha, ha, ha. But we'd know, Kay thought, Michael and I, we'd know—finally—where we stand. It would be a relief, such honesty.

He was saying: "I think there's something alive back in there."

In there, through the dark room, at the far end, a fluttering of feathery grey light. They entered the other room, this without a door, the door off its hinges, propped against the wall. Louder, the banging kept up. There was a smell, earthy, muddy, moldy— more mineral than vegetable, more vegetable than animal.

Michael tripped and dropped the flashlight. The narrow beam rolled across the floor. Kay retrieved it, she scoured the floor—there, the culprit: a loose brick. Michael gave it a peevish kick and it clinked against a stack of white paint cans.

"Can I have the flashlight back?" he said.

She handed him the hammer instead. He looked at it. He sighed. He sighed so much these days, his silent sighing, his loud sighing, his infinite patience, it meant so much to him to be patient with her.

The object ahead of them shifted back and forth in the beam of light. It was a cat, she could now see. Caught some-how. Caught in a trap. The trap had jammed against the window frame. And the banging was the animal's ceaseless attempt to escape through the window. The cat's front left leg was in the trap and the leg was already sheering off, exposed bone and flesh. In not too much time the cat would succeed in pulling its leg off. It hissed, a withered, whispered protest.

An hour later they were waiting in the vet's, the cat mewing and spitting and scratching but safe inside a Walmart tub. Kay had dumped out the quilts, using one of them—quite lovely, hand-made—to throw over the cat and wrangle it and the trap into the tub.

"The doctor is with another patient," the receptionist said, and Kay thought this quaint, a dog or cat as a patient. Did they wear little gowns that flapped open at the back; did they sit for chilly hours on a paper-covered table with year-old *People* magazines?

Loud droning from the lumber yard next door periodically piqued into a high squeal as the blade cut loose another log. Kay could see a light fog of sawdust, and how, if the window were opened, this would enter and lay like a fine dust on the surface of everything. Michael was on his iPhone, scrolling through his many important messages, so she picked up a loose copy of a newspaper, the local *Caledonian-Record*.

She always read the local papers, old habit. In Nairobi, she'd spent hours scanning the obituary pages, the faces of those "Promoted to Glory." The obituaries were in a kind of code: "sudden death" usually meant a car crash or violent mugging; in a young person, "long illness" meant AIDS. There were often multiple obituaries for the same day, which suggested a large accident, a bus or multiple collision.

The Caledonian-Record's pages were dominated by drugs, domestic violence, child abuse, ATV accidents, and minor fraud cases. There was a new drugs task force, a town clerk was facing charges of obstruction of justice for refusing to turn over property tax collection records, a local high school teacher had successfully scaled Mt. McKinley, "The biggest challenge of my life!"

On page two, above the police blotter:

Rescued Toddler Lived in Home with Moldy Food and Dog Feces
Mother Charged, Ordered To Clean Up Before Seeing Child

BY BRADY WILTON Staff Writer

SHEFFIELD—A toddler found wandering nearly naked on Potter Road Monday in freezing weather lived in filthy conditions, surrounded by dog feces, and had curdled milk to drink, Vermont Police say.

The boy, two and a half years old, was rescued by Sheffield Selectman Bill Morris and his wife and another passerby, Feller Morgan, and then police and the state stepped in to find the child's mother and take the child into state custody. The boy, dressed only in a dirty diaper, was found after 11 a.m. on Potter Road when the temperature on a state police cruiser was 26 degrees, Trooper Denise Polito said in her report. The boy was shivering and his lips were blue.

According to Polito, the child's mother, Michelle Whitehead, 23, of Sheffield, didn't know that her boy had gotten out of her trailer and walked away.

Whitehead told police she had just checked on the boy 15 minutes prior to when police knocked on her door in an attempt to identify the child. Trooper Polito said the boy had been gone from the trailer an hour and a half by the time they talked to the boy's mother.

Whitehead pleaded not guilty this week in Orleans Superior Court—Criminal Division to reckless endangerment and providing false information to police.

Whitehead told police she was taking prescription drugs, including a painkiller called hydrocodone, Lorazepam for anxiety and Cyclobenzaprine, which is a muscle relaxer. Syringes and a small amount of heroin were also discovered on the premises.

Judge Henry Van der Linde ordered Whitehead to clean up moldy and rotting food on the counters and scattered around the trailer and to clean up the dog feces in an indoor kennel where she was keeping a dog before being allowed to see her son in her home.

Why were they always smiling, Kay wondered, the children in abuse cases? No matter what was being done, what horror visited upon them day after day, these children still smiled for the camera. She looked closer at the boy. She could not detect fear. Perhaps compliance? *Smile for Mommy.*

Kay studied, then, the sullen face of Michelle Whitehead. In pleading "not guilty," what part of her child's suffering did she think wasn't her fault?

Michael suddenly spoke: "Ah, dammit."

Kay put down the paper.

"I've got to get back there."

She said nothing.

"Tim's come down with some kind of virus." Michael furrowed his brow. "They're airlifting him out."

Was this true? Because she suspected: you just want to get out of here. Away from me, from us. To be there. With her.

Now Michael reached out as if to touch her, to put his hand on her wrist. What would his touch feel like? Warm—sweaty in this summer heat? Damp and warm? Or oddly cool and dry, papery? Ghostly. But he retracted himself, his hand awkwardly hovering above hers.

At last, he lowered it to the armrest.

Sometimes, she could see the small of his back, his smooth shoulder. Just fragments, fluttering like prayer flags in her memory. I used to cast myself open for him, she thought. I ached for him. But now I cannot remember how I *felt*—the urge to rut and the rutting itself, against bathroom sinks, on beds, on floors, in hotel rooms. And love, hot, blind, fierce: wanting to be inside his skin. Back then—three, four years ago? Back then, we inhabited the same bodies as these that have not touched in a year. Not even a public gesture.

She studied the floor, white, clean linoleum, the faint scuffing of claw marks, some dog in a panic.

"When are you going?"

"This afternoon. A late flight out of Montreal."

Barbara will be there, Kay thought. Barb waiting for him in the Montreal Airport Embassy Suites in lingerie, a red peephole bra, just to make her ridiculous.

"And the children?"

Michael rubbed his face with his hands. "Sorry. I'm sorry, Kay."

"Sorry?" Kay began, because that was as far as she could get. She could feel the weight of the hammer in her hand again, the coolness of the cellar. She looked out from herself at the large woman with the little fluffy dog and the man with his ancient black lab that had a plastic cone around its head and a massive growth on its ass.

He was staring at his phone. He wasn't reading anything. He wasn't rifling through his messages. He was simply staring at the keypad. At last he said, "I know it was important for us."

Then the receptionist chirped in: "Mr. Ward, Mrs. Ward? Dr. Berry will see you now."

They'd never had a pet. In London it was too much hassle; in Nairobi, they'd been too busy. Freya had finally given up her campaigns for a bunny, a gerbil, a guinea pig, a kitten. On this, at least, Michael and Kay were in agreement.

Kay was surprised by how much the examination room looked like their pediatrician's—the table, the strong natural light, the expert in a white coat.

"Hi, I'm Dr. Berry." A small, neat, dark-haired man in glasses, he glanced at the thumping, hissing tub. "Cat caught in a trap, you said?"

Michael nodded, lifted the tub onto the examination table. "It's not ours. We found it in the basement. We're just renting for the summer."

Dr. Berry lifted the lid, pursed his lips. "That leg's going to have to come off. Feral, by the look of her." He put the lid back on. "Where you folks from?"

"London."

"But you're American?"

"We've been away a long time," Kay replied.

Dr. Berry glanced at her, very briefly. Then back at Michael, he spoke specifically to Michael. "You want to know the cost of the amputation versus the cost of euthanasia?"

"Sure. Yeah. That sounds reasonable."

"A grand for the amputation, 200 bucks for the other thing. What do you do in London?"

"Film."

"Movies? Famous people?"

"Documentaries."

Dr. Berry nodded, continued speaking only to Michael. "Thing is with the amputation, then you've got a three-legged wild cat that you're going to have to domesticate somehow because in the wild a three-legged cat will last about a day before some coyote scoffs it, and *poof*, there's your grand gone."

"Kill it," Kay said. Now Dr. Berry peered at her, almost startled that she had spoken.

"Yes," Michael nodded. "Best thing."

"What kind of documentaries? Anything I've seen?"

"Mainly Africa."

"Wildlife? My wife and I love Discovery."

"Political stuff," Michael said. "Wars. Corruption."

Dr. Berry's entire body swiveled toward Michael and away

from Kay, his hands braced against the examining table. He was deeply impressed. "Africa. Wow. That must get hairy."

"It can," Michael agreed and Kay just looked out the window at the lumber yard, the arboreal carnage, the severed trunks turned toward her, row upon row, stacked a dozen feet high, oozing with sap.

BEN SURVEYED HIS HOME, SUCH AS IT WAS, BET-
ter from the inside than the out, where the aluminum siding
was coming loose, a corner piece clacking in the faintest breeze.
From the outside, it was the kind of place that in a hurricane
broke open like an egg, a rotten, festering egg. Inside, however, it
might be cozy, when the heater was working, or it might be cool,
if all the windows opened and were not, instead, permanently
sealed with marine sealant. It might be homey with Jake's toys,
his clothes neatly piled on the chair. It might even be Shevaunne
who'd washed them and folded them, carefully paired the socks,
excised the stain from a cherry pie she might have made.

She stirred on the sofa like a creature in the mud, a mutant,
pink mud-puppy. Eyes still closed, she groped for her cigarettes.
"Get me a coffee, willya." He ignored her, started in on the
dishes that she might have done, in that alternative world, but
had not done in this actual one.

"Fuck you," she mumbled, coughed.

Whatever his intention, it had not been this.

Months ago, back in April, he had been coming out of the
Colonial Motel in Littleton. Things had gone well with Slim in
the over-heated motel room with its fecal-hued decor; they'd
shared a brief celebratory joint, the operation running very
smoothly, the tight teamwork, the logging truck up to Favreau's

in Quebec. Slim was pleased. He had given Ben an ounce of coke and Ben'd demurred; he hardly ever did the stuff. But Slim pressed the baggie into his hand, "C'mon, man, I don't have a box of chocolates."

He'd been coming out of the motel. Two women smiled at him, waved little waves, their impression of normal. We're just normal gals going to a normal motel room in the middle of a normal day. Their wrists were thin as twigs. Behind them, a tiny fellow scampered low like a fisher cat, pointy teeth, glinty-eyed.

The word was out, the junkie Twitter, Tweeker, Insta*gram*. And they had been shifting in and out of the motel parking lot, tramping, shuffling, scuttling up and down. They looked like junkies. If you wanted to cast a movie with 20 junkies, this is as far as you'd have to go. Even the recently washed ones looked unkempt, hunched over their empty stomachs, and something about their eyes, restless and hinky. They smelled like dandruff, and compost, as if their constipation, the shit impacted for weeks in their colons, was off-gassing.

Ben had been coming out into the grubby April daylight, stubborn cold from the White Mountains slapping him across the face. The snow curdled on the verges, drawing back from the debris it had hidden all winter: beer cans, dog crap, syringes. He'd been heading for his truck, stepping off the curb, when a Pajero pulled to a stop. Right there, right in front of him. Junkie car, he knew instantly. The expired registration, the missing muffler—errands the owners just never got around to because they were too busy stealing morphine patches from cancer patients or ripping off the farm stands along Route 2.

The woman, the man got out. They didn't have on coats. They were wearing sneakers. Her sweatpants were bright pink but dirty. Their faces were grey, like mushrooms in the cellar. Ben barely noticed them. Except he did. He gave the woman a second look.

Because she was looking at him, an energy passed between

them, some kind of human code—and he would remember this with absolute clarity, like a particular color, even though it was happening at a micro level, below sound and light and even thought, down in the earth of the mind. She was *telling* him something, willing him to look, look. Her eyes catching his, shifting away, then back, then away, ahead, into the building. She stumbled at the curb, muttered some obscenity, clearly it was the curb's fault.

He'd said to himself, *Please don't*— She and the man were behind him now, *Please don't*— He'd heard the motel's front door open. *Please don't*, he'd thought. *Please don't let there be a kid.* But of course there was a kid; the woman had been trying to tell him. With what was left of her smacked-out brain, with some remnant of her mother's love, she'd left him in the car, her child, her asset. She wasn't selling him. Yet. She wasn't that far down. Yet. The "yet" was out there, she could perhaps glimpse it in the distance like a dark tower, and therein the dark walls lay all the terrible things she was capable of.

She had dropped her gaze and walked past Ben. She had stumbled. She had cursed the curb. She and the man had gone into the motel to score. Ben glanced into the Pajero and saw the child. He was sitting in the middle of the back seat, no seatbelt, a hat and a jacket, filthy and too big. He was five, Ben reckoned, his eyes erased, gone like a war child, pin pricks.

Ben had been five miles along the I-93 when he'd realized he knew the woman. A long time ago. The foster home in Gilman, not a bad place. Shevaunne. Shevaunne, he'd never known her last name. Shevaunne had been her family's mattress until finally a teacher at school noticed the scab on her lip wasn't a cold sore but syphilis.

The boy, that boy. Ben felt himself gag. He could smell sour milk. Do not turn around. That boy, that child, broken doll.

The next exit was six miles ahead.

Do not turn around.

Do not turn around.

Do not fucking turn around do not open the door, the words all running together, overlapping, lapping, lapping so it was three or four voices all at once in his ears stereoscopic, do not do not open open the door the door do you hear me Benben you don't mind Momma partying do you, Benben.

He'd smelled the sour milk, the sourness of three days, the curds and the whey.

He knew the boy knew the smell as he knew hunger's metal coiling and he knew about the door you must never open, the turning around you must never do Benbenbenbenbenben.

He'd exhaled and inhaled, breath ragged as an asthmatic. He'd checked the mirrors, no cops. He'd swerved into the left lane, into a pull-out used by the plow trucks, and looped back toward Littleton.

I am turning around, he thought, I am turning the fuck around.

And it was just that, the car turning, going back the way he'd come, not the entire Universe upending, the planet tilting on a new axis. He was just one man, in a truck, turning around.

At the motel, he'd staked out the Pajero. After 30 minutes, Shevaunne—it was her, he was sure, even 20 years later, even with her brown teeth and ratty hair—and the man got back into the car; they were laughing, light of step having done a nip to take off the edge.

They'd stopped at McDonald's on the way, food for the boy, celebratory milkshakes for the grown-ups, onto the highway, exiting for Concord; then, from Route 2, a side road, a dark wood, the house within it moldering, stained, the dirty snow banked up against the windows where no sun came and no sun was wanted. There was a broken plastic climbing gym half-buried in the snow. It looked so like the house from Ben's own childhood, he was sure he could enter and turn left down a hallway, into the first bedroom and see his mattress on the floor with its Captain America sheets.

The junkies got out of the car. When the boy did not immediately comply, the man jerked open the door and yanked him out. The boy fell in the snow. The man shouted at him to get up. Ben waited for the kick—he was sure the kick would come. But Shevaunne stepped forward, took the boy's arm, and led him to the house. They went in, the door shut, the lights did not go on.

For a week, Ben watched the house. Shevaunne and the man were too preoccupied to notice him parked on the road. They came, they went, sometimes with the boy, sometimes they left him alone in the house for hours and hours, a day, two days. Once or twice the boy came outside and wandered around the yard. He found a stick and started hitting trees and then the stick broke and he went back inside. At last, the man left by himself. Ben followed him until he saw him turn onto the interstate. Then he doubled back to the house.

For a while—a dozen minutes?—he waited, considering the outcomes. Because the moment was upon him. The best thing was for him to drive away, forget it, he had his small life. But he got out of the truck. He walked up the cracked asphalt drive. He walked forward, not backward. He had momentum.

"Hello?" he called, knocking on the door.

The door was open.

"Hey, hello?"

He could hear the low murmur of the TV. His mother had loved, loved *Cops*. "Like home videos, eh, Benben," she'd say with a chuckle, tousling his hair. She'd watched the screen intently, imagining she might one day see someone she knew. From Ben's perspective, she'd known them all, every loser, meth-head, crack-head, smack-head, face down, perp-walker, always wearing flip-flops and cargo shorts, tatts and tank tops. They were the same; they were interchangeable. Paulie, Rickie, Dickie, Bill, Jed, *do not turn around do not turn around who do we have here?*

"Shevaunne?" Ben's voice intruded into the still house. No one moved much in here, the air stiff with the smell of microwave popcorn and unwashed hair and cheap coffee.

"Fuh? Wha?" He heard a garbled yelp from the back room.

"Shevaunne? I'm an old friend. Ben, Ben Comeau. I'm at the front door."

She ambled out. From a distance, in the poor light, she looked pretty, she looked young, but when she came closer he could see how her mascara and eye-liner were smeared, seeping into the cracks around her narrow eyes. Her hair was limp, greasy.

"Wha? Who the fuck'r you?"

"Ben Comeau. The home in Gilman? Mr. and Mrs. Bailey, you remember?"

She tilted her head, which put her off balance and she staggered. "Ben?"

By now the boy had slipped along the hallway and hovered behind her. He was small, feral, and gave the impression of being difficult to catch.

"You had zits." The memory focused her, an image she could grab on to. "They were seeping." Her eyes were so narrow, he couldn't see the color, he thought blue. "Whaddya wan, Ben?"

He glanced at the boy and she smiled a little smile as she reached out to touch her son, her hand on his head. "You a kiddie fiddler?"

A reasonable question—though, was she asking or offering? "No."

"Some church thing? You wanna pray or some shi?"

"I want you to come and live with me, you and the boy. I'll take care of you."

"I don think so." Her voice was lazy and slow. She was in the easy hammock of her high.

"There's a good school for him," Ben gestured to the boy. "He'll have regular food."

"Get the fuh out," she said.

But Ben would not. He had turned around. He was not all ruin. There was sunshine and fields of flowers. He had turned around, he had opened the door. This was why he had come. He knew she was watching him, trying to figure him out, if he was a freak or a weirdo and how much longer it might be until her boyfriend got back. He looked directly back at her, "And I have a steady supply for you, Shevaunne."

She had shrugged her junkie shoulders. She had all the loyalty of a plastic bag on a windy day.

The house emerged through the fringing green of sheltering maples. It was calendar pretty, with its high, peaked roof, dormers, and white clapboard siding. Already, Kay referred to it as *home*—she and Michael were coming *home* from the vet's—though they'd only been here two weeks. What might it be like to live here, to possess this summer beauty? The views tilted south across rough fields and dense green woods, not another house for miles. Dawns unfolded in silence broken only by birdsong; so quiet she could hear the *snap-snap* of chickadees' wings as they flew to the bird-feeder. It was the opposite of London with its hard angles, its miserly slabs of light.

The monthly rent was cheap, and Kay had wondered why the house hadn't already been taken. According to an email from Alice, the caretaker, it had no internet and extremely poor cell phone coverage, and "people want that nowadays." This lack of communication had, ironically, proved the main attraction to Michael. They would play cards as a family in the evening, they would take walks and read books. With the children at day camp, Michael would have time to work on his latest proposal and Kay to write whatever it was she was writing. They wouldn't be distracted by the siren song of internet news and Netflix.

That had been the idea, the promise.

But here was Michael, sitting beside her, catching the very last bar of reception on approach. He always wanted her to drive so he could tap-tap-tap his phone. The past few nights, she'd heard him talking in the bathroom, murmur murmur. He had to stand on the toilet, twisting his whole body at an odd angle to get even one bar. How did he contort himself like this for so long? She couldn't make out the words or even his tone, and she couldn't creep up on him as the floor boards were too creaky. He would mumble on and on, whomever he was talking to—Barbara?—never seemed to reply.

A few feet ahead of the car, yellow butterflies clustered on a puddle in the middle of the drive. Kay slowed, and when the butterflies did not fly off, she braked.

"Stop," she said.

She turned off the engine. Michael didn't hear her or wasn't listening. He kept tapping. She slammed her hand on the dashboard. "Stop tapping!"

His finger poised mid-air, he sighed.

"What are we going to do, Michael?" *Michael.* His name was hard on her tongue. It was what she called him now, not Babe or Love. They'd gone full circle back to the formality of Christian names. Only it meant something entirely different now.

He looked ahead, a long moment, then down at his phone. Kay could see his finger twitching; he was in the middle of a text. "I'm arranging a cab," he said, and with two more taps, pressed send.

They sat. Kay did not start the car. She watched the light sifting through the maples, the yellow drifting butterflies. She and Michael hadn't come here to save their marriage, they'd come to end it.

The taxi driver was a grizzled man who smelled of cigarettes and wheezed as he tried to lift Michael's heavy black Peli case. Michael took it from him, easily swung it into the trunk. He was physically strong. He used to lift Kay like that and toss her on the bed and fuck her.

"Daddy!" Tom lurched forward again, wrapping himself around Michael's leg. Kay glanced at Freya, her dark and judgemental eyes, and felt relief that it was Michael letting her down. Freya, who stored the wrongs done to her like candy during Lent; she'd binge on it one day, all that injustice, all that blame.

Afternoon was tilting into evening, a powdery apricot sunset. The looming maples slowly lost their dimension, turned inky and solid against the darkening sky. There was no wind, and far, far off, the sound of the interstate, a murmur upon the air that you had to listen for. Kay pried Tom away from Michael, lifted him into her arms because she still could. "We'll Skype as soon as we can."

Michael got in the taxi, he waved, blew kisses to his children. For the briefest moment, he looked at Kay, and Kay had no idea what she saw in his eyes or what he intended her to see. The taxi moved off, down the drive, and Kay could discern Michael's head, already bent and intent on his phone.

BEN TOOK JAKE TO THE LAKE.

"I'm taking Jake to the lake," he sang, his hands on the wheel, the boy beside him, now early July and three months of good food and clean clothes and a Big Wheel.

But still Jake did not speak. He had no voice. For so long no one had listened.

Ben took his hand, enfolded it like a small, soft mouse. They walked toward the water. It was a perfect afternoon. The hills curled around the lake, a green embrace. The water held the sky, as if a piece had fallen. Sky was somehow liquid, the elements all merging into one—air, water, light—even the trees seemed aqueous in the heat. Only the earth beneath their bare feet remained solid, dark, what held them to this place and time.

They reached the water. Jake hesitated. He stuck out a white toe, not quite touching the water, so it seemed accusatory, like a pointed finger. Ben stepped forward, the water up to his shins, smiled, "Feels good." Jake followed; ankle deep, his grip tightened. They eased out a few more feet, and he stopped.

Ben bent down and picked him up. "I'll hold you. I won't let you go."

They waded out, the boy clinging to his hip. "It's not so deep. You can still stand here. You want me to put you down?"

A shake of the head. So Ben held on, squatting down in the

water, submerging the both of them to their chests. Jake gasped at the cold, squeezing Ben's shoulder, both panic and delight. In the water, he became weightless, he might float away, so Ben held him tighter. He could smell the boy's skin, his dark hair. He felt an odd punching in his chest, almost like lust, and he wondered if this was what pedophiles felt, the beauty of the child, the ease of destruction—a kind of terror at one's own power. *What have I done*, he thought, *this is what I have done*, and he was clear again, as the boy began to smile, to laugh, a foreign sound, like a migrant bird blown off course.

How quiet the night. Tom and Freya had spooled in all sound, they sucked it up, hoarding it in their cells. Sound slept with them now, needing its rest, so that in the morning, it might again reverberate with force: singing, arguing, things dropping, breaking, feet always running, questions firing, *Mum, Mum, Mummy*. Kay could almost feel the pressure of silence upon her ears, like a plane descending. She had her own silence now; she was not pleading or nagging, admonishing. She did not hear her own voice rise with the words, *Where are your shoes hurry up we're late pick up your towel*. She did not have to find the way to say *Michael* that did not accuse or accost or echo.

She tidied away the last of the dishes, wiped down the sink. Two small lights winked in the valley below. The darkness made distance immeasurable, irrelevant. There became here, hills and stars in atomic continuity with the lawn just beyond the window. A plane's lights blinked overhead, and she imagined Michael, 30,000 feet above the Atlantic. He would have had his meal. He would be working on his laptop in the halo of his overhead light. Barbara was beside him, her arm touching his, the unfussy touch of their intimacy. Or she was waiting for him in Amsterdam or Dublin, wherever his flight hubbed through. She was issuing a flurry of ardent texts. She was shaving her legs.

And Michael was moving away, away. Kay had a strong

impression of this separation, of the white house around her and the steel plane around Michael, the movement of the plane, the counter movement of the earth and the house upon it, so that she, too, was moving away from him.

She stood still, observing the kitchen around her, the true house barely visible beneath the chaotic, sticky overlay of her family. The people who lived here lived here impeccably. If things were noise, then they lived silently. In Michael's absence, she began to notice; for it was as if their marital arguments, both spoken and furiously internalized, had created a white noise, filling the space.

Now she saw the bookless, dustless shelves. The effort to empty the rooms, not just of things but of *their selves* seemed more than was necessary for a summer rental—though Alice had assured her that the owners lived here year 'round. But how they lived: traceless, immaculate, mute, tidy as white mice, ceaselessly washing their neat pink paws.

For instance, there was no crap drawer of mystery keys, desiccated rubber bands, scratched sunglasses, an odd sock, batteries of indeterminate charge. Nor was there a closet piled with hurriedly folded bedding, nor bags of clothes long intended for Goodwill. The cutlery was arranged, the plates stacked, the towels arrayed. The flashlight had its hook by the door. The aesthetic was of rigid order.

The walls were bare but for a fading photograph thumbtacked above the sink: a cabin by a blue lake in a bowl of green hills; a perfect summer day. And in the back of the hall closet, Kay had found an old phone, dusty as a relic. There was a jack in the wall, but no connection.

She switched off the downstairs light and turned for the stairs. When Michael was here, she'd been the last one up, and she had done this—the turning off of the light. Now she hesitated, considering the lock of the door. She had never locked it. She had liked the feeling of not locking it. They were living where they did not need a lock. They were safe. Safe as houses, safe as unlocked houses. Wasn't that what country people smugly asserted: we don't need to lock our doors.

For who would come this way, so far out, along the pitch-dark dirt road to a house with nothing in it. Nothing but warm blood, she thought—she thought as a little joke, like watching *Jaws* before swimming in the sea, and so she did not lock the door.

"I want to strangle you and hang you off the balcony." Marco's idea of sweet nothings. He's behind me, in me, twisting my shirt around my throat. I lean forward to do another line and he grabs my hips and thrusts hard. The feeling of him deep and the hit of damn good coke are like I've imagined God: an absolute and precise sensation of being alive.

And we are alive, handsome Marco Morales and I, we are most definitely alive.

Three hours before, we were dead, face down in the earth with guns to the back of our skulls and the smell of fear and everything extraneous ceased. It was like being in a tunnel, the most focused I've ever been. Three hours before, we'd been in the heart of the North Pole. General Christmas was certainly good for jokes. He kept us laughing, oh ho ho ho. The Nightmare Before Christmas; *here comes Santa Claus, here comes Santa Claus, right down Santa Claus Lane; he sees you when you're sleeping, he knows when you're awake; etc, etc. Marco and I, nosey, nosey journalists, were chasing a story about how the Museveni government was supplying his archenemy with arms to perpetuate the war. As long as General Christmas was a threat—stealing children, hacking off their limbs if they were naughty—the US government would continue to supply Museveni with money and weapons to fight him. My sources had told me that the Christmas elves were armed with new American AK-47s. They could only have gotten them from the Museveni government.*

And, indeed, they were armed with AK-47s. These AK-47s were pointing at us, as we sprawled on the ground.

Fear is many different sensations. It is being in an elevator that suddenly drops a few feet; it is your jeans getting tighter around your thighs as the muscles swell with the adrenaline you might need to run away; it is absolute clarity and complete occluding panic. You are certain you will survive; you hope their knives are sharp. You are afraid and incredibly brave; you are accepting of death; you will do anything to stay alive.

As I lay there, my sound and vision narrowed in. The excited voices of the Christmas elves muted and I heard the faintest stamping, little marching. It was a trail of ants, moving to the left of me, between Marco and me. He was watching them, too, marching through the dry, red earth.

Suddenly he made a coughing noise. I realized they'd kicked him or hit him, and they were still doing so. I watched the ants and considered the millions of years that had gone into their design, the trick of evolution to produce something so deceptively simple as the ant. A leopard or dolphin you could see the effort. But an ant was a child's drawing, three little dots and six little legs.

Someone started tugging at my jeans, trying to pull them down over my hips. I had never been raped and I wondered now how you died from rape, as women do. If ten men fucked me one after the other, how was that different from ten lovers in ten weeks, men whose names I couldn't remember and maybe had never known. How can ten penises kill you?

Some of the ants were carrying bits of litter. Ants clean up, they keep the planet clean. Ants will be part of my cleaning, when my body is done. The ants and the flies and the scarabs. I felt my body, then, like a cloak, my flesh upon my bones, my skin firmly encasing my flesh. Mine, I thought, all that I ever owned.

My jeans were down by my ankles now, exposing my bottom, just this part of me, reducing me to this. But also the men reducing themselves. All we are is machines fucking each other to reproduce. They were scared, too, these boys, these boy-men of General Christmas—these Christmas elves could die any day and they probably would. They were like salmon who ejaculate upon dying.

The first one clambered on me, putting his knees between my legs and spreading them. What if I lived? What if I had his child? My stomach contracted hard, as if I'd been punched, and my legs tried to draw back together, my vaginal muscles clenched. It was all instinct. I breathed out, I breathed in. Did the second one care that he was putting his dick in another man's cum? And the third and the forth, weren't they disgusted by all the fluid?

But the improbable happened: they ran away. They just left us, Marco and I, and when we looked up they had vanished back into the bush. They'd taken our bags and our shoes and our sunglasses. There was a little trail of peanuts and raisins. The stash of GORP I kept in my bag must have burst open.

Marco and I sat up. I pulled up my underwear, my jeans. They were immediately itchy, as bits of dust and dried grass had become embedded in the fabric. We avoided eye contact but I could see out of my peripheral vision that Marco had blood on his face. For a few moments—minutes? seconds?— we just listened to the sound of the bush, the cicadas, weaver birds twittering inanely. Then, the sound of a vehicle, coming fast. We stood. Should we run and hide? The old axiom—the enemy of my enemy is my friend, is complete bullshit. The enemy of my enemy is simply the more ruthless motherfucker.

But we didn't move; a mutual, unspoken decision. Hiding seemed futile and would put us in a vulnerable position. No one wants to be found cowering in the bushes—you can't help but look furtive, suspicious.

Three military Land Rovers pulled to a stop. Twenty Ugandan government soldiers unpacked themselves and surrounded us. The commander, thin and tall with scholarly wire-rimmed glasses, appraised us, asked a few brief questions. We didn't mention the attempted rape, we simply said we were journalists. He ordered his men into the bush, leaving four to guard us or protect us—we couldn't know. Within minutes, there was shouting and shooting. The government soldiers ushered us to cover behind the Land Rovers.

I longed for a cigarette. Not a mere craving, but bone-squeezing need, almost like that moment before orgasm when you think it won't happen, the sensation begins to recede, and you feel a great angry need for it. Marco was uneasy, too. I saw him dabbing compulsively at the gash on his head. Without his camera, he had no way to interface with the situation.

After ten minutes or so the shooting stopped. There were shouted commands, scuffling, grunts of pain. The commander and his soldiers ushered six of General Christmas's men—boys—into the clearing. One was clutching his stomach where blood bloomed like tie-dye over his yellow t-shirt. Obediently, they knelt down. Very quickly, very professionally, the commander unholstered his side-arm and executed them. The last—a teenager, maybe 16 or 17?—looked at me in confusion, as if he did not understand what dream he was in and how he might get out.

"Mama," he said—not imploring me, as a generic mama, but the word drawn out, softly, as a child addresses his mother: *"Mama."* PAP! *He fell face first into dust.*

THE MOOSE HAD BEEN THERE FOR THREE days, ghosting among the birches. Ben watched her through the kitchen window. Her great head hung down as if weighted; from time to time she gave it a slow shake. When she'd first appeared, she'd walked in circles, stumbling, falling to her knees then hefting herself back up. She had stopped moving now, her legs braced out, like those of a saw-horse, stacked ergonomically on her bones. The coyotes knew she was here. Ben had seen them slinking across Ed's fields, yellow-eyed and sly; he'd heard them calling out to each other in the evening. She was waiting for them. They'd tear the velvet of her muzzle. They'd eviscerate her, coil by coil.

Ben grabbed his .30-06 from the top shelf of his closet. He walked past Shevaunne asleep on the sofa, the TV mumbling *and our next contestant*, her mouth open with little snores coming out. Even the hot noon light blasting through the bay window and heating the interior of the mobile home like a convection oven didn't wake her, merely raised a sheen of perspiration on her forehead. Shevaunne slept like a cat, an opportunist, at all hours and on numerous surfaces, sometimes even the floor, and she woke up with the imprint of the bath mat on her cheek. He stepped over an empty 16oz Dunkin' Donuts pumpkin spice latte and out the back door.

The moose acknowledged Ben but did not move away or flinch, and he could have gone right up to her, put the rifle right up against her skull. But she was a wild thing dying a wild death, he did not want to belittle her. He shot her from 50 yards, a clean shot through the heart, and she went down on her knees with a kind of relief. She was dead by the time he got to her.

It took several hours to butcher her, there was so much meat. When he cut off her head and sawed open her skull, he knew what he would find: the smooth brain sprouting clusters of worms, like a potato left in the bottom of the box too long. The worms had laid their eggs in deer excrement and the moose grazed on the grass nourished by the deer scat; the worms traveled from the stomach to the tender, soft brain, and, relentless, voracious, they ate it. Nature was not benign.

The meat of the moose, however, remained untouched, and she was a gift to Ben: a winter's supply of free protein. He'd teach Jake to enjoy even the liver cooked with onions, the heart and kidneys in a stew. Some nights he'd go over to Ed's, beers and a couple of flank steaks for the barbecue; there wouldn't be much to say, the honey-combed conversation of men: trucks, huntin', the cocksuckers in Montpelier who made up new regulations for dairy farmers.

When at last the moose was fully stripped, when she was the essential arc of her ribs, when she was joints and hooves and pelvis and the flies were a veil around him, Ben felt the weight of himself, his lumbering, earth-rooted body. He envied the animal's transcendence.

He walked back into the house. Now—again—he saw the Dunkin' Donuts cup. He picked it up, considered it carefully. There was no point in asking Shevaunne. She would lie. She lied without even knowing she was lying. She lied when there was no point—what she'd had for lunch or if the sky was blue, lying not merely from habit but as the state of her being. She was a sack of lies, bloated with lies, even her snores were lies.

He put the cup on the counter where she would see it, and she would know that he'd also seen it, his bloody handprint upon it.

She opened her eyes and screamed.

She continued to scream, hyperventilating, scrambling up the back of the sofa, a panicked animal, her eyes on him and full of horror, and, at first, he did not know why. He imagined she could no longer tell the difference between sleep and dream; the lying had so infused her that a door was not a door and a nightmare was real.

Then he realized he was covered in blood. "It's from the moose."

Did she think he'd killed someone? But she would not listen. She kept screaming, so he stood immobile, his hands raised and open-palmed in surrender.

Her own hands covered her face, and she gulped air. "Jesus fuckin' Christ, Ben. Mother of fuckin' God, Ben."

"The moose. I shot her and butchered her."

Shevaunne's scream segued into a coughing spasm, the wheezing protest of her tar-lined lungs. "I need a cigarette, man, I need a ciggie," and she searched frantically on the sofa, among her nest of covers, for her pack of Marlboro Reds, her green lighter. Her hands were trembling, and he was amazed at her fear, it was the only emotion un-dimmed by heroin, her fear was pure and uncut as truth.

He left her still searching and jibbering. He ran the shower and watched the water spiral shades of pink and crimson down the plug hole, and he thought about the pumpkin latte and how it came to be inside his home.

A mile past the town hall, they passed a weathered house with a shed tacked on the side. Freya sung out, "Sad bunnies!" And there they were, rows of cages, stacked one atop the other, little white rabbits, white as Easter bunnies, with pink ears and soft, virginal fur.

The first morning they had passed this way, Freya had said, "Bunnies! Oh, look, bunnies!"

And Tom had wanted to know if they could get one.

"We can't take it back to England, love."

"No pets! That's the rule," added Freya.

But Tom implored, Tom still believed if he asked for something over and over again he would get it. "Just for the summer, then. We could give it back. Oh, please, Mum."

Freya frowned, "They shouldn't put them in such small cages."

And Tom: "Just for the summer! Please, please! I'll take care of it, I promise."

"I'm going to sneak out at night," Freya had stage-whispered, "And let them out."

Sad bunnies.

Today, Tom asked: "What are all the bunnies for, Mum?"

"They're for eating," Freya declared. Kay shot her a look in the rear-view mirror.

Tom's eyes flew open. "People eat bunnies?"

"Yes," Kay confirmed and braced herself. The next ten minutes would be questions.

"Mum?"

"Yes."

"Have you eaten bunny?"

"Yes."

"What does it taste like?"

"Chicken."

"How do they cook it?"

"Like chicken. It's just meat."

What do you do with the fur, do you eat the ears, do you eat the bunnies with vegetables, roasted or what, are the bunnies afraid, why not just eat chicken, does it hurt the bunnies to die?

Sometimes there were lots of bunnies. Then, a day later, only a few. The shed had a door, and the door was open, a white extension cord leading inside.

Today there were many bunnies. Tom strained against his seatbelt, trying to see.

"How do they kill the bunnies, Mum?"

"They smash their heads," Freya offered up. "On the edge of a table."

"Freya!"

"It's true."

"How do you know?"

"Okay. Wow, you're right, Mum. They cuddle them to death."

Kay finally caught her daughter's eye in the rear-view mirror, a gaze too certain for an eight-year-old. "Your brother's only five, Freya. Maybe we can just not talk about certain things in such a graphic way."

"But I want to know." Tom leaned forward. "How do they kill the bunnies?"

"They probably do bash them on the head. It's very quick."

Freya made choking noises and Tom lashed out at her. "*Kakakakaaaakka*," Freya continued.

"Freya! For God's sake!"

"Sorry!"

Tom was mournful. "Sad bunnies."

"I wonder when Dad will be back."

Kay turned up the radio, the station Freya liked, just to make her quiet.

Kamp Wahoo was one exit down the interstate, on the outskirts of the small town of East Montrose. There was no West Montrose, no south or north or even Montrose. Perhaps there once had been, when the area was prosperous from wool. East Montrose had four churches along a half-mile strip—the old wealth shown in their brickwork, the height of their steeples. Now, all but the Congregational was shuttered.

A dozen fine, old homes introduced the town on either end; a few were even now in good repair. Layered back from the main road—the congregants who knew their place—were smaller homes, quaint at first glance, but Kay began to see the shabbiness each time she passed: the peeling paint, the missing roof shingles. This wasn't disrepute, merely an indication that most people here didn't have 20 grand to repaint their houses. They were working the low-paying jobs of a rural economy. A few cars were offered for sale in front yards; their wheels had already been traded for something more necessary.

Railroad tracks hemmed the town on one side; freight trains shuttling up and down the eastern seaboard to Canada only 50 miles north. The Connecticut River bordered the other side, and was famed to Freya and Tom for its ice cream stand, Foxy's.

Many of the old brick buildings that comprised the center of town appeared empty, the store fronts blank-faced or FOR LEASE. Aside from two fabric shops selling quilting and knitting supplies, there was a drug store, White's Supermarket, the Gas n' Go, and a bar, the Dirty Ditty. Side roads Kay had yet to explore suggested other options, though not many: a thrift store, childcare, various social services, fire and police, perhaps a dentist.

Past the park, at the other end of town, Kay joined a line of cars funneling down an avenue of cedars. In its term-time incarnation, Kamp Wahoo was a small private school, an old farm house and barn converted into classrooms and a gym. From June through August it was the domain of Phoebe Figgs, an energetic, loud woman who understood the symbiosis of order and chaos. Certain kids wanted to sit and draw pictures all day or make necklaces from only pink beads; Mrs. Figgs never interfered. But she also organized water balloon fights, and then let them play out with borderline *Lord of the Flies* intensity.

Freya and Tom, used to the constraints of London, of uniforms and private school, adored her. Every day they ran from the car, forgetting Kay in an instant, hurling themselves at Mrs. Figgs, who expertly rebounded them toward the warm Pop-Tarts and chocolate milk that counted as the inclusive camp breakfast.

Kay drove home the long way, by Claremont Hill, a narrow, winding road, past fields and dairy farms, where the hills layered into the horizon with perfectly diminishing clarity until they seemed to dissolve, the pixels fragmenting into sky.

Turning into the driveway, she noted a pick-up parked several hundred yards inside the gate. She slowed down, stopped even with the truck, old and battered, rust like cancer from bumper to bumper. "Hello?"

No one answered.

She got out of her car.

In the truck bed were chains and traps. She glanced through the cab window at beer cans and fast-food containers. There was a gun rack with no gun.

"Hello? Hello?" She banged her fist on the side of the truck. "This is private property."

Kay turned and he was right there, a foot behind her, silent as a fairy-tale troll in a filthy ball cap. She could smell him: old sweat, slept-in sweat. He pushed past her, ran his skinny hand over the side of his truck where she'd thumped it.

"Who are you?" she challenged. "What are you doing here?"

His age was difficult to determine, given the unkempt beard, the appalling teeth. He could be 50 or 70.

Seeming to ignore her, he walked back into the thick bramble. There he collected his bounty, hefting them onto his shoulder: two dead coyotes. Their grey bodies hung limp, crude, bloody gashes across their forepaws where they'd been caught. He'd shot them at close range, a careful bullet through the eye to avoid damaging the fur.

"What are you doing here?" she repeated.

He passed her, answering her stupid question by swinging the dead animals into her face, so close that she could see the texture of the fur, matted with burdock, but also flecked in a tweedy multitude of greys. Deeper in, the root fur: a golden hue.

"I've children," she protested. "I don't want guns and traps."

He still did not reply, tossed the coyotes in the truck.

"Do the owners know you're here?"

Now he laughed, bearing his speckled gums. "The owners," he snickered. "The owners." Then, as he opened the driver's door, he assessed Kay—a long, slow slide of his eyes that had nothing to do with sex.

When he'd reached his conclusion, he slammed his door, gunned the engine, the truck jumped forward. Given the narrowness of the track, he nearly side-swiped Kay's rental car; but he kept one set of wheels high on the verge, mowing down the brambles, and bounced off toward the main road.

"Hello? Alice?"

"Yes?"

"Alice, it's Kay Ward." Kay stood on the toilet, angling her head against the window to keep reception. Her hands were shaking; she was angry.

"Oh, yes, hi."

"I'm trying to get in touch with the owners of the house."

"Is it the kitchen tap? I'm so sorry, Al's been meaning to get up there, but his arthritis—"

"No. It's not the tap. Someone's trapping coyotes up here."

"Coyotes?"

"Yes, coyotes."

"That'll be Ammon."

"I'd like Ammon to stop."

"Well, coyote season is year 'round."

"Then perhaps he could trap when we're not here? Next month?"

"The coyotes do a lot of damage to the deer population if you let their numbers get out of control."

"Do they? The thing is, we already had to put down a cat that was stuck in the house with a trap."

"Oh, dear."

"So it'd be great if I could talk to the owners, and they could ask Ammon, you know, to take a break while we're here."

"Just a moment, please."

Kay could hear Alice cupping her hand over the phone, a muffled exchange, a long silence. Then Alice's voice, soft and hesitant: "I don't know where they are right now."

Kay shifted her weight on the toilet seat, careful to keep reception. "Do you know who might know?"

"They keep themselves to themselves."

"But surely someone—"

"No, no one."

"No one?"

"Like I said."

"Do you know Ammon?"

"He won't be no help."

"Maybe I could talk to him."

But Alice had hung up.

In the hall, Kay stood on a chair and unscrewed a light bulb. She grabbed the flashlight from its designated hook and stepped down into the basement. The flashlight in her mouth, she screwed this bulb into the empty socket, jogged back to the top of the stairs and flipped the switch. The basement blasted with light, almost blinding in its whiteness. Now she could see the workbench with scrupulously labeled and ordered drawers. The metal shelving holding only the two Walmart tubs. The floor, the walls, all glossy white, gleaming, clean. The word *surgical* came to mind.

Kay ran her hand over the workbench—not a trace of dust— and pulled open the "Screwdriver" drawer to reveal screwdrivers ordered by size, aligned. Another drawer held chisels and files, the same perfection of order for six further drawers.

There's something special about tools, she thought. Duct tape, zip ties, chisels; they have their secret menace.

She shifted her focus to the two plastic tubs: the quilts and "Union Bank 2009–2016." This was surprisingly heavy—heavier than one would think for five years of bank statements.

Embracing the tub, she leveraged it to the floor. For a fraction of a second she checked herself. Michael had once said she was the type of person who saw a black garbage bag on the side of the highway and wanted to know what was inside. And at any rate, it wasn't the financial information she wanted, but names. She opened the tub.

Inside were recipe books.

Heavily used, the pages were warped by egg or sauce or flour. Additional recipes from magazines or on notecards were stuffed inside so that the bindings bulged. She began to sort through them; the worn books were oddly comforting, with their patient, objective prescriptions, their luscious photographs.

Was it the wife who liked to cook? Cakes, cookies, pastries, pies, barbecue; most especially, she loved to cook Mexican, four books, two in Spanish, two in English: *La Comida Yucateco*, *The Best of Tex-Mex*, *Comidas Nutriciales para La Familia*, *Beyond Enchiladas*.

Just as Kay was about to put the cookbooks away, *The Joy of Cooking* burst its seams, disgorging dozens of clippings of recipes. As she stuffed them back into the book, one in particular caught her eye—it was handwritten:

Hello Maria! You said how much Frank and the boys loved the fudge. This recipe is super easy, just make sure you store it in the fridge. Hope to see you soon! Candice.

Maria, Frank, the boys.

The names immediately yielded faces to Kay, as if she'd found photographs. Maria was dark-haired, Frank and the boys blond, sandy complexioned. The boys had freckles, they were lean from running around outdoors. Like Frank. Frank worked in the woods, on the land, he cut the firewood. He was a useful man. Handy. He made things with his tools. Maria was softer-edged, a woman with a name ending in a vowel, whisking eggs in a bowl. Up here on this hill, where they kept themselves to themselves.

Kay put the note back. She drew a breath. There were pivots, she knew. You didn't suddenly find yourself in a war zone or a marriage or a basement ransacking someone's stuff and wonder *How did I get here?* You got there in increments, decision by conscientious decision, turning left or turning right. You couldn't be sure where you were going, only that you were going, you were choosing to go. Methodically, then, she searched the house.

But the closets and the drawers remained empty or ordered, the shelves still had no books, the walls were still bare. She was reminded of the house in Nairobi when she and Michael had left it, emptied, abandoned, just a structure—wood, plaster, glass.

Looking around her now, Kay wondered if Frank and Maria had moved out and Alice simply didn't know or was being discreet. Perhaps divorce, those long winters, cloistered in by the snow. Perhaps financial hardship.

But: why leave the tools? The handmade quilts, the cookbooks? The photograph above the sink? Because these things mattered most? Or because they mattered not at all?

She thought of the empty villages of northern Uganda, the abandoned towns of her previous life: the extraordinary stillness of the air because the dust, unstirred by humans, had settled so completely. You could tell how much time people had had to flee, days or minutes, by what they'd left.

At last Kay came to the hall closet. She reached in and took out the phone. It was decades old, the kind with the curly cord attaching the handset to the base. The base contained a voicemail mechanism. Kay plugged it into the electricity. The phone's memory-stored menu popped up on the handset: *play message, answering system, directory, call log, ringers, settings.* There was no recorded message, and the directory was empty.

Again, she considered the strangeness of absence, it was systematic, like a crime scene wiped clean of every single fingerprint. Except: the call log yielded two numbers.

She found a pen, scrawled the numbers on the back of her hand. Upstairs, on the toilet, took out her own phone, dialed the first. A woman with an accent—probably Latino—answered, "Guadalajara Grill, how may I help jew?"

Kay hung up. A Mexican restaurant. She thought about the cookbooks, the plethora of Mexican food, the name—Maria.

She dialed the second number.

A man, this time: "Comeau Logging."

"Sorry, wrong number," she mumbled, even as she Googled the name. The Northeast Kingdom Chamber of Commerce listed the address: 5899 Jones Farm Road, Lost Nation; the proprietor, Benjamin L. Comeau.

Suddenly, the phone rang in her hand. This startled her, not just in the present silence, but as a sound she hadn't heard in the weeks since she'd left London. No one had rung her. Summer had flung the few people who might have phoned her to other corners, Ibiza, Provence, Cornwall. She stared at the phone for a moment. Michael. Michael. Michael. The ringing stopped. He didn't leave a voicemail.

There was a better part of her that wanted to phone him back. His voice might reassure her: *I haven't left, I've only gone away, we'll work this out.* And she might extend to him, *I'm sorry, I'll try harder, come back, I'm here.*

But there was a thick membrane around that other Kay; she was a shiny doll in a package. Her imaginary presence was a rebuke to the Kay who squatted on a toilet like a gargoyle, her hair tangled in a messy bun, lacking the courage to answer a phone call from her husband.

Jones Farm Road was not on the way to Kamp Wahoo. Kay could not pretend to be taking the scenic route to collect them. She was deliberately driving in the opposite direction into this high, open landscape. Pastures tumbled into woods, rolled up against corn fields, a crazy quilt loosely stitched with old cedar fencing.

As she drove on, the theme of the landscape seemed to change; or maybe she was paying attention. Here, she now saw, was poverty, not just hard times. Old farms struggled against the elements. A huge red cow barn sagged and slouched amid a debris of farm equipment and muddy cows. Fence posts tilted like drunks and plastic covered the windows.

Further on a scatter of mobile homes, trailers, and dilapidated houses. Dogs on chains, piles of junk, old cars, tires, plastic toys. Kay was used to African poverty, refugee camps and shanty towns; she'd almost forgotten people could be poor in America. The lushness of the Vermont landscape obscured such despair, made it almost photogenic—*rustic*.

Quite suddenly, *5899* flashed up on a fencepost—a mobile home tucked in a birch grove. She braked, then realized she could easily be seen. She drove on, another quarter mile, the road bisecting wide plowed fields, where it dead-ended. A murder of crows shrieked at her from a tree as she turned around. She drove back, slowly, aware that people around here surely knew each other, knew every car.

From what she could assess on her approach, the home was not well tended. It certainly was not the business office of a thriving logging concern. There wasn't a vehicle, but the door was open, and a boy of five or six was riding a Big Wheel around the house, all stamina and focus. Then, just as Kay was passing, a woman came out. Kay only glimpsed her, she was slim, wearing pink sweatpants and a pink tank top.

"Jake!" she yelled. "Get the fuck in the house!"

She clocked Kay's car. Kay swiveled her eyes straight ahead, assumed a befuddled expression, she was a wayward tourist trying to find the Great Corn Maze.

OCCASIONALLY, BEN SPECULATED ABOUT SLIM'S
private life. He must be rich after 30 years as a dealer, but he still
ran the Dirty Ditty, still drove a burgundy '91 Mercury Grand
Marquis. Somehow he got it past state inspection, even with
Bondo around the wheel wells. The vehicle was so old it had a
cassette player, and Slim still had cassettes: Motörhead, AC/DC,
very early Nine Inch Nails. Guns N' Roses was playing at lullaby
volume. Was Slim married, did he have children? A cat, a dog,
a fish? Ben imagined he owned a Caribbean island, and one day
he'd just vanish from East Montrose. The Dirty Ditty's gum-
eyed regulars would show up, but the door would be locked,
they'd wait mewling like abandoned kittens in the stairwell.

Ben and Slim were parked at a pullout on Diamond Hill
opposite the old cemetery, one of Slim's favorite meeting places
because he could see cars coming in either direction and he could
peruse the old gravestones. The compilation of loss refreshed
his perspective on life's ephemeral nature, he'd said. But also:
time absolved all sins, even drug dealing. The children affected
Slim most. "Infant boy, died 1823," he'd tell Ben. Or, "Ester
Rose, 1801–1805, Thou art in Heaven. Tragedy."

Slim lit up a Cool, exhaled as he spoke. Nonchalance was
important to Slim. "Tried vaping the other day. Thought, ya
know, the modern thing, gotta keep up with the times and all.

But it's not the same thing, is it? I slept with a girl with fake tits once. Didn't realize till I got her home, they looked great but it woulda been like tryin' to tit-fuck a couple of basketballs and who wants that?"

Ben nodded, who indeed. But Slim wasn't looking to parley, he did not care for anyone else's ideas or opinions. He was not a friend, not even an acquaintance. He was a drug dealer. And, so, by association, was Ben. Ben wanted to excuse himself, he didn't *feel* like a dealer, or how he imagined Slim to feel: sly, confident, wary, mercenary. In the beginning, he'd been resentful that he'd had to do this, but people had worse lives, people had cancer, people lived in terrible countries with terrible wars. Now he felt pretty much nothing, he didn't even try to get his head around the irony of being a heroin dealer. Generally, he considered irony the universe's most powerful force, stronger than gravity. The most ironic thing that could happen was usually what happened.

Slim was tapping his fingers on the steering wheel, though— Ben noticed—not in time to the music. "We gotta problem, Benito."

A car drove past, a ferrety old man in a battered Subaru Outback with a big mutt-dog riding shotgun and *Bernie for President* stickers all over the bumpers. The dog glanced at Ben and Slim as it drove by and let out a self-important bark. "NPR-listening mother-fucker," Slim mumbled, then barked back, a sudden wild, manic lurching and Ben smelled the panic smell of Slim's sweat.

When the car had gone and silence resumed, he turned to Ben, his voice calm again: "Feds."

Slim had endured because his instinct for narcs was exquisite; he could smell them on the wind like a turkey vulture scenting carrion. Ben listened up.

"Some new task force." Slim sucked his Cool. "Undercover bitches."

Did Slim mean bitches as in women agents, or, in a more purely misogynistic sense, that all undercover agents were *bitches*?

"Your friend, Frank," Slim said.

"Frank, yeah?"

"You trust him?"

"Frank is not going to talk to the cops. I guarantee it."

"Guarantee?" Slim snorted. "He dead, then?"

"I've known Frank a long time."

Slim merely smoked his Cool, tapping, tapping out of rhythm. "The other guys?"

"Ed and Moses?" Ben shook his head. "They're solid."

"All I know is this shit is deep undercover. Jacques Cousteau, like."

"You want to hold off?"

"Nah. We've gotta shift it now. This week. Get rid of it. No phone calls, no connections. Eyes on, Benito, eyes on. We do not get careless. But we shift it fast."

"Gotcha," Ben said.

"Oh, yeah," Slim reached into his glove compartment and handed Ben a brown paper bag. "Per your request. You would not believe the range of merchandise available. You can even get rabbit piss. The internet, eh? They're catheterizing bunnies. There is some sick shit out there, man."

Ben took the bag, made as if to pay. But Slim waved him aside, "It's on me. It's got a trace of THC." He started the Marquis, the engine rumbled, throaty, well-oiled and tended. "Agnes Gillman, 1842–1869," he went on. "Baby's buried right next to her. A real heartbreaker."

After Slim had gone, Ben waited in his truck—20, 30 minutes, watching the woods, listening. Deer couldn't stand still for more than five minutes, and a person got shifty before that. Chickadees, squirrels scrabbling in the understory, a downy woodpecker looping over the cemetery. There was no one here, Ben was sure, but he waited another ten minutes, just the same.

The old man and the dog passed the other way in their Subaru. DEA agents, Ben mused. But that was the point, wasn't it? You couldn't tell. They weren't going to show up here in suits and cheap ties, like Jehovah's Witnesses. Some felt-shoed liberal and his dog in a clapped out Subaru, pretending to listen to *Fresh Air with Terry Gross:* the perfect cover in rural Vermont.

Grabbing his backpack, Ben got out of the truck and entered the cemetery's small gate. The stones were lopsided, some had fallen over. He walked among them. Dead babies, dead children, Vermont's hillsides were their catacombs. They had once died of disease and cold winters; now they were punched in the head, thrown against walls. Or their deaths were slower: spite, meanness, left out with the dogs.

Ben looked around at the trees, the dappled light, waving leaves, the grass under his boots, tightly woven, newly mowed. Someone kept the graves, trimmed the weeds, remembered the dead. He found Agnes Gillman and her dead baby. He slid his fingers under the gravestone, listened hard for the sound of a car, the crack of twig under-foot. Nothing, silence. He pulled on latex gloves, lifted up the granite, took hold of the first plastic-bound brick, slid it into the backpack, then the next, the next, all six, all six kilos. Why kilos? This was a joke he had with himself: only drug dealers and Canadians used metric, and Canadians used Canadian metric. As he replaced the headstone, he felt the desolation of Agnes. She'd only been 19.

He drove to Ed's, he kept checking his rear-view mirror. It was a bad feeling, nervy, like tweeking. He remembered his mother once, after a bad eight-ball, the carpet burns on her face from peeping under the door. The windows of the motel were all blacked out, but there was a quarter-inch gap under the door that let in daylight. She'd been convinced Satanists were coming to get her for their next human sacrifice, so she knelt on her elbows and knees for hours, moving her head back and forth, back and forth on the crusty shag rug, watching every shadow.

You watch the shadows, Benben, the shadows coming in here, the shadows moving too fast.

It was easy to lose the ability to tell fact from fear, and it was easy to see patterns. Patterns felt safer than the random. It was also a matter of self-importance: to put oneself at the center of a scheme just because that felt better than redundancy. Still, Slim's fear crawled all over him like ants. Cops. Undercover bitches.

Ed was tinkering with his chainsaw carvings. Seeing Ben, he turned off the saw. "Howya?"

Ben pulled to a stop, nodded to what might be a giant, angry squirrel. "Looking good," he said.

The carvings were an idea Ed'd had to make extra cash. He set up a display at the local fairs carving the sculptures, Indian heads, turtles, and such, attracting mostly lost children and solitary men in camo. He was nimble and quick with the saw, but he had no flair, no "eye" as the arty people called it. He made the bear's head so big it looked deformed; the turtle's shell too small, a mutant. That didn't matter with Ben, Ben didn't need a frigging artist.

Ed smelled strongly of iodine from cleaning the teats of his dairy cows. It was a smell that never wore off; you couldn't wash it from your hands. After backing the truck up to the cow barn, they unloaded the drugs into garbage bags as the radio played country and Western for the cows, and they stored the bags deep within a stack of hay bales. It wasn't hard work, but the afternoon was hot, and they were sweating.

Ed clapped his hand on Ben's shoulder, "You want some Newman's Lemonade? I just opened a fresh tin."

"Sure," Ben replied.

They turned toward the house as a Ford Focus with out of state plates drove past, heading fast back toward the main road. A woman, Ben ascertained, coming from the dead end, coming from the direction of his house.

"Lookie loo," said Ed.

Ben watched the car until it turned the bend, out of sight.

Freya and Tom were waiting outside Kamp Wahoo with Phoebe Figgs. Kay was 20 minutes late. "I'm so sorry."

Phoebe had been with 60 children for more than eight hours. She was unimpressed. "Pick up is between 4 and 4:15."

"It won't happen again."

But Phoebe looked like she knew otherwise.

On the way home, they stopped for ice cream at Foxy's. Tom, with his Moose Tracks, leaned against her, and Freya, with her vanilla chocolate dip, sat close enough for Kay to place a hand on her thigh. Freya didn't move away, she softened, put her head on Kay's shoulder.

"Mum, when can I get my ears pierced?"

"When you're 11."

"But Najma already has hers done."

"Have we already had this discussion? I seem to remember—"

"Please, pleeez, Mum, everyone has pierced ears. I'm like a freak."

Tom mugged: "When can I get my ears pierced?"

"I think your nose." Freya pinched it for good measure.

Then the phone rang.

Kay knew who it was.

"Mum, Mum."

She should tell him about Ammon. She should say, "You

know that trap? I met the kook responsible." She should tell him about the basement and Frank and Maria. They would have a chat, a conversation, back and forth, they would wonder, they would puzzle over it, conclude together.

"Your phone, Mum."

Tom tapped her thigh.

Freya grabbed her handbag, rummaged inside. "It's probably Dad."

The ringing stopped. Freya held the phone aloft. "It *was* Dad."

A car drove past, a dog leaning out the window, smiling and barking, tongue out. Kay watched the dog. Who was to say it was well-treated at home? Only that moment of being mattered, the open window, the smells striating the air, the rush of wind on its fur. The car turned into traffic, abandoning Kay to herself and the dark, oily matter that filled her.

She smiled at her daughter. "We'd better call him back, then."

"Daddy!" They said when he answered. "Daddy!" How complete their delight.

"I'm learning to dive," Freya told him. "I have to go up on the diving board and it's really high, and the first time I got water up my nose, and it was, like, the worst ice cream rush ever."

When Tom's turn was done—a long story about a child at camp who'd choked on a carrot stick and Mrs. Figgs had hit him on the back and the carrot popped out all covered in green gunky stuff—he handed the phone over to Kay. "Dad wants to talk to you."

"Hello." She wondered if the children would note her formal tone.

"I'm sorry to ask you this." He didn't sound sorry. What did sorry sound like from Michael? "But I need you to pay Pearl Street Digital. Take it from the general account. I'll send you an email with the details."

"Of course, no problem."

"How are you?"

"Fine. We're all fine. And you?"

"Delayed in Schipol. Severe winds over the Sahara. Flights canceled."

Kay wondered if this was a euphemism for a boutique hotel in Amsterdam, two days with Barbara, wandering the canals arm in arm.

"I'd better go," he said.

She didn't hang up right away; she was certain there must be something else to say. He was still speaking, but it took her a moment to grasp that he was not speaking with her, his voice muffled.

Accidentally, he hadn't disconnected the call. He was saying, "Has Morton got those permissions yet?" to someone else.

To Barbara?

Has Morton got those permissions yet?

His life out there, his Action Man life of permissions, permits, locations, sandstorms in the Sahara. While she groveled on her knees disinterring apple cores from the sofa. Did Barb, in her chic Italian culottes, know what happened to a doll's hair if you held it over an open flame? Did she know it wouldn't go nice and curly; rather it would shrink and wad in a stinking mass and the doll's face wilt like old wax? Did she know how to comfort a child holding this Burn Victim Barbie? The pathos required?

Kay swallowed hard. Her bitterness appalled her. She ushered her children toward the car. As if there was urgency, purpose. But there was only dinner and the savage mortality of motherhood.

Sam and I slept together a number of times, we were casual lovers, there was never an obligation. The first time: in the Sheraton Hotel in Kampala, 2001. We'd come back from the north, child soldiers previously employed by General Christmas being returned and reintegrated into their villages. It was a powerful story of forgiveness and redemption: these children, who'd committed atrocities, who'd had atrocities committed against them, trying to navigate their way back to normal life. Their communities were terrified of them. Everyone was deeply traumatized. But the kids just wanted to go to school and play football.

My whole career had been so steeped in the human propensity for violence that I'd overlooked the equal pull toward contentment. People really do just want to get up and have a cup of tea and feel the sun on their faces and know they won't be raped today, they won't eviscerate or behead today, they'll just hang out with friends and talk about the weather and watch sparrows pecking at bread crumbs.

We had no desire for each other, Sam and I. Stumbling into the Sheraton's lobby, we were filled with sadness and hope, utterly polarized emotions. We were used to anger or cynical disgust, but the hope was like a dare. We'd been caught up in the kids' resilience, as if a nine-year-old really could come home from war and study geometry, and his aunt wouldn't look at him through the blood-stained filter of her memory: what he'd done—what he'd had to do—to his mother and father, the glint of the machete, the thud and slice of a blade against skin and bone.

It's a simple choice, the returning children seemed to say: choose life, choose peace. I remembered a quote from Simone Weil—"Love is a direction, not a state of the soul," and I repeated it to Sam, that the children of Gulu proved it was all direction, all free will. I could read his mind, how he wanted to say, "Let's come back next year and see how it's gone to shit when the kids can't find jobs and the trauma starts to leach out in its insidious, inevitable way." But he didn't, he swallowed the cynicism and took my hand, and we very calmly went to his room.

K ay stopped herself. Even without shutting her eyes she could see the scene, she and Sam, the hotel hallway with its lurid carpet, its missing light bulbs, the smell of old room-service food—always French fries. The hotel, with its history, so that it was more than a hotel: a shrine, a memorial. It didn't matter that the carpet was new, the walls repainted, that the country had had two different presidents since. Memory couldn't be erased so easily, especially here on the top floor, she and Sam, strolling, a little drunk, not looking at the fire door at the end of the hall that led directly onto the roof. Because there was video footage of Idi Amin swimming contentedly in the hotel's pool, surrounded by sycophantic white businessmen. Those men knew Amin threw his victims from the hotel roof. Sitting at the poolside bar, they could hear the screams. One of them complained about the noise.

She and Sam, opening the door to his room, couldn't quite pretend that the past had not happened because it had.

Shall I write about Sam and I? She wrote.

The sex was terrible. Shall I confess how the story never made it to print, "Too much child soldiers stuff," our editor declared, because The Sunday Times Magazine *had just run a piece about child soldiers in Sierra Leone with sexy black and white photos of ragged, dead-eyed boys carrying weapons that weighed more than they did.*

A photograph of a 14-year-old former Christmas elf learning to sew could not possibly compete. Her gonorrhea-scarred uterus, her nightmares, her tremors, her astounding bravery—these were not visible to the camera.

So the story—The Truth—remained the stolen children, the violent children, the horror, the exciting, rubber-necking horror of General Christmas and his mirror-shaded cohort. It confirmed and conformed the Africa we created and continue to create with every story.

Afterward, Sam had tears on his face. We should never have had sex, only held each other, my head on his shoulder.

Or—Or—I could make up a romance, a daring love affair, Sam and I? Isn't that the better story? Not a lie, exactly, but a harmless rearrangement of the facts. I should throw in a road block, scary black men with guns, and how we traded Sam's Rothman cigarettes for our lives. Fear makes you horny, an atavistic desire to fuck, having survived near death, or in the face of it, or in spite of it, or surrounded by it. Someone— name lost, face unremembered, a fellow hack in a bar—suggested this was why soldiers rape. It's a desperate response to fear, the same force that sent us scurrying to our hotel rooms with bottles of tequila and condoms—the relentless irony of being human: death and life, horror and pleasure, linked together like little plastic beads.

I've never had so much sex as when I was in dangerous places, and it didn't matter with whom, Sam, Marco, Rick, the waiter, the interpreter, a dozen other men I hardly remember. It was sex, like food, like water, brusque and impersonal, good, bad. No apologies were necessary, no regrets, no lies, no promises, a cigarette instead of a kiss at the door.

There was simply no time for introspection, certainly no time for love, nor weeping. No time, we were too busy with deadlines, with arranging travel to the next story, competing with each other, lusting and drinking and sleeping on beds or floors, in airport lounges, in bars.

And now I have time, lots of it. And no fear. And no sex.

I have a lovely view. My children go to Kamp Wahoo where they are fed Fluff sandwiches and Pop-Tarts and come home reeking of chlorine and sunscreen. They tell me about a boy with his arm in a cast who's not allowed to swim. And I'm writing because Sam told me—because Sam, not Michael, saw the problem: "Write, write, you have to write. Whatever happened, whatever happened then, there, you have to write, even if you make it up, the truth will be there just the same."

The white walls, the dark night. In here, out there. These demarcations amplified her solitude. She sat at her desk. She stared at the screen. Nothing happened. She lifted her hands to the keyboard, she lowered them. She took another sip of wine. And another. As a journalist, she'd never been wordless; the stories had been outside her, all around her. In a sense, they still were: the dozens of notebooks she'd retained, now stacked on the desk and under it. She could pull any one open and know the story, Goma, Addis Ababa, Lokchoggio, Mogadishu. And more than the story: the dust, the light, how a cockerel always crowed at dawn and there was always a lone dog barking in the night, *woof woof woof*, like a satellite pinging in hope of a response. She used to put a dirty pair of underwear on the very top of her suitcase so light-fingered baggage handlers wouldn't pilfer. She could bargain with taxi drivers in French, Swahili, Amharic and Arabic. She knew smells. Jasmine on the trellis outside a hotel window in Kinshasa, wild grass after a thunderstorm in the Serengeti, the different smells of smoke—wood, garbage, bodies. The notebooks were stained: wine, beer, grease, mud.

"What are you writing?" Michael asked when she'd first established herself in a corner of the living room in London. Because there had been offers. At first. Articles, the odd book review.

But there just wasn't sustained work, freelance or otherwise, the newspaper world was going-going or gone, journalists were like whalers and chimney sweeps. Bloggers had taken over. An agent, a friend of Michael's, had urged her to consider a memoir, "Lynsey Addario, but with more sex and drugs." She wondered how this person knew about the sex and drugs. Perhaps she'd been infamous.

"Write," Sam had said. "You have to write."

As if she were tunneling, a prisoner digging with a spoon. As if there were a direction, a place the words would take her. Rather than mere habit: the prisoner tries to escape because he is a prisoner, it's what prisoners do.

She sat, her ass turning to cement in the hard wooden chair in the white house in the dark hills. She preferred discomfort while writing, it kept her leery.

At last, she pushed herself back from the desk and stood. The back of her legs had gone to sleep, her hips ached. She stretched and wandered into the bathroom, climbed up on the toilet to check her phone. There was only a text from Michael: "We need to talk." Oh, they would talk. Who would have the kids on the weekend, who would keep the house, how would they divide his money.

Leaning back against the tank, Kay felt the coolness of the porcelain through her dress. She wasn't looking, merely gazing when she noticed an incongruity in the beadboard paneling below the towel cupboard. She peered. Indeed, there was a vertical seam in the wood. She got up off the toilet, crossed the bathroom, and knelt on the floor: a door, about three feet high and the same across.

It was impossible to pry the door open with her fingers, so she scouted around for a tool and selected a nail file. She ran the blade up, discerned two hinges on the left side. On the right, a little inside latch that gently popped.

The space was small, more like a cubby. It was empty. Kay

stared into the dark. Why was the latch on the inside? It made no sense unless someone was locking themselves in. And did that somehow make more sense?

Crouching down, she edged herself in. She felt like a child. Perhaps this was just the compression of space, making her smaller and at ground level where adults seldom dwelt. Surprisingly, she could sit up, almost comfortably, even though her legs were bent, either cross-legged or loosely folded. It wasn't as claustrophobic as it first appeared. She shut the door, and the darkness was almost complete.

She could hear her breath, she had tremendous awareness of her body in the dark, her proprioception heightened, the boundary of her skin, the bones of her face and hands. She felt oddly calm, insulated.

It was impossible to track time in such dark, but she felt she'd sat quietly, meditatively, for a dozen minutes before she became aware of the sensitivity of her fingertips. Her hands were on the floor, and she could feel the grain of the wood, the precise ridges—and this despite the heavy surface lacquer. Slowly, she traced her fingers out to the walls of her enclosure, and up, across the surprisingly rough texture of the paint. The tiniest globlet rose like a mountain from the plain to her touch. The intimacy was almost sensual—as the tightly focused attention to the detail of a lover's back or neck.

She traced the edges and corners of the enclosure, in front of her, around her, and down. And here she discovered a divot in the wallboard. Twisting her body to reach behind her, she found, further along, a hole, big enough for her finger. She stuck her finger in, wiggling the tip on the other side. Leaning in, she tried to see. She sucked her finger, wetting it thoroughly, then stuck it back in the hole. She felt the air, the space beyond. She withdrew her finger, and sat quiet and still, safe and unknown. She was soft-edged darkness, blurred around the edges like a charcoal drawing.

The moment she cracked open the door, the bathroom light leapt in at an accusatory angle. As she began to unpack herself, she saw it: scratchy strands of writing just over her left shoulder on the wall.

DIRTY SQUEAL SQUEAL
DIRTY PIG SLIT YOU OPEN

She touched the words lightly, as one might hieroglyphics, or perhaps, braille. They weren't carved in or painted on. The writer had used indelible black marker. There was nothing to be gained by her touch, except to confirm the existence of the words. She couldn't feel with her skin what was between them, inside them. That required another sense altogether.

Sitting back on her heels, she considered: who. Frank, Maria, the boys? She considered: why. A joke, an angry child, an adult. A man. She tried to think objectively. The awkward handwriting looked childish, but might not necessarily be that of a child; it was difficult to write evenly at such an angle. The words were aggressive. SLIT YOU OPEN sounded like a rape. And it was something men did, they slit open women, children. A woman, on the other hand, would have written with more self-hate: SLIT ME OPEN I'M A DIRTY PIG.

Frank, she thought. Frank. And Frank is, perhaps, not well in the head. Frank is, perhaps, in a mental hospital or at a treatment center. Which, perhaps, accounts for Alice's reticence.

Carefully, Kay closed the door. She moved the laundry basket in front of it, because, God knows, Tom and Freya wouldn't go anywhere near it. The laundry basket emitted an impermeable force field, repelling children and their clothes, so they were forced to leave them all over the floor instead.

At dawn, a doe and her two fawns grazed in the field beyond the lawn. Kay paused in her making of breakfast, the soft-boiled egg Tom wanted, the toast severed of crusts for Freya. She admired the doe's grace, the absolute precision of her movements, her ceaseless vigilance. Her entire reason for being alive was her children.

Dirty pig, squeal squeal. The words skittered into Kay's brain. They were like spiders, she could feel them, up there, above her, in that odd little cupboard. They were too near the children, they might escape, crawl out. Kay felt a swipe of panic. Absurd.

The fawns leaped and twisted and bucked, they charged and nuzzled, then stopped and aggressively jabbed their mother's udder with their damp muzzles, even though they didn't need her milk anymore. Sometimes, the doe stepped forward to discourage them and they shimmied away from her in the damp grass, leaping in the silken warmth. They knew nothing of winter, they did not even suspect.

Kay went up the stairs, the narrow, steep stairs almost like a ladder. At the top, she peered into the bathroom; the laundry basket was as she'd left it, the secret cupboard completely hidden.

What would Michael say, had he seen it? Dismissed it? "People are strange," he would have said. "That shouldn't surprise you."

But why these particular words? This malevolent haiku—rather than a banal scrawl of "The Patriots suck" or a cursory rendering of a vagina or penis. It was a code, it meant something more than its words. And why the cupboard, the secret recess, locking from the inside?

She moved on past the bathroom door, the floorboards creaking underfoot.

Sun edged around the heavy cotton curtains in the bedroom, illuminating her children as they slept in a froth of white sheets and stuffed animals. Kay stood over them, loving them. Now was the time to love them, when they would not shy away, when the wrong thing would not be said and the juice would not be spilled and the story did not need to be written. They were hers in such moments, completely. She touched Freya's blond head, Tom's smooth back. "Wake up, my darlings, wakey wakey." Tom turned instinctively toward her, curling his body around her thigh like a snake seeking a warm rock.

JAKE WAS PROPPED IN FRONT OF THE TV, SOME-
thing loud and angry. Ben hated the TV. He'd have been outside,
in the woods, despite the black flies, the deer flies. If Jake was
his child he'd turn off the TV, he'd take him out. And he will,
that is what he will do when he becomes Jake's guardian. It was
in the woods that a boy could find what he needed to get by,
he could learn his resilience. But Jake was leery, Jake was timid,
the TV had been Jake's stalwart companion for the many, many
hours of his mother's nods. Ben kissed the boy on the head. "I
love you."

Shevaunne stood out on the deck smoking. When she saw
Ben, she stubbed out her cigarette, pushed open the screen door
and came inside. "I got the test today."

"I know."

"Obviously I'm not going to pass."

"Sure you are." Ben showed her the brown paper bag he'd got
from Slim and took out a plastic packet about the size of take-
away soy sauce. The label read *Willow Bend Supplements*.

She screwed up her face. "Is that piss?"

"You had a toke," Ben confirmed. "It would look suspicious
if you were totally clean."

She snorted. "Don't you know they watch you?"

"That's why it's in this little plastic bag. You store it in your underwear."

Shevaunne regarded the packet of urine for a long moment. "I don't know," she said at last.

He stood near her, close, almost like a lover. "Yes, you do."

Freya's missing sneakers, a blue sock, a green pencil, a yellow pencil, a spoon, three inter-linked paperclips, a peach stone, a *Harry Potter* CD now badly scratched, paper cut into dozens of pieces, a red hair tie, 16 pennies, a pink t-shirt, a rubbery carrot less three bites, books, an empty reel of Scotch tape, an orange sock.

Kay dutifully collected these items, the maternal choreography of bending, gathering, no longer nuts and berries but bits of LEGO. She shoved the vacuum cleaner under the sofa, under the chairs, across the floor. The machine began to falter, so she opened the canister. The bag was reusable. She lifted it out, walked to the trash and emptied the contents. Amongst the dust, the indeterminate debridement of Frank and Maria's living, was a single pale-blue disposable surgical bootie.

For a moment, Kay simply held it. As an objective fact, it was nothing. She might describe the specific blue, the texture of the material, the elastic binding the whole together. When she touched it, nothing happened, it exuded no smell, and she was not psychic, she had no visions. But she had found it. It had been there to be found. In a way, the house had provided it to her. As it had the cupboard upstairs. *Look here.* The house was revealing itself, coyly. Not, of course, in a crazy, Stephen King way, Jack Nicholson leering down the corridor of a haunted hotel. The house wasn't *doing* anything. But there was a tilting. It was as if her family had so changed the house, shifted the habit of its gravity, that revelation became possible. Objects slid free. She stuffed the bootie in her pocket and went out to the car.

The Town House was a house like the house on the hill she was living in, Frank and Maria's, a house like other houses on hills or in valleys or towns. You just couldn't tell from the outside what was inside, what was underneath. General Christmas, for instance, had been an excellent shop-keeper, he kept his prices low, the shelves well-stocked. He even extended credit to his poorer customers for things like gin and matches.

Kay walked up the wheelchair ramp, there was only a screen door so she pushed this open. The office was pokey, the antique computer with its dusty screen probably still ran on DOS. A large scroll of maps hung on the wall behind the desk. No one was at the desk.

"Hello?"

Along one wall, a huge vault displayed folios and leather-bound land records. She eased around the room to the maps, flipped through them. A topography of the town, a county map, a state map, a property map demarcating the property boundaries. Kay found Frank and Maria's land. WILSON, it was written. Wilson, Wilson, she knew now.

On the desk lay a copy of the town report. She flipped through: the school budget, the road budget, financial statements, property transfers. Under the property taxes section was a list of delinquent payers and the amount overdue. Kay was surprised at this outing, it seemed shaming; everyone knew you hadn't, or couldn't, pay.

"Can I help you?"

Kay turned, abandoning the report.

The woman was dark-haired, apple-cheeked, wearing a floral sundress. She smiled, "I'm Nadine, the clerk here."

"And I'm Kay Ward, hi." Kay returned the smile. "We're renting the house up the road. *The Wilsons*. Frank and Maria."

"Is that AirBnb? I hear a lot about that these days."

"No, it's not AirBnb, we found out about it through another site."

"Lovely views. Tough in the winter."

"I can imagine. Wow, winter, I mean, maybe I can't imagine. Um, Nadine, do you know how I could get in touch with Frank and Maria?"

"Alice would be the person to ask. She's caretaking the place, right?"

"She doesn't know." Kay was cheery, a cheery visitor. "What a beautiful part of Vermont this is."

"It's not called the Kingdom for nothing," Nadine enthused.

"My husband and I are thinking we might buy a place here, we've really fallen in love." Kay made a vague gesture to the property maps. "Do you know what's for sale? The Wilson's place, maybe?"

"Oh, you'd be better talking to a realtor. But as far as I know Frank's not selling, no."

Kay noted the exclusion of Maria from ownership. "Do you usually see them around?"

"Not unless he comes in here."

Again, the singularity of Frank. Kay glanced again at the property maps. She could make out the road, the boundaries of Frank's land—Frank's not Frank and Maria's. It comprised nearly 300 acres buffered by a state park, no neighbor for a mile in either direction. She thought how the thick woods must absorb sound. "And you have no idea where they might be. Family? Vacation?"

Nadine cocked her head. "He has a cabin up north."

"A cabin?"

"Derby, Granby? Not far from the border. His mother's family were from there, old Québécois."

"And Maria's with him?"

"Maria?" Nadine was alert now.

"His wife."

"I don't know her."

"Their kids?"

"I don't know."

"Where are they?"

Nadine's lips opened, then closed. Thin, with the faintest trace of peach lipstick.

Kay pressed on, her voice light, airy. "When did you last see them—Frank, Maria, the boys?"

Nadine pulled her chair closer into the desk, putting it firmly between herself and Kay, her shield. "I've already told you I don't know where they are but I'm sure they're just fine."

But Nadine wasn't sure, not 100 percent. Kay could see the tiny fissure in the facade of certainty she'd tried to maintain. And not just now, right now, but before. Maybe for quite a while Nadine had sensed the Wilsons were not all right. This was a small community; Nadine knew most of the business there was to know: who was delinquent on their property tax, who was selling their land, who was buying, who was building, who had special-needs kids, who had disabilities, who applied for state heating aid. Nadine was not sure; Kay heard the lightest inflection, 20 years as a journalist had tuned her ear.

As a mother, she was merely late.

LACEY WAS A LARGE WOMAN, HER UPPER ARMS like boiled hams, she dressed meticulously. She wore bright blue shoes, and she kept her hands well, she had pride in her dainty extremities. She had a large folder open on her desk, the morning light shining directly on it like an annunciation—Shevaunne's life: the record, exclusively, of her misery, her addiction, her failure. Normal people did bad things and didn't get caught and those bad things could be forgotten or forgiven and then they evaporated. But people like Shevaunne could never shake them off, the folder got thicker and heavier, the gigabytes or whatever on the computer swelled like over-hydrated cells. The good that Shevaunne did—there must be some, the simple act of not abandoning her son at the interstate rest area while she got high—these were not accounted for.

Somewhere, Ben reckoned, the Department for Children and Families must have a folder on him, a faded green folder such as this, with a label on the side, *Benjamin L. Comeau*. And inside, a photograph of his blank child's face, his shuttered eyes, the clear skin of his seven-year-old self. There would be the story of Benben, their version, succinct, factual, reports from doctors and shrinks, foster parents, schools, assessments from a dozen caring women like Lacey. He'd really been no trouble, he'd adjusted, a bright boy, scholarship material. He wondered if Lacey had already found the file, read it; if it would somehow count for him or against him in his bid for guardianship of Jake. He was in the system, once and always, its ward, its product.

Lacey regarded Shevaunne. "You're aware that you missed your last drug test."

"I had the wrong day, I, ah, I wrote it down wrong. It was my fault, yeah," Shevaunne nodded, licked her lips.

"And your P.O., Officer Feldman, wasn't able to find you at the address listed here in Concord."

"I moved in with Ben. Ben, here. In April. May? Was it May, Ben? And I meant to tell Feldman. It's just been, you know, I'm staying out of town, Ben lives out in Lost Nation. I'm out there so I can stay clean." She began to jiggle her left foot.

"And will today's test be clean?"

Shevaunne glanced at Ben, he did not reciprocate. "Yeah, I'm clean." Then she bit her lip. "But I had a little toke and a beer."

"As long as it was 'little.' But it shouldn't happen again." Lacey flipped to another page. "And where is Jake at the moment?"

Shevaunne's drifting gaze suggested he could be anywhere, in the car by himself, under a bed.

Ben leaned in. "He's at the daycare. Little Feet."

"And he's enrolled in school this fall?"

"Yes," said Ben.

"Where?"

"East Montrose."

Lacey nodded, returned her attention to Shevaunne. "He was supposed to start last year. You had him registered in Concord. Why didn't he go?"

Shevaunne looked at the floor. "I forgot." A long moment passed, Lacey purposefully leaving the space. At last Shevaunne looked right at Lacey, "I know I'm a shit mother. And that's why I'm here with Ben, so he can be Jake's guardian. I mean—in case—" she gave a little laugh. She was very convincing, thought Ben. "We all know what'll happen to me. Eventually."

"We don't know that."

"I'll stay clean and go back to school and get my GED, and what? Work in Dollar General? Sure."

"People do. People have jobs, they raise their children."

"People," Shevaunne made a little noise, possibly a laugh. "Junkies are not *people*."

"To this office you are, to the legal system you are."

"That's sweet."

"Nothing to do with sweetness." Lacey shuffled more papers. "It says here 'Father's whereabouts unknown.' Any ideas?"

"Dead. Or jail be my guess."

"Do you have a name?"

"Sure," Shevaunne obliged, and Lacey dutifully picked up her pen. "Junkie Dickhead."

Lacey simply put the pen down, swung back to Ben. "And, Ben, anything going to come up in the background check?"

"I've got bad credit, some legal stuff."

"What legal stuff?"

"Fraud, trespass."

"Any convictions?"

Ben shook his head. "Not yet."

"But pending?"

"It's on appeal."

"Can you give me the case details?"

Ben shifted in his chair. "Guy called Paul Steiner. Didn't like how I logged his land."

Lacey continued: "Otherwise, I see four years of military—Marines, right out of high school?"

"Yes, ma'am."

"Honorable discharge. Right? And between then and now?"

"Alaska, Colorado. Just worked whatever jobs. But I'm from here, guess I was always going to come back here."

"Your own business, the logging. And how's that—aside from Mr. Steiner?"

"Pays the bills. Mostly."

"Stable?"

"For logging. For 'round here."

"Why do you want to be Jake's guardian?"

He wasn't a relative, he wasn't a family friend; he was a guy from Shevaunne's sketchy life. A creep, a predator, potentially. He couldn't, therefore, use words like "love." On the other hand, Lacey was aware that he was Jake's only real shot at staying out of the over-crowded foster system if Shevaunne fucked up. If. When.

Ben said, "Just give him a home he can count on, regular meals, school. A quiet, safe place." He raised his eyes to hers, just a moment, before dropping them again. "What I didn't have."

Lacey fluttered her pretty hands over the folder, shutting it. "And you're aware that Jake suffered trauma with a previous male in his life?"

"I assumed. Something made it so he won't talk."

"You should be aware of the severity of the incident."

Shevaunne stood up, moved to the window.

"Jake was placed in foster care two years ago," Lacey began. "Shevaunne lost custody for 18 months. He had been found wandering along the railway tracks, poorly nourished, covered in lice and bed bug bites."

There was more, Ben could tell.

"Shevaunne?" Lacey glanced at Shevaunne, as if for permission. Shevaunne shrugged. So Lacey turned the file toward Ben, her pretty painted nail arrowing to a specific paragraph.

Please don't, he thought, *please don't let there be—*

Lacey's manicured index finger arrowing to the words. Ben read. He read. He sat back in the chair.

Lacey folded her pretty hands, moving on. "The guardianship hearing will probably take place in a few weeks. We have to go to court and make a clear case because Ben isn't a relative. Until then, Shevaunne, you've got to see your P.O. and go to meetings and submit to your tests and those need to be clean. If we have to take Jake away before the hearing, it will endanger Ben's bid for guardianship. You could lose your son for good this time. Is that clear?"

"Yes," Ben said.

Shevaunne still had her eyes out the window and Lacey shut the file. "We have the home visit scheduled for two days' time. Is that still convenient?"

"Absolutely."

Outside, Shevaunne and Ben got in the truck.

"I still don't get it," she said.

Ben put the keys in the ignition. His hands were trembling; he did not want her to see.

Shevaunne went on. "I keep trying to figure you out."

He finally found the slot, jammed the key in, the engine roared.

"Like, come on, Ben. If you wanted to fuck me that would be one thing. Don't ya wanna fuck me?" She glanced at him almost coyly, shifting her arms so her breasts squeezed upward.

Suddenly, he lashed out, his hands at her throat, his thumbs pressing upward against her jaw. He felt her life, he felt the pulse, her neck thin as a chicken's, the delicate bones, the pale blue veins of her. She tried to pry him away, but he held her until she gargled and fretted and little flecks of white spit gathered at the corners of her mouth. Then he let her go. "I would never fuck you. You make me sick."

"Be sick then," she held his gaze. "But I need my bump."

The spring peepers and their bright kettle whistle in the wetlands; a car on the mountain road—a drunk, maybe, taking the back way, the night way. Kay gazed out through the window above the kitchen sink as the dark moved in, soft as moss. Only the black silhouette of the hills retained relief against the star-lit sky; all else compressed into blackness. She took the hammer and butted the tap to turn it on.

Alice had carefully placed the hammer there; she had shown Kay and Michael the force necessary to turn the old iron tap on and then off. "My Al'll be up to fix it any day," she'd promised. Did it mean something, this broken tap, in a house of scrupulous repair? This house of coded secrets.

The water surged out warm on Kay's hands, into the sink. A miracle fluid, miraculously made warm. She added the soap, frothed the bubbles. Other women had stood here, as she did now, a long line of women, a matriarchy, connecting back through this ritual of washing dishes, this solitary task.

She imagined those other housewives—the many wives of this house—their feet right where hers were planted, their hands as hers, dipping and sponging, caressing the plates and cutlery. They were not all resentful. Some liked the peace, and others had only the expectation of such work, they were born to it. Maria? What about Maria? Poised here in front of the mixing bowls she'd used to make Candice's fudge. Maria treating herself to a lick of the sweet batter. Maria, who said, "Frank, honey, you need to fix this sink." He kept everything else fixed.

The hammer lay there by the tap. Kay touched it. The hammer, the hammer. She turned it in her hand and put it down again. Marriage was like a hammer: you could build things with it or bludgeon each other to death. Marriage was like a hundred different things, but similes ultimately failed, because marriage was the air around the hammer, the air which held all words and deeds and feelings, breathed, thought, intended, everything unseen, everything existing and no longer existing, history, prehistory, dinosaurs, pond scum, star dust, the boundless, shifting, unavoidable, choking air of every single, merciless day. She had believed in the iron and steel of marriage, the substance, dense and defined, the bitterness, sourness of her sweat and words across the dinner table, the sunless steppe of their bed.

But marriage did not exist as a weight and a shape, it was a wish thrown into a well.

She knelt before the cupboard but didn't open it. She had a suspicion the writing wasn't there, she'd imagined it, projected it.

Slowly, then, she ran the nail file along the seams and popped the latch. The latch worked so fluidly, mounted by a careful, precise craftsman, the kind who kept tools in perfect order. The words were there, each expressing its own discrete menace.

DIRTY SQUEAL SQUEAL
DIRTY PIG SLIT YOU OPEN

"Hello, Frank," she whispered as she edged herself in, on her hands and knees, now pressing her eye to the hole in the wallboard. There was nothing to see, darkness thick as felt.

"Mum?"

She startled. Why hadn't she heard him? The floor was a minefield of creaks, and somehow Tom had traversed it without a sound.

"Mum, what are you doing?"

Trying to block the writing with her body, she began to slither out.

"Just thought there was a leak."

"Oh," Tom said, believing her, because he believed grown-ups, he was five. "Can I see?"

"It's not very interesting, love. Just some pipes."

"But can I see?"

Crawling out completely, she shut the door, replaced the laundry basket. "What are you doing up?"

"I had to pee."

He shuffled forward, pulled down his pajama bottoms. She wondered at what point she wouldn't stand in the room with him when he peed. And at what point she'd never see him naked again—that body she'd grown, birthed, bathed, wiped, caressed. She'd taught him how to urinate, how to clean his foreskin because Michael had been away. And yet it would be Michael who'd share his nakedness in years to come, man-to-man, pee-ing in the woods. Nothing prepares you for the retraction of intimacy, she thought. Just as nothing prepares you for the way it slams into you like a cast-iron skillet.

"Mum," he spoke over the steady tinkle. He was very serious. "Do octopuses pee?"

"I don't know."

"If they do, won't it just float up and get in their eyes?"

"They live in quite a lot of water, so maybe the pee would just disperse."

"What does *disperse* mean?"

"Float away. Like if you pee in the pool, there's such a little amount of pee and such a lot of water."

"Hamish says they put special stuff in the pool so if you pee the water turns blue and everyone can see."

"Grown-ups say that so kids won't pee in the pool. But there's no dye."

Tom turned, looked up at her. "Really?"

"Grown-ups said the same thing to me when I was your age."

"When's Dad coming back?"

Because he was always there, even now, in the middle of the night, in the middle of a discussion about pee.

"I don't know, love. Maybe not until London."

"Can't we stay here? I don't want to go back."

She knelt. "It's not always summer here and the winters are very long. It gets very, very cold.

"We could have a fire."

She kissed him. "Off to bed. You need your sleep for camp."

His lean brown back, she watched, the shoulder blades protruding slightly, the dimples where the top of his buttocks tucked against the sacrum. He was miraculous.

Now she heard his footsteps on the wooden floor, the creak of the old bed as he got back in. She felt a sudden rush of fear, as she used to when they were babies, asleep, and she'd convinced herself they weren't breathing. For how soft a baby's breath, how vulnerable the child in sleep. For other children had slept in those beds, those sheets. Where were they?

Where, Frank? Kay thought, returning to that faint tremor in Nadine's voice. The simple solution was to go to the police, express her concerns, and wipe her hands of it. But she wouldn't—for the same reason she wouldn't tell Michael: it was a story, she was possessive of it. She wanted to open the black garbage bag all by herself and see what was inside, right down inside.

It was difficult to type holding her phone above her head and Kay wondered how Michael had managed for all those hours, tapping and whispering. What dedication. To whom? Barb? Barb*ara* as Michael called her, exotic accent on the final syllable.

After several awkward and unsuccessful configurations, she sat on the toilet's tank, wedging the phone against the window. She glanced through her emails; there weren't many aside from "Pearl Street" from Michael, possibly because she'd posted an automatic reply: *We're on vacation in a remote location with no phone or internet. It may take me a few days to respond.*

Scrolling on to Skype, she trawled through her contacts, Julian, Marco, Teddy, Gina, a dozen or so people she didn't remember or didn't remember friending or who'd been part of her past life. Teddy was recently married, a glamorous German countess, so he was off the list. Marco? It had been too long; she didn't know if he was still single or even where he was. She'd heard vague rumors that he'd gone off the rails and was teaching history at an elementary school in the Hebrides. Gina. Was in Afghanistan for Reuters. But Sam, for instance, Sam, of course, *available.* She hit video dial, it rang twice, and there he was, un-ironed, un-shaven. They peered at each other.

"Sam!"

"Kay, darlin'."

"How are you, Sam?"

"Better than not at all. And you?"

"Good, yeah, well, we're all well."

He squinted at her through the camera. "Where the hell are you?"

"Vermont."

"Vermont?" he looked perplexed. "Don't they make a lot of cheese there?"

"Ha. We rented a house for the summer."

"I can only see white tile. Are you sure you're not in an asylum of some kind?"

"The bathroom. I'm in the bathroom. It's the only place I can get reception."

"You look great."

"It's the high pixilation. I've only got one bar of reception."

He pushed his forelock back, appraised himself in his own image. "I look like shit."

"Shit from a goat's ass."

"With diarrhea."

"And a weeping STD."

They laughed, it was so easy.

"Tell me about Vermont."

"The kids love it. I'm writing."

"Good. That's good, isn't it?"

She might imagine she was there with him, sitting in a coffee shop in London or Addis, their coats slung over the back of their chairs, half-eaten pastries on the table. How it had been for years. They were always half-flung from the broken world into the civilized one, the dust still on their shoes. She peered in at him.

"Where are you?" she said, instead of answering his question.

"Ali's."

"Christ, Ali's! I can't believe it's still there. How is Ali?"

"Bitter, cantankerous."

"And what's the story?"

"South Sudan."

"Ah."

"Ah, indeed," said Sam. "Aahhhh. As in, 'Open wide, this won't hurt.'"

"At least it's still considered a story."

"They put Kanye West on the cover and me on page 36." Sam shifted in the light of Ali's Carpets and Internet and Kay could suddenly see his age. They'd been babies when they'd met, mid-20s, young, thrusting journalists, they strode across the continent. Sam's face was lined now, bags beneath his eyes.

"I heard about the Magnum award. Congratulations."

"Sure," he shrugged. "Only I'm not going to take that picture anymore."

"But you will."

He raised his eyebrows. "Nope."

"Because you care, Sam, you care."

"I'm going to become a professional ping pong player."

Kay laughed. Then realized Sam was waiting for her to finish. "Oh, my God, you're serious."

"I got into playing at a refugee camp near Kigoma. Turned out I have natural talent. I've been getting into shape."

"What kind of shape?"

"Shape. Toned muscle. Svelte. I'm svelte." He smiled. "The resurrection of svelte self."

They looked at each other, but she could only see this fuzzy version of him; his eyes were out of focus like the rest of him, and it wasn't a metaphor, it was just poor bandwidth.

"Hey, Sam, I need to run something by you."

"Sure."

"I think something's happened in this house, to the owners."

Sam's image froze for a moment. "What did you say? The link dropped."

"In this house. The people who own it. I think they might be missing."

"What do you mean, 'missing'?"

She outlined the story—Ammon and Frank's cupboard, Alice, the surgical bootie. Sam leaned back, arms crossed, "You know what I think?"

Kay waited.

Skype made a little *whoop* and Sam vanished, a black screen, then a message popped up. *Please wait while we get your call back.*

He came back, he was saying something about camping.

"What? You're breaking up."

Sam flickered, the video went out. Instead, Sam typed a message:

They're camping in Alaska.

She dialed again, several times, but the connection kept dropping out. And then Sam was off-line. The generator had broken down or run out of fuel or Ali hadn't paid the phone bill and Egypt Telecom had cut him off. Sam was pushing back his chair, finishing his dark, sweet Arabica coffee, he was stepping out into the street, into Cairo, into the blare of horns and nightlife, tea-sellers and pick-pockets, the air so thick with diesel fumes he could feel it brush against his face like an animal pelt.

For 15 years, she'd been stepping out of that door, into that street, writing, documenting, reporting. All those words, all those miles. She wrote about one war, and when it stopped or the editors lost interest, she waited for another. She'd felt so necessary, the work so imperative. Now the dirty, hot roaring world carried on without her and the Wilsons were camping in Alaska. Or they'd gone to a beach house in Maine. Or even simpler: to their cabin in Granby so they could rent out this house for money.

She slid down off the toilet's tank, sitting on the lid, pressing the phone to her forehead. She could not account for what she felt: an unhinging. She was not so certain of the seam between fact and narrative. Words were malleable. This house may be secluded or isolated, it may be haunted or merely empty. It was a matter of the adjective. The interpretation was hers; the words were spells. The Wilsons were in Alaska, they were keeping themselves to themselves. Or they had disappeared—they had dispersed, floated away.

And here she was, keeping herself to herself. If she and the children disappeared, how long would it be until Michael noticed? A month? Six weeks? He was on his way to a remote mining camp in Côte d'Ivoire, there'd be no internet. He might call on the sat phone from time to time, leaving message after message. He'd believe she wasn't replying out of pique. No one was expecting to hear from her. Parents, friends, anyone who emailed her. *We're on vacation in a remote location with no phone or internet. It may take me a few days to reply.*

HE HEARD SHEVAUNNE'S TV THROUGH THE

thin walls. *You always you never you don't love you cheating bitch you broke my I hate I love I never you always never—* The soundtrack to her life was the hearty laughter of strangers, the violent haranguing of jilted lovers. She could not stand silence, she could not stand solitude—those long, cold minutes when she had to live with herself.

He thought about what he'd read today in her file about Jake. What had been done made beating a child merely dull. The report didn't say if Shevaunne had been directly involved, but that did not matter. She was guilty. She had carried on living with the man who hurt her son, scoring with him, until Jake was found and the cops were hailed and Shevaunne went to prison.

How readily she'd come with him, just the whiff of smack, and she got into his car with her child. He'd thought, then, that she was just a junkie and neglect of her child was the worst of it, malnourishment, filth, sour milk. But *the consistency*—he recalled the words—*the consistency of abuse.* And the precision of it. How particular, how thoughtful. And consistent. Day after day.

Through the walls he heard her snuffling sounds as she turned in her sleep. She slept so well in her vast cavern of sleep, the sleep of the innocent. She was innocent, heroin made her innocent, it was the junk, the smack to blame. But she knew exactly how much a boy of five was worth. And to whom.

Ben began to wonder how he could live with her through the long months to guardianship. But this was part of a larger question: why she lived at all. Her body sucking oxygen, the blood cycling obediently through her veins. Nature culled the useless, but humanity was brimming with it.

When she first moved in, he'd hidden the bills. No one would get far with his credit card details, but junkies would steal anything, sell anything, even the screws you had the TV screwed to the wall with. He remembered his mother removing the light bulbs, the shower curtain, the sheets, and selling them to a tweeker who would sell them on to a different motel across town. Ben kept the bills in an envelope taped to the back of the fridge. He kept other papers here, the logging manifests, his gun licence. This was no guarantee she wouldn't find them. She might notice faint skid marks on the floor from where he'd moved the fridge. Junkies were cunning.

He was so deeply in debt, he was tens of thousands in debt, the repairs on the equipment, the cost of the new processor, the small-business taxes, the insurance, the property taxes, the hospital bills from five years back when the crummy lifter broke and a log cracked down on his head, serious concussion, ambulance, overnight in the hospital, high deductible, 15 grand owed. He added up all the years it would take him to pay off his debt if he continued to pay the minimum—297 years.

Carefully, he placed all the bills to his left and discarded the envelopes on the floor. Then he divided the bills into three piles. One pile had red letters or heavy block letters and always exclamations, words like FINAL and COLLECTION AGENCY softened by imploring notes, "If you need assistance please, please, please contact our customer service agents *please*." Then he added and subtracted, he moved one bill to another pile, like a shell game. Perhaps he could phone Visa once more, perhaps they would give him another month. Or he could reduce his pay-ment. Again. Thousands, thousands and thousands. He could not make the numbers stretch or shrink. Numbers were solid, like stones, pebbles, boulders. He was buried under the weight of them, a grave.

He wrote out the checks. He was particularly careful with the check for the feller buncher: he left out his signature. It had been a year since he last did that, so he could probably get away with it. If he was nice to Juanita or Susie in customer service—"Jeez, I'm so sorry, ma'am, I forgot to sign the check? What a dumb mistake"—he could get another two weeks without the late pen-alty, the 24.9 percent screw-you interest.

The light on the ceiling created a cocoon, softly spun around him. He could not see out into the night. He imagined Ed down the road sitting at his kitchen table, wondering how he would pay for a new baler. And all along the road, through town and across the country, kitchen table lights connected people like him, the bill payers, with their cups of coffee, their check books and calculators, the cold pits in their stomachs.

When he paid what he could pay, he carefully put stamps on the envelopes. Then he took the outstanding bills, tapped them into a neat stack, and put them back behind the fridge.

This next shipment would be his last, he knew that now. He couldn't trust Shevaunne or "undercover bitches." Things were shifting, Slim had warned him. He hadn't cared before. Prison might even be a relief to be stripped of all responsibility—three hots and a cot. For a moment Ben simply stood. Anxiety prick-led up his arms, swarmed across his face with special heat, then down through his chest, clamping around his groin so he felt his sphincter tighten.

He went into Jake's room. He sat on the side of the bed, watching the sleeping boy. Children reveal who we truly are, he thought. The best and the worst we are. They bring us home to ourselves. He lay down, curling his body around Jake, as if in a storm, he would take the brunt of it on his back.

We were driving across the South Sudanese border to Moyo, having heard that General Christmas was forming an alliance with the Sudanese People's Liberation Independence Front—or SPLIF, which was hilarious, except for the dead people, huts burned, girls (of course) raped. But by the time we got there, SPLIF and General Christmas had squabbled; he had sulked off back to the Congo. Sam and I were itching, having picked up fleas in a shepherd's hut.

Sam caught one and showed me: it was fat with blood, its abdomen the size of a pumpkin seed. I examined it. "How do you know it isn't a bed bug?"

"Bed bugs are fatter, rounder, with shorter legs. It's definitely a flea."

As we drove on, I began to feel them crawling all over me, at first assuming it was my paranoia. But then I glanced over at Sam, and two monster fleas crawled out of his shirt, up his neck. I pulled open my shirt and saw three meandering across my chest. "Son of a bitch! Stop!"

Sighting a deserted spot, Sam pulled over and we got out. We tore off our clothes, shaking them, slapping them against the ground. Within seconds, several dozen people had materialized from the bushes. I considered how we appeared to *them: two white people taking off their clothes and dancing around, possessed or deranged. Certainly, we were entertaining, for the crowd began to hoot and laugh, grown men bending over in fits, children howling and falling about. Sam released his inner stripper and shimmied for the crowd, pranced and gyrated, but when he approached his new fans to shake hands, they ran away screaming.*

"See what happens when you take your clothes off!"

"Ach, Kay, they're just jealous."

We got back in the car, which was still full of fleas. Within minutes, we were covered again. There was nothing we could do; the car was infested. At the next village, Sam bought a large bottle of the local gin and began rubbing it over himself. I grabbed the bottle and took a swig, arguing that if it couldn't prevent flea bites it could at least alleviate their effects. Six hours later we were in Juba.

Through his connections, Sam had upgraded us to the Hilton, a cathedral of marble and glass built on a former slum. We staggered into the gleaming lobby just after dusk, filthy and stinking of gin. A contingent of Chinese investors looked at us in alarm; the receptionist retained her tourism-school smile as she stretched her arm as far out as she could to hand us the key.

Sam turned to me, bewildered: "Is there something wrong with me, honey?"

"You're just a bit dirty, dear," I fussed him with my hand, dust lifting in a cloud around him.

We made the elevator, the doors shut, and we began scratching madly. Just as I had put my hand into my trousers to itch my crotch, the doors opened. A man was standing there. He was tall, Caucasian, carrying a digital camera. He calmly raised an eyebrow. "I'll take the next one." The doors shut gently.

Sam snickered, "Your future husband."

A shower when you are filthy, sweaty, and tired is better than the best sex. There is something deeply sensuous in getting clean, you attend to your body as a lover might discover you, a process of increasing focus. I stood under the stream of hot water, watching it turn brown as it swirled down the plug hole. The water soothed my skin. I lathered the fragrant hotel soap, behind my ears, between my toes and fingers, in my belly button. It took five minutes for the water to run clear, three shampooings to clean the dust from my hair, then I stood like a supplicant at the altar of hot, clean water. Drying myself, I discovered I was covered in flea bites; I counted more than a hundred on my abdomen, constellations over my thighs and buttocks. I looked like I had the pox.

Sam was already at the bar. He'd bought me a whiskey on the rocks. He was very merry. He admitted he'd counted several dozen bites on his ass.

"How do you see your own ass?"

"In the mirror. Angle the door mirror in and you get the reflection of your backside off the bathroom mirror."

"But why, Sam, why did you want to see your own ass?"

"It's better than the front view."

"Oooo. You sound like a woman, all self-critical."

"You ever heard of mirror balls?"

"Do I want to?"

"It's an affliction of middle-aged men. You can't see your balls anymore except in a mirror."

"I'm so glad I don't have balls."

"Me too."

We were giggling and drinking when my future husband walked in. Sam nudged me in an obvious way so that I spilled my drink, then hailed him over.

"Hey." Sam offered him the bar stool next to me. "Can we buy you a drink?"

The man laughed and took the seat. "I'm Michael," he said.

"And we're just colleagues," Sam pointed to me. "Not even friends. She's totally 100 percent available."

"My pimp," I smiled. "He takes 20 percent, just so we're clear."

Michael looked at me, and I realized he had not stopped looking at me since he'd entered the bar. I have since wondered if this is his trick, his shtick, how he makes all women feel special, how he makes Barb feel. He focused absolutely as if every movement I made fascinated him; it was an almost anthropological inspection. He studied my hands on the glass of whiskey, the pale freckles on my cheeks, the V at the base of my throat. It was weird and sexually thrilling.

After three hours of drinking and bar snacks, Michael and I left Sam chatting up an Ethiopian Airlines flight attendant. In Michael's room, he peeled off my clothes. With his fingertips he touched my flea bites, and then he leaned in, connecting them with his tongue. In the morning we said goodbye, good luck, we didn't trade emails or numbers. He was heading to Djibouti and me with Sam back to Nairobi. I did not think of him again.

Then, a year later, we bumped into each other in the arrivals hall in Lagos. He was with a crew on his way to film the Ogoni oil fields, I was covering the memorial of the execution of Ken Saro-Wiwa. We were familiar, we were like old lovers. We immediately went to my hotel room, to bed.

"I have a map of your body in my mind," he said.

"The flea bites? I looked like the London Underground."

"No." He laughed and put his face against my belly. "Your topography, valleys, hills, slopes."

I believed him, I still do. Whatever the lies and obfuscations of our marriage, we were true in that beginning. I never imagined that those plump hours of happiness and room service would have to last us for years and years. How we would one day scrape the bottom of the jar, scrape and scrape until love was just gone, the last of the strawberry jam.

He asked me to the wedding of friends in Paris. And I invited him to Lamu for New Year's Eve. How glamorous we were, how we grabbed the pendulum as it swung us lightly away from the slums and the war zones and the refugee camps, from the blood and the stinking latrines. We were journalists, we never stayed too long.

The rain slapped fussily on the windshield. Kay peered ahead, hunched behind the wheel, a little old lady trying to see. Logging trucks, milk trucks roared by, regardless. It was like being in a car wash, hit from all sides with tides of water. Kay clung on.

"Mum, do you still love Dad?" This from Freya in the back.

"What?" Kay said, though she'd heard.

"Dad. Do you still love him?"

"Freya, sweetie, I'm trying to drive."

"But it's a simple question, it's not algebra."

"Love isn't a thing that is or isn't."

"What does that mean?"

"It doesn't stop or begin," Kay attempted.

A silence. Then: "So you don't love him."

"That's not what I said."

"He loves you."

He does not, Kay thought. She caught Freya's eye in the rear-view mirror: "We love each other, we're married, it's just some-times—" Another truck sped past, its wake breaking in a wave over the windshield.

"You don't even sleep in the same bed."

"Frey—"

"Are you getting a divorce?"

"Jesus Christ! I am not having this conversation anymore."

"One-dollar fine!" Tom sang, shattering Kay's hope that he hadn't been listening.

At Kamp Wahoo, Tom ran through the rain into the building, forgetting to say goodbye, but Freya slipped her arms around Kay, kissed her cheek. "I love you, Mum." And the slightness of her arms, the scent of her, the crumb of toast caught on her lip: how Kay wanted to hold on, press tighter, pull her daughter back into her body. But that wasn't the point, the point was letting go before Freya pulled away, the point was timing the moment of release so she didn't cling to her daughter.

There.

Freya spun toward a group of girls sheltering under the porch; they turned to greet her. Freya made friends so easily.

At White's, she roamed the aisles, list in hand. She'd had to learn how to shop, how to cook. Before children, food had appeared or been acquired in finished form. On assignment, she'd eaten what she needed to achieve sufficient caloric intake, street food, snacks. If there had been no food, there were always cigarettes and Coca Cola. Or she had been staying in hotels with room service and buffets. When she and Michael had lived in Nairobi they'd had a cook, as well as the *ayah* for Freya, and Kay simply gave the cook the money, he did the shopping, he produced the fine meals.

Kay struggled to move beyond macaroni and cheese, and if she did, she was castigated by her children.

"Can I have my spaghetti without any sauce?"

"I don't really like chicken."

"Spinach kind of looks like snot."

In such moments, she felt the urge to take the perfectly good, nice, healthy, organic food that she'd ceded an hour of her life to making and shove it in their ungrateful mouths. *Don't you know about the Syrian refugees? The children of South Sudan?* It was an absurd idea that if her own children ate their food it made anything better for those ravaged people. She often ate the food herself, so obscene the sight of wasted food in the garbage.

Did other women feel like this about their children—the sharp rush of resentment? Did they covet such moments of righteousness? *Damn you, eat the food!* The carefully dressed mothers she saw at the school gates or at the camp drop-off under Phoebe's gimlet gaze, kissing their little ones goodbye: what did they hide, shameful as bulimics in the dark? Did they stand in a cellar, hammer in hand, staring at the back of their husbands' skulls?

Kay had never found a way to speak to them—really speak: the intimate language of coffee and a warm muffin, heads bent, attending. She felt too rough, too loud and unfashionable. What had worked for her as a journalist in Africa was clumsy, gauche in London. Who she had been before was like an old coat, hung by the door, out of season.

She decided to take the back way along Claremont Hill Road.

The rain obscured the view. She felt narrowed in, just the road, 20 feet ahead, herself in the capsule of the car. And because of the rain, she was driving slowly enough to see a pick-up parked on the side of the road, and a man looking under its hood. Poor bastard, broken down in the rain. She slowed even more, and was therefore able to distinguish the logo on the door of the pick-up: *COMEAU LOGGING*. She pulled over, wound down the window.

The rain spat in her face. "Can I give you a lift?"

He looked up at her, the rain dripping off his baseball cap. He was in a t-shirt and jeans. The muscles in his arms flexed as he moved. His eyelashes were thick as a girl's. He studied her car, bumper to bumper, as if it was unusual in some way. Then he came over to her, wading through the rain.

"Thank you, yes, you can," he said. She watched him jog around the car. But he didn't get in. "I don't want to get your car wet."

"I have children; you can't ruin it more than they already have." She reached over, pushed open the door. "Besides, it's a rental."

And he was there, filling the passenger seat, rain dripping off his hair. "I really appreciate this. There's a mechanic just up the road."

She put the car in gear, pulled out into the road.

He took off his hat, pushed back his dark, wet hair. "It's the connecting rod."

"That's something that connects things, right?"

He gave her a grin. "You're not from around here."

"London."

"Canada?"

She nearly laughed, but caught herself. "England."

"The Queen, tea at four?"

"Something like that."

"You're here on vacation?"

Their eyes held just for a moment. She turned back to the road, but she felt his gaze lingering.

"With my family," she said.

"You having a good time?"

"Great."

"Just up ahead."

She saw the sign, Mort's Auto Works.

She pulled in, stopped.

"I'm Ben," he extended his hand.

"Kay."

"Like *K*, an initial?"

"No. I'm not that cool. Three whole letters. *K-A-Y.*"

"Thank you for the lift, *K-A-Y*."

He started to get out of the car.

"Ben?"

He turned, perhaps a little too eagerly. And she asked, perhaps a little too eagerly.

"Ben, do you know Frank Wilson?"

He was expecting a different question. His face was still and she could see the effort of the stillness. "Frank Wilson?"

She smiled, perhaps a little flirtatious. "Yes, Frank Wilson."

He tilted his head. "Why are you asking about him?"

"We're renting his house."

Ben waited for more.

"The thing is, we're having a problem with this man trapping coyotes."

"Ammon," he said.

"Yes, apparently, Ammon. Do you know Ammon?"

"Yeah, I know Ammon."

The way he said this, she wished she could replay again and again, to better hear what the casual tone belied, the multiple chords within the words: what he was actually saying. *Yeah, I know Ammon.*

"I thought Frank might ask him to stop. Just while we're here."

"I'll talk to Ammon."

"I'd like to get in touch with Frank myself."

Ben swung his long legs out of the car. "And why do you think I know Frank?"

"Your number's stored on his home phone."

Ben held her look, bland, polite, incurious. "Is it?"

"And Frank?" Kay went on. "Is he at his cabin?"

Ben turned back around now, fully toward her. "His cabin?"

"Is he at his cabin?"

"I wouldn't know."

"Ben," she touched him now, her hand on his arm, she hadn't meant to. "Is he dangerous?"

"Ammon?"

"No. Frank. It's just, I don't know, maybe being in his house and not knowing him or where he is, he and Maria. Sorry. I'm not explaining myself."

He smiled, quick, confident. "I'll talk to Ammon about those traps."

He rose up out of the car. Kay watched him for a moment, he was impervious to the rain.

HE SAT IN THE CAB OF HIS TRUCK. THE RAIN refused to let up. He glanced out at the hay fields, whoever owned them had started to cut and now the hay was soaked on the ground. The landscape was pretty here, gently rolling, and the farms in good condition. Family money, he reckoned, or a savviness for state aid. Summer people liked this Vermont, this Maple Avenue, this Sugar Shack Lane and Daisy Meadow Way. He double-checked the address he had, he was nearly there, another quarter of a mile on the left.

Hadn't Frank disconnected the land line years ago?

This woman, this Kay, what did she want with Frank? "Is he dangerous?"

Ben thought about how he'd seen her on the road right there by his house, and now she just happened to be passing him in the rain. She asked about the cabin. He thought about her elegant wrists, the deep hollow at the base of her throat, because he'd seen that about her, too. She wanted something, all her questions. *Eyes on*, Slim had said.

He pulled his phone out, dialed, and Ammon answered.

"The traps at Frank's place," Ben began.

"Ya met her, then." Ammon snickered, almost as if he could detect the trace of lust in Ben's voice. His Doppler for human weakness tuned to the most sensitive frequencies. It was Ammon's special gift.

"Can you clear them out?"

"Why?"

"Just clear them."

Ammon didn't reply right away. Ben could hear him drinking, then a soft belch. "Ya tellin' me whatta do, Benny?"

Ben said nothing.

"I know about the kid, saw ya with him."

Even now Ammon cast a special kind of fear.

"Ya wanta be a dad now, Benny?"

Ben hung up. He felt like vomiting.

At the top of Silver Birch Lane, he reached the quaint summer cottage. He appraised the red cedar siding, 30 grand's worth, and the white painted gazebo, probably hand-crafted by some local *artisan*. Then he got out of the truck, stood for a moment so he was good and wet, before stepping onto the front porch. He took off his ball cap, held it in his hands. He found this attitude of humility effective. People associated good manners with honesty. He knocked on the door of Theodore Morse.

"Justa sec!" from inside, an older voice. Mr. Morse was old, which was good, and the barking of a big dog. Also good.

Dogs always liked him. All he had to do was remain absolutely calm because dogs were drawn to calmness. They scanned you with their noses, a 3-D hologram of smell, and they'd store this in their brains so you would always be familiar. Initially a friend, always a friend. Dogs don't make assumptions, but in the long run they're lousy judges of character.

The dog barked, desperate to get a whiff of the stranger at the door.

Soon the door opened a crack, a 70-ish man peered out, grasping the collar of a large pointer who leapt and snapped.

"Hello," said Ben. "I'm Ben Comeau."

"Sorry about T.J."

"I'm fine with dogs, I love dogs."

The man let T.J. go and T.J. made a bead for Ben, wildly sniffing his hands and jeans. "He's a beauty."

Purebred, Ben had already noted, an expensive breed. The dog was sitting now, pressing his head against Ben's thigh. Ben moved his hand very slightly onto the dog's head, just the smallest amount of pressure so the dog knew its boundaries. The man noted, "He likes you."

"My pa said I have a way."

Pa. My pa. The irony ladled on so thick, it almost became a joke. Sure enough, the man stuck out his hand. "Morse," he shook Ben's hand firmly—the cultivated handshake of a successful businessman. "Teddy Morse. My wife Evie, she's here somewhere. We just bought the place this spring."

Ben nodded. "I was sad about Old Mac."

Teddy Morse smiled, unsure.

"The previous owner," Ben clarified. "He'd been born in this house, got pneumonia, he's in The Pines now."

Instinctively, Teddy glanced at the grove of Scotch pines to the south of the drive. Ben laughed warmly, "Oh, ha, no, I mean The Pines in town, eldercare place. But looks like you've fixed this place up, very fine."

"Well, Ben?"

"Mr. Morse, I'm sorry to just show up like this, but I know you're summer people." He edged toward shyness, lowering his eyes often so Teddy Morse wouldn't know *summer people* marked him, how he and Frank had scoured town reports for owners with addresses in Boston or New York. "My family used to own the property next door, where the Wileys live now? A long time ago, 200 years, my family owned this piece, too. Sheep, in those days."

Teddy nodded.

"The reason I'm here is that I know your woods haven't been forested for a long time—20 years, in fact. Because my pa and I did the job back then. You've got a lot of deadwood and over-crowding that's affecting the health of the good trees. It's also a fire hazard, especially with summer predicted to be dry. Mac let the woods go, he couldn't keep up, especially after his son moved to Florida, and they're in bad shape."

"Oh," Teddy blinked. "We don't know much about woods. You'd better come in."

Ben stepped into the mud room. How nice it was, hooks and drawers, white paint and a contrasting trim of sky blue. He started to take off his boots. Golden manners, humility.

"Goodness, don't worry about that," Teddy urged him on. "Evie? Evie? Nice fellow here, Ben, local, wants to talk to us about our woods. Can you bring us out a pitcher of that sterling tea you make?"

And so it would go, Ben laying out the land for them, how he was personally connected to it. Sometimes he threw in intimate knowledge of a unique bear—"Ol' Clubfoot"—or the famous eight-point buck: "A lot of us have seen him, but he's smart; there's a reason he's lived so long." In some versions, the buck vanished and reappeared *as if by magic* directly behind the hunter, *no way* he could have moved that quickly, which begged the question whether he was even real or an Abenaki shaman's spirit. Other times, Ben would talk about logging the land with horses, and how this was "real" logging, and he'd bring his pair up here except one was lamed from a botched shoeing.

Regardless, the woods now owned by Teddy and Evie Morse or Betty and Sam Goldman or Zack and Mitch Bradley were in bad shape, they needed thinning, tending. In the old days, woods took care of themselves, but now—now, with invasive plants and the whole predator chain amok and climate change—*now* you had to take care of the woods. Curate was a word rich summer people loved. He wasn't logging, he was *curating.*

When the conversation came, gently, to the matter of price, Ben demurred. "I'd have to look at what's there. I couldn't just give you a number." He explained the complexity of which mills took which lumber and for what purpose and how some had closed down due to the economy and, first off, he'd have to determine the quality of the lumber. He'd always add, "It's personal for me, I've got to admit, I've loved these woods since I was a boy, and they once belonged to my family, so whatever I come up with, cost-wise, will be close to a net figure, just my expenses and a couple of six-packs for the boys."

And then, just to completely lull them into trust—these summer people, these soft-pawed city-folk, these *flatlanders* who loved their token locals, collected them as if they were a set— toothless old dairy farmer, buxom farmstand maid, rugged logger—Ben would add in Frank.

"I'll be working with Frank Wilson, the county forester. He'll oversee my work and make sure I'm complying with the forestry plan you've agreed upon with him. He's a great guy; he loves his trees." Ben would then smile, twinkly-eyed. "And sometimes we even argue because he won't allow me to cut something I want to cut. He'll always err on the side of conservation, while the logger in me'll see a tree as money."

Evie brought the tea, ice cold, lemony, delicious. She was beautiful, Ben noted, the kind of honest beauty women took on only in their fifties, when the game was done. Of course, Evie had money. Not many local women kept their looks: bad diet, lack of dentistry, addiction, and poverty made sure of that. He thought of Shevaunne and how she'd look in ten years, the lines around her lips puckered like a cat's asshole, her veins like old spaghetti. He thought of how she'd look if she had Evie's life.

He was watching Evie. He was murmuring how lovely—how *lovely* the tea was and what a *lovely* job they'd done with the house because he knew the effect of a rough-looking guy using feminine words. And he was noticing a duffle bag, packed and ready to go.

"Well," Teddy was smiling. "When do you want to begin?"

"That's up to you."

"We're just heading back to Boston now. We won't be back until—Evie, love, we're in the Vineyard next weekend, right?"

"And then we've got the Bentleys wedding in Ardsley. So not until that third weekend of July."

Ben turned thoughtful. "Frank's son, Frank wouldn't tell you this, but his son is special needs, so he's pretty strict about being home on the weekends. But..." Carefully, humbly, as if Frank's special-needs son weighed on his mind—that cruel, blind bad luck, the love and dedication required to parent such a child: "Would it be all right if we came up during the week? He could look around and just send you the report? Email, hardcopy, whichever works best for you."

Like a deer catching scent of the hunter, Teddy hesitated. Good. That moment of doubt would make his fall into trust that much more thorough. Ben sited his shot. "Or, I'm sure Frank could come up on a weekend and go over the report. If you could give him time to make arrangements for the boy. He has a sister who sometimes helps out."

A few years ago, when he and Frank had first got going on this scheme, Ben had laid on a story about Frank's wife needing dialysis. But he'd learned it was better to leave out anything too heavy-handed. People didn't like to feel guilty. It was better to hint at an honest, earthy family struggling together to make ends meet.

"No," Evie said. "It's fine. Don't bother him. We trust you." She smiled at him, an expensive, sexually neutral smile, as carefully constructed as the one he gave back to her.

"Thank you, ma'am. I think sooner would be better."

Evie was looking at his boots, worn from work, his strong hands. "Why don't you just start tomorrow?"

"If you're sure?"

"Then we won't have the noise when we're up here." Teddy was in now.

"There's some paperwork—"

"I'll get a pen," Evie wanted to be helpful, as was her nature.

By late afternoon, the rain had eased to a sniveling drizzle. In Kamp Wahoo's entrance, Freya stood by a pile of unclaimed towels, water bottles, and shoes, while Tom swung from the monkey bars in the playground, oblivious to the weather. Weren't the bars too slippery, thought Kay, would he fall? Her attention shifted closer in, back to Freya.

For a moment Freya regarded her mother with an almost haughty air, like a chauffeur, a low-level employee. Then she began to cry, her face scrunched up, her eyes averted. Kay reached out, but Freya shrugged her away, strode off to the car.

Over her shoulder Kay saw Phoebe Figgs looming. "We need to talk."

Tom threw his arms around her hips, almost throwing her off balance. "Mum! Do you know that caterpillars change their skin five times before they become cocoons?"

Kay leaned in, kissed her son. "No, I didn't know."

"Their skins don't stretch like ours, so they have to get rid of them like a snake. It's called an instar, right, Mrs. Figgs? After five instars they become cocoons and they turn into goo, just total goo, and then the goo becomes a butterfly. Isn't that so cool?"

"Yes, love, that's amazing, isn't it. Run along to the car. I'll be right there."

As Tom sprinted to the car, Phoebe handed Kay a business card. "After seven is best."

On the way home, both children fell asleep. Kay regarded them in the rear-view mirror. Tom looked more like his father. He would have the same narrow nose and unruly hair, the same length of bones; and Freya resembled her, sufficiently pretty, with Kay's eyes, almond-shaped, shades of green and blue and gold, traceable through several generations of family photographs.

Just as she slowed to turn into her driveway, Ammon's pick-up burned past her and out into the road. Without hesitating, she stopped, jammed the car into a three-point turn, pulled out into the road to follow him. In the back, Tom and Freya remained fast asleep, drugged by Doritos and chlorine.

Ammon must have seen her in his rear-view mirror, yet he made no effort to evade her. After several miles on the mountain road, he turned left onto a side road, and after another mile through hay fields, veered right down a wooded track. Here, Kay had to drive slowly, the low-slung undercarriage of her rental car jarring and grinding against the potholes.

After several hundred meters, the track opened into a small yard. Ammon's old truck complemented the rest of the rusting, decaying junk: long-defunct snow mobiles, a log splitter, aluminum livestock troughs, haphazard piles of wood, steel, plastic. There were also two constructions, like gallows, slung with chains that Kay guessed were for hanging dead animals—deer, bear, coyotes; and not far, a steel cable slung between two trees for the drying coyote skins.

A farm house reared out of this debris—more concept than form, as if the wind had spun around one day and thrown bits of plywood and old, broken windows together. A blue tarp comprised the roof; the siding was gone along the north exterior wall.

The door was open.

In the back of the car, Tom and Freya slumbered on. Kay got out, picked her way across the grass and up the rickety steps. There was an animal stench coming from the occluded interior. She entered.

"Ammon?"

In a dim corner, an enormous mound moved and grunted. "Mind 'im," Ammon said and dipped an empty coffee tin into an open bag of cat food by his chair and chucked it in that direction.

It was a pig. Bloated, vast, and tusked, the pig shuffled toward the scatter of cat food. "He can move faster than ya think if ya piss him off," Ammon warned as he opened himself a beer and leaned back. His chair was a recliner covered in a hide-all-sins brown corduroy. Kay noticed the dainty chintz print of the sofa and scanned the room for a sense of Ammon's history. Who, for instance, might have been responsible for the chintz? Every surface and inch of the floor was obscured by an accretion of litter, including—from the smell—pig shit; so opposite to the Wilsons, that it almost became the same thing: a purposeful obliteration of anything personal. She wondered, now, if this said something about Ammon himself: that his scruffy varmint was not default, but a careful obfuscation.

She also wondered about the pig. *SQUEAL SQUEAL.*

Ammon lifted his beer to her. "I got the traps."

"Thank you."

"So ya can piss off."

"I want to know about 'The Owners.' About Frank."

Ammon's blue eyes glittered. "Frank?"

Kay knew she was here only because he'd let her follow him; he wanted to talk, he had something to say. So she kept going. "About his family. Where are they?"

"Ya nosey, hey."

She took a $50 bill out of her wallet. It worked with customs agents and soldiers in Africa, why not with Ammon? For a long moment, he stared at the money, almost disbelieving. Then he leaned forward and grabbed it, slipped it into his shirt pocket.

"Frank's wife was a wetback. Had enough and took the kids back to where she came from. Build a wall, I say."

"Had enough of what?"

The pig grunted, shuddered, and Frank pelted it with another round of cat food. "Frank's a leaker."

"What's a 'leaker'?"

"Had some weakness in his structure. Leaker, leaky boat. His father was a mean fucker."

Kay tilted forward, flattering him with her attention.

"State took him away, gave him back, took him away. Back an' forth. Could say that made it worse."

"You know Frank well, then?"

"Well enough."

She watched him, he watched her, both trying to see in.

"And the house, that's the house he grew up in?"

Ammon nodded. "Back since his mother's family had it for Christmas trees, 1940s, thereabouts."

"The Québécois?"

"That'd be them."

"She had a cabin, too, his mother. Do you know where that is exactly?

"Ya investigatin' Frank, then?"

"Just trying to find him."

The pig snuffled while Ammon ruminated his answer. Kay wondered who decided that pigs go "oink." Perhaps dainty pink pigs did. This one spoke from deep inside; it would roar if it could. It regarded Kay with tiny, bright eyes, pin-pricks of reflective light in the dark cavity of its corner. The writer in her considered the pig must be a metaphor, but for what she was not yet sure.

"That boyfriend of yours. Ask him."

"What boyfriend?"

"Oh ya had him runnin' to whine to me pretty quick."

"Ben?"

"Mum!" A panicked wail set upon the air. Ammon raised his beer to her as she turned out the door.

Tom was standing by the car, tears streaming down his face, Freya's arms around him in comfort. Seeing Kay, he rushed to her, simultaneously hitting her and hugging her. "Where were you where were you?" He was breathless, sobbing with genuine terror at the coyote skins, the chains, the animal gallows. "I woke up and you weren't there, I was shouting for you and you didn't answer, where were you where are we where are we what is this place?"

Freya was quiet and compliant for the evening, kind to Tom, reading him a story and helping him with a jigsaw puzzle. As a reward, Kay let them watch a heart-warming movie she'd saved on her laptop about a rescue dog and a little girl who'd lost a leg in a car accident. As soon as the opening credits began to roll, Freya and Tom leaned in, open-mouthed, beguiled. They'd been without TV for two weeks.

She kissed their heads and took the phone to the upstairs bathroom.

Phoebe answered after the first ring.

"Phoebe, hi, it's Kay Ward, Freya's mom."

"Oh, Kay, yes, thanks for calling. How is Freya?"

"She's fine, a bit quiet."

Freya had hit another child in the head with a full juice bottle. Phoebe hastened to add that the child wasn't hurt—it was just a juice bottle, but she was concerned about "the tenor and intention of the attack."

Kay took a breath, answered carefully. "I'm not excusing her behavior, but was there any provocation?"

"The other child can be challenging, and it's likely she said something to Freya. But Freya hit her really hard. I think she would have kept on hitting this other girl if one of the counsellors hadn't intervened."

Oh, Freya.

Kay looked out through the window at the gauzy green evening. "Maybe there's some adjustment issues. It's so different here to London."

"Sure, I can imagine."

"What do you want me to do? Should I withdraw Freya?"

"No, no, that's not necessary. I think she was a bit shocked herself. However, if there's an escalation, we'll have to revisit the issue."

Even before Kay hung up she was aware of Freya on the stairs, about halfway up. She could just see her shadow, and how it hovered, well in earshot, then stepped carefully back down three stairs. Kay put the phone away, flushed the toilet and washed her hands. As she came out of the bathroom, Freya was making a show of trotting up the stairs.

"Oh, hey, Mum, Tom has a piece of popcorn stuck up his nose."

Kay regarded her daughter's innocent face, seeing both the innocence she feigned and the innocence that was real.

"Does he? Silly boy. Let's get it out then."

SHEVAUNNE SPRAWLED ON THE SOFA, KICKING
back a 24-ounce mug of Dunkin' Donuts pumpkin spice iced
coffee. Jake's face was about two feet from the TV screen, angry
people shouting at each other, the swear words bleeped out, so
their argument was just a series of bleeps, incomprehensible.
Ben walked over.

"Don't you dare," Shevaunne shrieked. "Don't you fuckin'
dare."

He turned it off. "Where'd you get the coffee?"

She threw it at him, hitting him square in his chest, the cold,
sticky, stinking liquid splattering his face and arms. He stepped
toward her, but she was already up, off the sofa, moving with
speed and urgency.

"I'll call the cops," she was yelling. "Jake, call the cops,
Mommy's in trouble. 911, baby, 911."

Ben watched her scrambling toward the door, her pink jeg-
gings and fuzzy slippers, despite the heat, and he watched Jake,
eyes shifting from him to her, and back again. Not a question
of love or loyalty, merely a calculation. Whom did he fear less?

And he chose his mother, he ducked and ran to her and clung
to her thigh. Because deep down and against all experience, he
still believed there was a lever in her soul, and if he pulled it
enough times she'd love him back, she'd protect him, her most

basic duty. He was like one of those tragic little monkeys in an animal experiment that keeps pressing the red button for the nuts even though it gets a shock instead.

"Don't hurt me! Don't hurt my baby!" Shevaunne cowered, and Ben saw that she believed her own drama, she infected the boy with it. Even though Ben had never, never, ever hit or tried to hit. But he was a man—Jake had known Shevaunne's other men.

"Goddammit, Shevaunne. I'm not going to touch you." He kept his voice low, he barely moved, he tried so hard not to be frightening.

But Shevaunne sank to the floor sobbing, wrapping her arms around Jake. "Jake, Jake, my baby, my boy, don't worry, Momma's gonna make it okay, Momma's gonna make it all better."

And Ben remembered the sour smell of his own mother, her unwashed hair and body, she was lying on the bathroom floor, arms flaying like a beached octopus, "Benben, I love you my little Benben." He felt acid swirl in his stomach and scorch up his esophagus into his mouth, and he thought: this is what I taste like, inside.

He forced himself to look away, out the window, the last light gleaming through the birches, flickering, diffusing. He could see Ed's hay fields, unmown, the timothy about to go to seed. He wondered if Ed was having trouble with the baler again, and should go and help him fix it, and he drank in this thought to slow him down. The baler, the hay, the baler, the hay.

Shevaunne was whimpering, weeping, mascara dripping down her face so she looked like a sad clown, and he saw that Jake had crapped himself. "I'm not going to hurt you, Jake, or your mother. Ever." But he thought he might; he felt the capacity. So he stepped past them, out the door.

The evening was warm and soft, the light gone creamy. He should go back in and help Jake into a clean pair of pants. But what if he could never make it better for Jake? What if the scared boy grew into a scared man? The many ways fear twisted you, mutilated, amputated. Ben got into his truck.

As he pulled out he heard Shevaunne calling after him, a plaintive wail—"Ben! Ben!"—that morphed into, "Fuck you, asshole!"

He turned on the radio. He turned it off. He was thinking, where'd she get the coffee, who brought it to her, who's been in my house, or did she go somewhere when I was out? Because all of these options were bad, all of these options took her away from his control. He felt his perimeter fraying. He'd been so careful, so closely held in. So *clenched*. He stepped on the gas, the tires ripping up the dirt. He wanted to burn down his house, burn them both and then he would be clean; they wouldn't exist anymore and he'd no longer have to try.

Buying a six-pack of Bud at the Gas n' Go, he was nicely buzzed by the time he reached Island Pond. Few things in life are better than drinking and driving on a summer evening. He drove on north and east, the land flatter, wetter, so it seemed altogether another country. Different trees, different way the road moved across the earth, as if this were Canada already. The sky, for lack of bordering hills, arched into a high bowl, and he could see the sunset in all dimensions: the red and orange glow in his rear-view mirror, inky dark seeping up in the east. A scattering of early stars winked down.

He remembered Slim's little bonus from months ago, and had a hankering. He pulled over. He'd stuck it in a groove behind the ashtray—not failsafe, and he'd been careless to leave it there so long. All the better, therefore, to get rid of it now. He stuck his finger into the baggie and rubbed the white powder on his gums. Good coke, that's for sure. "Dessert," Slim called it, what junkies with extra cash took to top off their high. "Would you like dessert?"

Scrounging around the seat and, finding a plastic spoon from an ice cream he'd bought Jake, Ben tipped the coke into the spoon and sniffed. His brain lit up with Christmas lights, pretty, bright colors, some flashing. Better, sharper. He did another snort, then resealed the bag, took a long sip of his beer, and drove on.

Out here, there were no road signs. Either they'd been stolen by bored kids or there had never been any. No one complained, because locals knew the way, and if you weren't local and you didn't know the way, you shouldn't be out here. He was going slowly on account of moose and deer and his being increasingly wasted. But it felt good, his bones soft inside the casing of his body, almost as if he was blurring with the cool air coming in the window.

There were headlights in his rear-view mirror. He'd noticed them miles back, but he now realized they were still there, neither turning off nor speeding up. Going the same speed, on the same lonely road. Briefly, Ben imagined another man out for a drink and a drive. Then he imagined the man in the Subaru: his face was different now, not attending liberal talk-show chat— *That's an interesting question, Terry*—but intent as a predator. Kay, instead of the dog, sat in the seat beside him, a badge of some kind where she should have a heart. *Do you know Frank Wilson? Where is Frank? Is he at the cabin?* And so she was out here trying to find the cabin.

Abruptly, he veered off the road, a rough logging track, and cut the lights. He was sweating, regretting the coke, and now thinking how he needed to get rid of the rest of it. If he threw it out the window, they might easily find it, a little baggie smeared with this fingerprints and DNA. He certainly couldn't be caught with it in the truck. He stuffed it deep inside a beer can, and tossed that out, no one would give a roadside beer can a second thought. Then he hunched down, eyes on the side mirror. Moments later, the car cruised past. He couldn't determine the make, it was too dark, but the driver was in no hurry.

Ben waited for an hour to see if the car would come back. He drank the rest of the beer, the coke losing its edge to a meaner beer buzz. At last, he started the engine again, backed out onto the road. He was feeling more confident now. Even if Kay and Subaru Man found the cabin—even if, through the maze of tracks—they would not find Frank.

But no one was following him. No car from the darkness lurched out.

The darkness enfolded him, velvety and kind, and he drove by instinct, one road to the next, each one a narrower, rougher capillary, until he was on a grass track. And then the wide, black lake stopped him, almost a surprise.

When he got out of the truck, he swayed and righted himself. He could still hear the engine rumbling in his ears, but as it faded out, the insistence of peepers and woodcock faded in. It was cool here, chilly, and he should have brought a sweatshirt. He rubbed his arms and walked to the lake's edge, smooth and still and inky black.

"Hey, Ben."

Ben turned toward the voice in a kind of ecstasy, and in the moment of turning, he knew no one was there, Frank was not there, Frank was not there with the kerosene lamp and some hot dogs for the grill. Frank, like an old woman, chiding, "Ben, don't put the spoons in with the knives!" Frank, wiping the faucet with a cloth so that it shone like new, Frank admiring all they had created with scavenged wood and stolen time, a couch found on the roadside. They had been friends for so long, so deeply and intently, there was hardly a time before Frank.

The cabin was dark, sealed up; inside, the pans and plates, the cutlery and cups neatly put away as Frank always left it.

"Frank?"

Ben spoke the name aloud, absurdly, for he already knew Frank would not answer. Ben was hearing things, he was speaking things that were no longer. Those summers were gone, the boys they had been here amid the hills, the thickets and brambles, the silver lake smooth as mercury, the mornings they swam into, laughing, prevailing. They'd believed that even Ammon couldn't take it away from them.

He shut his eyes, and, tilting on his axis from too much beer, steadied himself against the truck. Was it better with his eyes closed or open? The squealing pigs, high-pitched, were moving about in an unnatural way.

"Frank." No question now but a sob through his teeth. And the glorious summer night abloom with stars that doubled on the black water, and underneath trout and pike nosed among the drifting weeds.

S he got out of bed, she could not sleep. She made for the
bathroom, flipped on the light. The light was too bright,
the walls too white. Were the Wilson boys afraid of the
dark? Was that why Frank painted everything white—an anti-
dote to the dark? The cans in the basement, the bootie was for
painting, Frank and Maria put booties on to protect their shoes
from the paint, and having painted their house they had gone to
Alaska. Camping. Or Maria had taken her sons back to Mexico.

Was it Frank who feared the dark? He was a leaker, he'd been
taken away from his parents, who could imagine why. Fear of
the dark is the first fear, never quite relinquished. She remembered Freya, all her terror of dark rooms, dark spaces. "There's
nothing there, there's nothing there, sweetie," Kay would say,
Michael would say, turning out the light. But Freya was sure of
what the dark contained, and how the boogeyman folded up like
a lawn chair when you turned on the light. You could not see
him, but he was there.

Perhaps Maria could not sleep, Maria running a bath in the
middle of the night, Maria staring at her face in the mirror,
nowhere to hide in the blast of 100 watts. Look at yourself, who
you are, what you've become for your husband, your children.
Maria, alone on the hill with her boys and Frank. "Hard in the

winter," Alice had said, the house bound in by walls of snow, too deep for the plow, this foreign, cold Yankee country.

When Tom had been a baby and they'd had to move to London and Tom did not sleep and so neither did Kay, she had learned about night; not the place you sleep or dream, not the place you leave, but the one you come to, wide awake at 2 a.m.

As long as Kay had walked, Tom would not cry, so she paced, hour upon slow dripping hour, she walked miles inside the room of night, across deserts, the Arctic ice, all the places she could no longer go. Tears leaked out of her like the milk Tom refused to drink, night's windows reflecting back to her the hunched, grey-faced woman holding a mewling baby. No one was watching, so no one could see the hunger of the baby; sometimes Kay felt Tom's tongue slip out of his mouth and into hers, seeking the interior of her, to suck her out like a raw egg. "You chose this," she heard herself mumbling. "You chose this, chose this, chose this."

Even after Tom began to sleep, Kay didn't. Three, four hours a couple of times a week, sometimes three days passed without sleep. In the daylight, Kay drifted, blurred, uncertain. When she spoke she had to listen carefully to make sure the voice was outside of her, not merely in her head.

But at night, she sharpened like a cat. Her heart picked up beats, rattling like a castanet. At night, she could see everything, even what wasn't there, hand-prints on mirrors, how sound rippled the air like water. If she shut her eyes, her heart jolted her with a sharp current; she must remain vigilant.

And she had sweated, a sour, acrid smell almost like fear; she smelled even during the day, she couldn't wash it off. She shuffled around the supermarket, smelling herself. Her eyes, contracted in their sockets like shy fish, ached. In the mirror, she looked over-medicated or under-medicated. People stepped away from her.

Until Sam—not Michael, not her own husband, father of her

children—came to say hello, to bring the children toys. He took one look at Kay—"Mary Mother of God, Kay, you look like an aborted baby left out in the rain"—handed over a bottle of Valium and commanded, "Sleep!" And she slept.

It had been a long time since she'd woken like this, eyes peeling wide, in the middle of the night.

She locked the bathroom door, clambered up onto the toilet. She waved her phone like a wand to catch the magic airwave. Two bars. She logged on to Google, began a deeper search for *Benjamin Comeau Vermont*. Scrolling down from the Chamber of Commerce listing, she skimmed over a few random entries with the names Comeau, an antiques dealer, a car dealer, Facebook pages, to a post: STATE V BENJAMIN L COMEAU.

CASES HEARD BY JUDGE THOMAS A. MURRAY
DATE/TIME/PLACE
WEDNESDAY, APRIL 4
8:30AM
COURTROOM 1

STATE VRS COMEAU BENJAMIN
203-4-16 CRIMINAL
PLAINTIFF, STATE (PAUL J. STEINER)
DEFENDANT, BENJAMIN L. COMEAU

Criminal could mean anything from murder to trespass. So she created an account with BeenVerified, paid the 20 bucks with Paypal, and within minutes had a full report. There was a bank lien on his house, a finance company lien on his logging equipment, and a scattering of lawsuits over the years—though none, apart from the one brought by Paul Steiner, had gone to court. It was currently under appeal.

She wrote *Paul Steiner* in her notebook. *Frank, Maria Wilson, Ben Comeau.*

"What are you writing?" Michael would ask, if he had walked in, seen her scribbling in this corner, this midnight. "What are you writing?" he'd asked in London, almost surprised that she wasn't folding laundry or unpacking groceries. No longer wars or coups but a piece for *Parenting* magazine about the pressure mothers feel to breastfeed or an interview with an organic egg baron for the business supplement of a fading broadsheet. "Interesting?" Michael would ask a few tepid questions, as if he'd read somewhere—some paint-by-numbers marriage manual—how to attend a wife whose career was now a hobby.

Ammon, she wrote.

Ammon, simply Ammon.

"Whose house was that?" Freya had wanted to know as they'd driven away from Ammon's.

"A local man."

"It's creepy."

Tom had quieted his sobs: "Were those dead dogs, Mum."

"No. They were coyotes."

"Did he kill them?"

"Probably."

"Why?"

"Some people like killing wild animals."

"Why?"

"The fur, they can sell the fur."

"But you said they like killing them." Freya paid attention.

"Maybe they don't like or not like. They just don't mind. I think it's different for some people, killing things."

"Like bunnies."

"Yes, Frey. That's a good point."

"How does he kill them?"

She didn't answer, and Tom thought she hadn't heard.

"Mum, how does he kill them?"

"Traps. He sets traps and the coyotes get stuck in the traps."

"And the trap kills them?"

Kay had taken a breath. What was she supposed to say? Should she withhold the truth? Is Santa real? The meat we eat, the clothes we wear, the forests we annihilate, the atrocities we commit every day just by breathing, the traps, the hammers, the bunnies. "No, love. They get caught in the trap, their legs get caught and they can't get away and he shoots them."

"How do the traps caught their legs?"

"Tom, my love," she had said. "I can't answer these questions anymore."

"But—"

Freya had put her hand on her brother's shoulder, and this quieted him. In silence, they'd driven back down Ammon's rough track, onto the road, and she'd chided herself for taking them there in the first place. She knew Ammon had a gun, people used their guns here.

She went downstairs and locked the door.

The land was wild, rough, torn, inhabited by people and their livestock who lived somehow. Eking, I thought at the time. What the word was made for: hungry little birds searching for grass seeds on the rocky soil. Michael and I had been meaning to come to this part of the country for months, but he had been trapped by his work, and me by mine, our many important commitments. And when we finally packed the car, it was as if we were eloping or playing truant from school. We laughed and opened a bottle of champagne when we reached the outer limits of Addis, and he made a triumphant show of turning off his cell phone.

For hours, shabby subsistence farms marred the land-scape, there were people everywhere, walking in columns along the road. Unless you've been to Africa, it's impossible to understand how many people there are, how many chil-dren—impossible to even begin to comprehend the scale of a billion people, six billion people, nine billion. Not dollars, not grains of sand, but individuals inhaling, exhaling, eating, shitting, hoping, eking.

Children defecated in the open, and everywhere was open. There were no trees except for the small groves of mercenary eucalyptus, all that was left, all that hadn't been hacked down and burned on cookstoves. The eucalyptus survive because their roots are so deep and so aggressive that they suck up moisture for up to 50 yards in any direction. Eucalyptus trees make it impossible for anything else to grow. Eucalyptus trees are an indication that it's already too late, the land is fucked.

Further out, five, six hours, the farms ceased, the land was too dry, too rocky even for the most optimistic or desperate farmer, and we had at last the feeling of space and sky—the Africa we were looking for. Arid, harsh, inviolable: where wild things lived by design and not default. We felt happy, then, the windows open, the dust and the heat, sipping from our bottles of water. We couldn't chat because of the loud rumble of the car's engine and the rough road. Michael looked at me, I smiled. We didn't need to speak.

We drove until late afternoon, and turned off into the bush, several hundred yards. We had imagined camping quietly underneath the acacia trees. We had imagined cocktails and stars, still dawns, trembling with the call of a mourning dove. Cooking breakfast on our little camp stove. We had expectations of solitude and nature. But then, but then—the people arrived. Always. The children, in particular, appeared within moments of our stopping, and they could not be persuaded to leave. They stood staring and tittering. When I squatted behind a bush to pee, they followed. After cutting up kindling, Michael left his machete against the trunk of a tree; a moment later it was gone. At nightfall, the crowd dispersed, only to reform just after dawn—a curtain of black faces in ragged clothing that blocked us from any view. We had to retreat to our tent to eat. We had to lock our car, peevish that the Out of Africa *fantasy to which we felt entitled was so rudely, thoroughly interrupted. And it was their fault, these ragged, TV-less people.*

As we drove further south into the Omo River Valley, the land became even drier and more desolate. Now, with regularity, spindly goatherds threw pebbles at our car. This began to enrage Michael. We crossed a shallow river bed that must have run fiercely in the rains but was now a remnant trickle. A boy threw a stone that hit the windshield, making a small pit in the glass. Michael slammed on the brakes and bounded out, up the river. The boy ran, nimble with fear, and scrambled up the steep river bank. From his perch, he began to laugh at Michael. Michael stopped exactly where the boy had been standing. There was a large plastic container half-full of water that the boy had been filling. Michael took out his pocket-knife and stabbed it repeatedly. After he had rendered it useless, he came back to the car. "They have to learn," he said.

I watched the boy in the rear-view mirror, emerging from the bush to examine his ruined container. It was most likely the only one his family had, the sole means of collecting water—it was an object of immeasurable value destroyed by a white man in a fit of pique.

Michael hadn't murdered or tortured. But the act was brutal. It told me something about him that I didn't want to know. The cruelty was so finely crafted.

For days I was distraught. We drove on, camping, hiking. But I could barely look at my husband, he disgusted me now; I slept with my back to him. Our marriage had been spur-of-the-moment, a lark, when we were on Lamu for New Year's Eve, and less than four months later I was considering divorce.

"Over a kid's bucket?" He was incredulous.

"Because that's all you see it is."

I left him.

But, but—I was pregnant, you see.

An accident, a broken condom. Michael sat with me for the ultrasound at the clinic in Nairobi. I assumed we'd agreed on abortion, and we saw the kidney bean inside my womb with its sprouting fetal pole, its tadpole heart. It meant nothing to me, that blurred echo from within. But Michael—Michael wept, he begged, so I leaned forward to love him, to agree to the pact of parenthood. Soon the baby who would be Freya made me vomit and abstain from hard liquor and soft cheese and war zones.

But—

What if I wasn't pregnant?

Not for another year, and I've changed the dates, a white lie to make myself look more honorable, and what if I admit that I forgot all about the boy. And what happened was this: Michael and I drove on, I glanced back at the boy, he was soon erased by the dust, just another poor African child, a prop, an extra in a grand set of Africa. *What if I felt merely a momentary disgust with Michael, a flash of concern that he wasn't who he seemed, he was a selfish asshole. What if I didn't care, really, that he was a selfish asshole, selfishness having value in our white lives; everything we did was selfish so who could call it selfishness, it was merely normal.*

We drove on—didn't we?—and the boy was erased by the dust, and in camp that night Michael and I made love, what love felt like then, burrowing into the other person, the exclusion of the entire world, and I never thought about the boy again.

Kay dried her hands. As she turned she had the sensation of Maria turning with her; she was two people, the way she turned and took the dish cloth and hung it over the rung along the stove door, smoothing the wrinkles. Any woman could do this, every woman did, the ritual choreography of the dish cloth. And then Maria would pause and regard the sunny, clean kitchen, how it was ready for the day: a sense of pride at the order of things. She understood that routine was an anchor, routine was putting one foot steadily in front of the other and not running or fleeing or dispersing.

At some point, in the winter, Maria became afraid, fear at first appearing like a mouse, shyly. The long, deep days, the strange light of the snow, and she began cooking extravagantly—complex dishes with marinades, requiring detailed preparation. Ingredients were difficult to source. She was able to get achiote from the Mexican restaurant; the produce manager at White's Supermarket obtained pablano chiles for her. She peeled and stirred and chopped, she baked and sautéed as Frank began to remove items from the house. At first, just old books, drawers of junk, she hardly noticed. One day she came home and all the pictures had been taken from the walls. One morning, she woke up and he was piling her summer clothes into the back of the pick-up. She watched him drive away, the bright bouquet of fabric lifting and subsiding as he hit hardened drifts of snow.

"Kay?"

She turned again, a slow pirouette.

"Sorry. I knocked. The door was open."

Even when Frank took the boys' skates and coats, their toys and games, Maria stayed because she believed it was an affliction of the winter, a passing season. She chased the fear back through its little hole, back into the walls. But then, he bought the white paint, not painting. Erasing.

At last Kay's eyes focused in on Ben. He was speaking to her. "Is everything all right?"

"I was—" she made a small sound that was supposed to be a laugh. It took her a moment. "I was not expecting anyone."

Ben stood in the doorway, his cap in his hands. She hadn't realized how tall he was. "I wanted to check that Ammon got those traps."

"He did. Thank you."

"Okay, then, well, good, problem solved." Ben put on his cap. "I'll see you around." He took a step back toward the door, she took one forward.

"Wait. Ben. Let me get you a coffee."

"Thanks but I have to be going."

"You know this house." The words sprang out of her.

He paused. "Yeah, I know this house." And bent down to pick up one of Freya's hair clips from the floor. He passed it to Kay, pressing it into her hand as if it had value.

"Maria liked to cook."

"Did she?"

"What's going on here, Ben?"

Ben crooked his head, as if he might see her better from a different angle. "What is it, exactly, that you're after?"

"Where are they?"

"I don't know."

"You do."

He took a moment. "But who are you that I should tell you?" His words were Michael's, were Sam's, a hard masculine backwall against which she might hurl her hysterical self. Ben went on, "I don't know you. You're not from here. You start asking questions about people, and those questions have implications, you have some kind of agenda, and I have to wonder, what could it be."

"Concern."

"About people you've never met?"

"Aren't you concerned about them?"

He turned away for a moment, looking around the kitchen with the same attention he'd given her car. "You alone up here?"

She looked at him. The question was loaded with menace or it was entirely innocuous. Ben was unreadable. "Yeah," she said. "My husband's away."

"You're a city person, then."

"It's not that. I'm not scared because I don't know how to milk a cow or whatever it is I need to prove my toughness here. I'm not scared." Her arms were folded tight across her chest, so she unfolded them to make the point. "I've been a journalist for years, in all kinds of hairy places, and I know something is wrong."

There was no recrimination in his voice, just a calm negation: "Frank and Maria—their lives are none of your business. You're renting their house, that's all."

Briefly, he tipped his fingers to his cap, "Enjoy your vacation." He smiled. Beguiling as a woman, Kay thought. For she felt the smile, where he'd aimed it, way down low.

She listened to the sound of his truck fade. She could hear it for a long time, clanking along the drive, then down the hill, around the bend. Odd how sound didn't work the other way: you couldn't, so easily, hear people approaching the house.

WHEN HE HAD FIRST TAKEN A JOB LOGGING
with Ammon in Victory, Ben had watched in amazement as the
machines pawed and bowed and laid waste to the forest with
scrupulous objectivity. The machines did not wince, they were
the mindless servants of the men who drove them. And most of
them were numbed with booze or amphetamine. The noise was
incredible—the whine of the blades, the rumble of the engines,
the crashing of trees. He'd seen a crow fly out from the trees
and alight on a pine, its beak open in terror and confusion. Wild
animals are so quiet, Ben had thought, they live their entire lives
as silently as possible.

Then Ammon threw a can of beer at him, shouted above the
din, "What am I payin' ya for, shitstain?"

Ammon pointed out that the foster system would abandon
him at 18: "Who else is gonna employ a high school drop-out
for 15 bucks an hour."

Back then, Ben thought he'd do it for a couple of years. The
money was okay, better than stocking shelves at White's or working the till at the Gas n' Go. So he learned to work the skidder
and the grabber, he learned the names of every tree, he learned
the mills, which mill took what lumber, and who paid the best.
He learned to seek out the suckers by reading the annual town
reports. Out-of-state addresses meant second-, third-home folks

who weren't around to check up on you. Those delinquent on taxes could easily be convinced to seek relief through Land Use Compliance.

Divorces, noted in the courthouse records, meant financial hardship for whichever spouse still held the land. Divorces had been Ammon's particular forte.

Once, he took Ben on a cold call to the house of a woman newly divorced. "Good thing yer skin's clearing up," Ammon had noted. "Ya scared people." Ben had seen Ammon smile to himself as he noticed the overgrown lawn, the four cords of wood unstacked in the drive. He'd knocked on the door, took off his hat, held it in his hands. Ben followed his lead. "Golden manners, humility."

Margot was a pretty woman in her early 40s, slim, delicately boned, bare foot. She was wearing a sundress that hinted at her figure, tightening against her hip bones when she turned. She looked tired. Ben didn't know much about what women did with their hair but he liked how she held hers carelessly up from her neck by a single silver clip. He stared at her neck. She smiled at them uncertainly.

"Hello there, ma'am. I'm Ammon and this is my nephew, Ben. We own a local logging operation."

Ben sensed a special emphasis on the words *my nephew*. He knew better than to contest.

Margot brushed a strand of her fading hair back from her face. "I don't need any logging."

"Ma'am, if you'll give me a moment of your time?"

She acquiesced with a fluttering gesture.

"I know this property. Used to hunt here when I was a kiddo." Ammon smiled, and smiling he could be handsome. "And I know yer woods. And ya've got overcrowding which'll lead to diseases such as Dutch elm, encourage pests like the gypsy moth, and could be a real source of fire danger."

And so she invited them in.

Ammon solemnly explained the distressing state of her trees. He showed her a piece of mildewed bark—Ben had no idea where it had come from, but Ammon crumbled it in his fingers and hoped it wasn't already too late. He offered to help with her wood pile. "The boy and I'll do it before we go. Won't take us but ten minutes. He's strong and good with his hands."

"No, no," she demurred. "I can do it."

She was planning to put the property on the market; there was no way she could keep it with taxes being what they were. But she definitely wasn't interested in logging it. She loved the woods too much, all the things that lived there.

Ammon nodded sympathetically. "I know how you feel. The woods is where I go when I need to think, it's church to me, better than any cathedral." Ben very nearly laughed, he thought Ammon must be joking. But Ammon had a glow about him, the light on his face and possibly even a tear in his eye. Margot soaked it all in. She offered them pie she'd just made. Ammon demurred. "We've got to be heading out. Promised my wife we'd be home in time." He flashed a look at Ben, and Ben picked up the baton.

"My aunt's got MS," he improvised. "The carer leaves at four."

Margot gave a little frown of sympathy.

As they drove away, Ammon muttered, "Horny bitch."

That evening, Ammon told Ben to go back to Margot's house and stack her wood.

Margot was surprised to see him. She was hunkered down in the vegetable garden, dirt on her hands, her hair stuffed up and held in place with a pencil. At first she wouldn't hear of it, she'd already said she could do the wood herself.

"I don't doubt that, ma'am." Ben looked at her more boldly now. She met his gaze then stepped back. Ben felt a rush of heat in his groin, and this rushed to his face. He blushed and turned away. She'd seen it, he knew, but she pretended otherwise, wildly brushing dirt from her dress. He was so used to people who would sneer or call him out—"Lookit Benny, blushing like a radish!"

A week later, Ammon gave him an envelope containing $15,000.

"Take this to that bimbo on Ridge Road. Tell her ya haven't spoken to me but ya want to help. She can have this and ya'll log her land with all the care in the world, ya bleed on about the baby fawns and the baby foxes."

As Ben headed for the door, Ammon grabbed him and undid the top button of his jeans.

Ben was about to punch him, quickly did the button up. Ammon grabbed him, undid the button again. "I'm no faggit, Ben, ya ken me. But ya just see, ya just see how she spins for ya."

He drove to Ridge Road, her car was there. He glanced at himself in the rear-view mirror. He had his mother's eyes, the green-blue with thick black lashes. He was never quite brave enough to look at his reflection full on in the mirror. He hardly recognized himself these days without the seeping mask of acne. Suddenly, it had vanished from working in the sun and though his skin remained lightly pocked, it was clear and clean.

Margot smiled when she saw him, asked him in. She was at the kitchen table, books and notepads spread out. "I'm an English teacher," she explained. "Where are you at school?"

"I dropped out."

She looked up at him. "How do you feel about that?"

Ben shrugged. "The classroom felt like prison."

"Yes, it can."

He was aware, then, that she'd clocked his undone jeans.

"Amm—" he corrected himself, "Uncle Ammon. He wants me to have the business, as it was my grandfather's originally." Ben felt the velvet smoothness of the lies, and how they could so easily be the truth that others wanted. "But ma'am, your woods need logging, and I have a sense it'll help you with your Land Use debt."

"Oh, the Land Use. Yes, my husb—" she made her own correction, "ex, he did all that. I haven't got my head around it yet."

Now Ben brought out the envelope, fat with money. "I haven't talked about this with my uncle yet. But I'm sure he'll agree. I can give you this right now and I can begin logging next week."

She took the envelope, glanced inside.

"Fifteen thousand," he said. "That's keeping my margins real tight. But I can manage it."

She suddenly came undone and wept, and he did not know what to do but put his hands on her arms and guide her to a chair. He knelt down before her and as a means of comfort he put his hand on hers. "It's okay, ma'am. You'll figure it out."

Her hand was warm beneath his, and he was also touching her bare thigh. Her dress had slipped up above her knee and he was directly touching her skin. He stared at her skin and the shadow of the dress where he could not see. He wanted to lean in and kiss her. He wanted to taste her. He could not think clearly. His heart was racing and he felt the heat all through him, so he was no longer sure if he was fantasizing or doing. His hand slipped off hers and to her thigh, the soft rose petal of her skin, and he pushed the hem of her dress aside and slid his hand upward. He was amazed by the heat of her body, by her skin, by the way the world funneled into this specific moment, all brutality and sadness was vanquished by the beauty of the feeling inside his chest and the softness and the outline of her panties, cotton with small flowers. He saw the faint bulge of her pubic hair against the cotton and he could smell her. She made a vain attempt to stop him, she muttered "no." He looked up at her, the lines around her eyes, the fine cut of her cheekbones, and when he leaned up to kiss her she kissed him back.

He was no virgin, he'd slept with Tina Vincent when he was

13 and Felicia Baumgarten whenever he needed to. But this was different. Margot took him to bed. She was both shy and carnal, nervous of what he might think of her body and yet at ease with the pleasure she took. He saw her every day for two weeks. He did not think that Ammon knew.

But Ammon, being Ammon, was merely waiting. He was doing paperwork, he told Ben to get him a coffee, and Ben did, and Ammon looked at him with his carnivorous grin.

"Ya learnin' something, horndog?"

Ben pretended not to hear—pretended to himself so that he could hold on to this good thing, this gracious, gentle thing for another few seconds.

"She know yer only 17?"

Ben kept his back to Ammon. "She knows."

"She could lose her job."

Now he turned to face Ammon. "Fuck you."

"That the best ya got?" Ammon tossed him the keys to the skidder. He used his quiet voice, "Better get up there and do the job I've paid for."

Ben was salt, he was crumbling, molecule by molecule. "Please," he said. "Please get someone else to do it. Ray or Jim."

"High grade." Ammon drank his coffee. "We've paid her for a high grade. Forty acres. Clear it. I've got Poulsen's wanting the chip."

It was good wood, quality birch and an old stand of maple. Other mills would be paying top dollar for boards. But Ammon was going to chip it out of pure spite. Narratives flipped through Ben's head, pages of a comic book, he would run away, he and Margot would run away together, California, Mexico, somewhere age didn't matter, one of those Pacific Islands, they would swim and eat mangos. Anything, anything but the sick, dead weight of the feller buncher's keys in his hand.

Margot heard the sound of it. The ripping, eviscerating, the crushing. She ran toward him. He refused to see her, he kept his focus, he didn't even look at the forest, just the gears, the levers. He wondered if she would call the police or if she would meekly accept the consequences of the choices Ammon had made for them.

At dusk, he turned off the machine and gazed about at the late-summer evening, the sky orange-hued and hazy with residual heat. With his t-shirt, he wiped the sweat from his forehead and took off his hat to scratch his hair. He was in a different place than where he'd begun the day. The earth was newly naked, its smell filling the air with the intensity of a spring thaw, as if already trying to forgive the assault.

He observed what he had done. He wanted to own it, to possess this act: what a man could do to a landscape in eight hours, to the trees that had taken a hundred years to grow, that had outlasted winters and diseases and droughts and ice storms. He severed them with a blade and ground them up into little pieces.

Later that year, a cold, grey November day, he saw Margot again. She was coming out of White's, the wind catching her hair, her skin pale against a red scarf. He felt trapped, standing up against his pick-up without enough time to either hide or face her. She walked right by him, before stopping, turning back.

"Ben."

He merely looked at her, trying to read her voice, her expression. She smiled. "How are you?"

"I'm okay, yeah."

She glanced at her watch. "You want a coffee? I've got half an hour."

He sat across from her in the White's café section, surely the least romantic place in the world with its plastic chairs and teetering stacks of special-offer items: tiny cacti, discount Halloween candy, spaghetti. How oddly formal he felt, how remote from her and from who they had been in her bed, in summer. He had seen her cunt, she had tasted his cum. Now she was overly cheery, babbling, regretting already—he felt—her invitation.

School was going well. She had some great students but the usual frustrations. "And you, Ben, what about you?"

His reply might be banal, a few words to hurry away the interaction between them. But, suddenly and despite himself, he said: "He's not my uncle. Ammon. He is a sadistic, lying douchebag and I hate him with all my heart." It took him a moment to realize he was crying, tears sliding down his face and plopping on the table.

Margot's face contorted oddly, the opposing tension of hundreds of tiny muscles busily working beneath her skin. The pale winter light showed every line. Then, surprisingly, she put her hand on his. "And yet you made me happy, and you will make someone else happy and you will be happy, and that will be your revenge on Ammon."

He held her hand, she held it back.

At last he withdrew.

She sat back and began to collect her things. "Crap, I'm late." She stood, he stood with her, a momentary misstep with the chair between them and he bumped into her. His hand went to her waist by instinct, her hand to his shoulder. They could have danced, they could have waltzed, he could feel the curve of her hipbone beneath the layers of her rough wool skirt.

"Get out," she said. "Get the hell out."

She detached from him. She flew out the door, a loosened thistle seed, her red scarf looping behind her. He was stunned, he was hurt, and also angry. Then he understood. *Get out, get the hell out.* Of here, of this.

But he was here, back here, nail-gunned to this particular corner of the map. Some faulty ideal had led him—the myth of home, Ammon offering him the business because Frank was going into forestry. Frank would have nothing to do with Ammon, and he did not need to, his mother had made sure of that. She'd put all her property into a trust for him, to be opened when he turned 21.

"You've been like a son to me," Ammon said grandly to Ben, and Ben had wondered if Ammon really thought he was like a father. Ammon had shown him the equipment, they'd walked around the solid, well-kept machines, and Ben had been pleasantly surprised—Ammon had generously low-balled the price on the equipment for him.

By the time he checked the registration numbers on the machines against the registration numbers on the bill of sale, it was too late, he'd committed his Armed Services loan. The real equipment was a pile of rusting junk and Ammon had laughed, funniest thing in the world, funniest thing since the pigs. "Didya learn nothin' from me, Ben?"

Ben made the best of it he could, which was mostly debt, lawsuits, and, finally, Slim. At times, he wondered at the predictability of his life, dead junkie mother, foster care, high school dropout, the military, debt, crime. It was inevitable, ticking boxes, and he'd missed every chance for escape. Get out, get the hell out, and he'd come back, right back.

Between the Dunkin' Donuts and an art supply store, the Guadalajara Grill in St. Johnsbury had bright turquoise paint around the windows. Inside, the late-morning sun illuminated the red leatherette banquettes. Frida Kahlo prints and tourist posters lined bright yellow walls. There were a dozen people, the late side of breakfast, their plates swamped with rice, beans, tortillas, and indistinct items in sauces.

Kay took a booth. A spotty teenager posing as a waiter handed her a menu, ubiquitous offerings—chimichanga, enchilada, burrito. The food could be awful or not so bad, though Kay felt it unlikely she would be pleasantly surprised. She ordered a bean burrito.

The bathroom was just past the kitchen. She got up, crossed the restaurant, and glancing in, saw a large, dark-haired, brown-skinned woman tossing meat about a skillet.

In the bathroom, Kay washed her hands and briefly examined her reflection in the mirror. The green-tinged fluorescent light highlighted her wrinkles and sun damage. She pinched the skin near her ears, drawing it back as might be done in a face lift. Perhaps she might cut open her face, pull tight the skin as if it were plastic wrap.

She turned to the left, examined her three-quarter profile, then let her hands fall, stepped back. How did she look to men?

Men had always looked. Ben looked and saw a bored housewife. He was right. She thought of his hands. What if a man never touched her again?

By the time she got back to her booth, her burrito was there, a log afloat in a sauce of brown mole, adorned with a single sliver of avocado. She called the waiter over.

"Is everything all right?" He sniffed as if he had a cold or allergies.

"The cook, what is her name?"

"Who?" The poor lad had a massive oozing pimple on the tip of his red nose.

"The woman back there in the kitchen cooking."

"Silvia?"

"Is Silvia from Mexico?"

He sniffed harder. "You immigration or something?"

"Gosh no! I just wanted to know how authentic the food is."

"They come down here from Derby sometimes. Total dickheads."

"Why are they dickheads?"

"They eat and then they come into the back and give us a hassle. You know, anyone with a tan."

By now the Guadalajara Grill was filling up with a lunch crowd, and the cook wandered out to fuss with the till. Kay watched her for a moment—Silvia, flicking through the morning's receipts. Kay should pay and just walk out; she should be on time to collect her kids and cook them fish fingers for supper. She felt the fulcrum once again: she had options, choices, a woman like her always did. So why did it feel so Pavlovian—was she obeying some inner bell? She stood up and went to Silvia, bill in hand.

"Hi, Silvia. Your food is great."

Silvia lifted her gaze to meet Kay. "*Gracias.*"

"Do you know Maria Wilson?"

Silvia glanced at the receipt, "Tweny-two sixty."

"I'm not trying to make trouble or anything. I'm just trying to find out if she's okay."

"An' jew are?" Silvia opened the till, pulling out bills, counting them silently, expertly.

"Kay. I'm renting the Wilsons' house for the summer."

Silvia paused, licked her fingertips, recounted. Then looked blankly at Kay.

"I heard she went back to Mexico," Kay continued.

"Jew say her name is Maria?"

"Yes."

"Well, honeee, my name is Silvia. Jew wanna know how is Maria, ask Maria."

"Is she definitely in Mexico, with her sons?"

Silvia was now tapping calculations into her tablet, muttering numbers, "*Ciento tres... cincuenta y cinco, once...*"

"Does anyone know for certain where she is?"

"*Catorce, dieciocho, noventa...*"

"Do you know?"

"*Setenta y cinco... Dios mío,* Gilberto!" She snapped her fingers and the pimple boy came slouching toward her. She spoke at him in rapid Spanish, stabbing a receipt with a short finger.

Gilberto spoke back. Kay couldn't understand the words, but his tone suggested that the answer was obvious, and Silvia—his mother?—was an idiot for even asking.

Silvia fired back at Gilberto, they went back and forth, until he pulled off his apron and stalked away, flapping a dismissive hand at her. Then she turned to Kay, as if she'd just appeared. "Jew pay cash or card?"

Kay brought forth her wallet, handed over a card. "I just want to know if she's okay, if she's safe, that's all. Not where, specifically."

Silvia's eyes narrowed. "Frank sen' you, eh. Jew tell Frank to *vaya* fuck heemsel."

"So you know where she is," Kay pushed on.

"That fuckeen crazy *madre*fucker he make her scrub the toilet every day and her kids to put on special clothes when they come in the house. And then the white paint. Fuckeen *loco*. Maria ees never comin' back, she gone, *hasta luego*, baybee. So jew tell Franco he need a fuckeen head doctor. That dude is messed up." Silvia handed Kay her receipt. "Got it?"

"Got it."

"And don' tip that keed, he sneeze in your salsa."

LACEY SAT DOWN ON THE SOFA, SHE SMILED AT Jake. "Hello, Jake."

Jake buried his face against Ben.

"Say hi to Lacey," he urged.

Jake pressed closer to Ben.

"It's okay, she just wants to chat. She's a nice lady."

Shevaunne brought Lacey a cup of coffee. "I also made some banana bread."

"Oh, no!" Lacey patted her thighs. "Not for me!" Then she turned back to Ben and Jake. "Let's talk about daycare. How's that going? Any issues?"

"He seems happy. He lets me drop him off, no tears," Ben said. "He's waiting for me when I pick him up. I don't know much about in between."

"Are you making friends, Jake?"

He kept his face away from her.

"Is there a special toy you like?"

Ben closed his arm around Jake. "How about that bulldozer I see you with all the time?" In truth, he'd seen Jake with it once, when he'd come early. Otherwise, Jake was always waiting, back-pack ready, shoes tied, sitting apart from the others.

Shevaunne offered 'round the banana bread; she had indeed made it, from a mix, purchased by Ben. But she seemed genuinely pleased with herself, as if she'd produced not Betty Crocker but a delicate French patisserie. Lacey hesitated, then grabbed a piece. "It just looks too good."

"I really enjoy baking," Shevaunne smiled. "Cookies, cakes, pies. The secret for a good pie crust is lard—you have to use lard."

Ben took a bite of the bread. "This is delicious."

"Thank you, honey."

At first Ben thought it was the bread, somehow Shevaunne had made banana bread that smelled like runny shit. For a long moment, no one said anything, though Ben could see Lacey had noticed the smell; she'd gently put the bread down beside her mug.

"Oh, Jesus," Shevaunne mumbled. "Oh for fuck's sake."

Jake felt soft in Ben's arms, floppy. "It's okay, it's okay." He scooped the boy up. "We'll be right back."

He carried Jake into the bathroom, ran the taps in the bath. Jake could not stand up, so Ben lay him down like a baby, peeled down his trousers, gently, gently, saying, "It's okay, it's okay, no one's mad." There was shit everywhere, an explosion all over Jake's thighs and genitals. Ben winced and heaved. The smell, the stench. Standing up, he splashed his face with cold water. Blinked hard, splashed again. But the smell had him. He remembered the smell, the shit and fear, the fear shit, a special combination. He kept his eyes open. He kept them on his reflection in the mirror, not there, in the dark behind him where moved the hump-backed and slow, their hot anticipating breath in the cool cellar.

Ben placed his hands flat on the countertop; he felt the heave jolt right across his shoulders, the bile in his mouth. He spat it out. He took a gob of toothpaste and rinsed it around his mouth. Jake had crawled away from him, inched into the corner by the toilet, crumpling into himself—he might keep crumpling into a smaller and smaller boy and eventually disappear. But in crawling, he'd smeared the feces all over the bath matt, all over the linoleum. Ben crouched down. "Jake, Jake, it's all right. I'm not going to punish you."

He lifted the boy up in one strong, sure movement and put him in the bath and ran it full with warm water. "It's all right, it's okay, we'll sort you out." Here he took the boy's shirt and jeans right off, the shit fragmenting and floating to the surface in clumps, like moss. "I love you. I will not stop loving you. I want you to know that." Ben washed him just with the water, then drained the tub, ran it again and washed him with soap. When this was done, when Jake was clean, he wrapped him in a towel, then took him to bed. "She's not going to take you away. I promise, I promise."

Jake was asleep, or perhaps simply lying with his eyes closed—he had not moved or spoken. Ben closed the door to his room, stepped quietly back into the living area. Lacey was already standing, handbag on her shoulder, her clipboard pressed to her chest. She sucked in a breath. "How is he?"

"Why don't you ask her?" he nodded at Shevaunne.

Shevaunne took a cigarette out of the packet, pointed it at Ben. "Kids have bowel problems. They have accidents."

He thought he would heave again so he looked away from her.

Lacey was at the door. "Let's reschedule? I have toys for him that might make it easier."

Shevaunne put the cigarette in her mouth. She knew better than to light it, so she spoke with it hanging from her lips. "Those dolls? I don't want him playing with those fuckin' *atonomical* dolls. They made him worse." Then she smiled, her teeth in a hard line. "No smoking in the house or the car, Lacey, don't worry."

Ben swallowed his reflux. Then he turned to Lacey. "We'll be here, whatever you need from us."

She nodded, gave a little purposeful nod to Shevaunne. "How are the meetings?"

"Fine. Yeah. Really helping me become a better person."

It would have been easy for anyone less vigilant than Ben to miss the way Lacey's eyes lingered on Shevaunne's. He watched her out the door, her dainty shoes tip-toeing across the dirt driveway. She glanced back, and he knew she was looking at the mold stains, the loose siding, very likely rodents nesting in the walls. What a place to raise a kid.

Before Lacey's car was even out the drive, Shevaunne had her hand in his direction, touching him, scraping him, her fingers like dry twigs. She smiled, dry-smoking her Marlboro. "Come on, I made a cake."

He reached into his back pocket, brought out the spindle of smack, and put it on the counter between them. She grabbed for it, but he held it fast with his fingertip.

"We have a deal."

"The deal is you're my dealer, I do what you want." She hung her arms from her shoulders like a puppet.

"The laundry."

"I will. After. C'mon. I can't do the laundry now, I'm all wiggy." She pouted while trying to retain her smile, or at least its jocular intent. He wanted to hit her. It was a craving, just to slap her, and then punch her and then maybe smash her head against the wall. She would make no sound. She would be more like a doll, and he would hit her and hit her and punch her and kick her. He would smash her and there wouldn't be blood, there wouldn't be any mess, because she wasn't a person, she would just be dead.

He took his finger off the spindle. She laughed and did a little jig.

M a'am? Do you want the paper?"

Thursday's Child

Thursday's Child is a weekly column in *The Caledonian-Record* featuring a child currently in foster care in the Northeast Kingdom, awaiting adoption. There are over 100 children needing safe, loving, permanent homes. This Thursday's Child is Jericho, 7.

Jericho describes himself as quiet and good but with a sense of humor. One of his favorite gifts is a joke book, and he loves to make people laugh. He also loves to paint, draw, and model clay, especially Sculpey because of the bright colors. When he gets the chance to be outside, he likes watching birds and squirrels and wishes to know more about the natural world.

In school, Jericho is supported by an Individualized Education Plan (IEP) as he has some learning challenges. While he has the capacity to be a strong student, Jericho suffers from voluntary mutism and can become easily distracted and unable to concentrate for extended periods. He struggles to interact with his peers, preferring to remain solitary, even non-reactive.

With a significant history of trauma, Jericho receives weekly therapy. His individual trauma-focused therapy is helping him develop confidence and expression. He is beginning to process his trauma through art and play therapy.

Legally freed for adoption, Jericho will thrive in a calm, stable home with a parent or parents who provide structure and clear expectations of engagement. Given his delayed entry into the schooling system and on-going learning disabilities, it is recommended that Jericho be in a supportive academic environment able to address his specific academic, social, and emotional needs. His therapy should also continue until further assessment. Jericho would very much like to be in a home with a pet, in particular a dog.

"Yes," Kay said, corralling it with the toilet paper, eggs, bread, Cheerios, dish soap, broccoli, butter, olive oil, pasta, organic chicken thighs, lemon, peaches, cherries, wine, cheese, organic yogurt, pizza sauce and pizza crust, low sodium soy sauce, organic tinned tomatoes—the bounty so casually available to her and her children.

She loaded up the car, sat for a moment in the stunning, tinned heat of the car. She should turn on her phone, she should check for messages, perhaps she should send some. But to whom? The heat, the sealed car was womb-like, impervious. Certainly, if she was ever to consider suicide, she would do it with car exhaust. Although she'd heard that it was more difficult now, to asphyxiate oneself, due to the smog controls on cars.

But it wasn't suicide she was considering—rather dispersement: the fragmenting of what had been whole, or had at least appeared whole. Break anything down far enough, and it's not whole at all; it's merely a collection of particles in specific and temporary proximity.

Jericho, she thought. A fetus grown, not aborted, and born, a baby given the name of an ancient city, an uncommon name—chosen, intended, not merely drawn from thin air. His parents had meant to love him. But children do not always obey, they do not understand, they will not be quiet.

At Kamp Yahoo, her children careened toward her, brown-limbed, well-fed, remnant paint under their fingernails, juice staining their t-shirts. They could be broken down, too. It took so little effort, only consistency, the breaking and breaking again and again into smaller pieces. What is done to children, she thought, shutting her eyes because such thoughts frightened her: you can't think them, you become inhuman, you can't even write them anymore. When she opened her eyes Tom was at the window, his mouth agape.

"Mum! Mum! I lost a tooth! I lost a tooth! Mrs. Figgs put it in a baggie for me." He held up the baggie with the tiny pearl of a tooth. "Do you think the tooth fairy will come? Will she, even if we're here in America?"

Freya leaned in, winked, "She'll have to pay in dollars, won't she, Mum?"

A LOGGER MUST KNOW THE WOODS HE LOGS,
he must map out the species of trees and note the vernal pools,
the marshes, the streams. He must take into account the con-
tours of the land, the steep slopes and ridges, ravines and dells.
He walks the property for days, marking the boundaries, tag-
ging the trees of value and those destined for the wood chip-
per. In walking, he sees the delicate lady slipper orchids and the
trout lilies and the sun dappling through the poplars. The ferns
grow richly on moist soil, sheltering tiny, delicate red efts. There
are bull frogs in the streams, newts and salamanders and six or
seven species of smaller frogs. The trees are private kingdoms
for owls, woodpeckers, nuthatches, chickadees, the kinglets who
all survived the brutal winter. And in the undergrowth—the
spiny bramble, the twisted bracken—here live the grouse, the
oven birds, the juncos. Garter snakes and milk snakes and toads
inhabit the leaf litter, the rotting logs, the moss-covered rocks.

Ben heard and inhaled this, the living multi-dimensions of
the forest. He knew it more intimately than the land's owners
who would never learn the dodge and dance required to walk
in thick woods. They were worried about ticks. They didn't like
the way brambles grabbed their clothing and skin. Mud sullied
their expensive hiking boots. Walking the woods, Ben found old
ruins, coils of rusted barbed wire, and the stone walls a farmer

took years to build a century ago. He often thought about those who'd first cleared the land, tree trunks the size of houses, it would take a year to clear an acre. Those men and women spent their lives clearing the forest, year upon year, peeling it off the face of the earth. And in exchange, the earth took them, took their children, year upon year. All that effort, Ben thought, all that fretting, and the woods grow back; not the big trees anymore, but a clear-cut can reforest in 30 years.

He found junk, too: messes left by other loggers—steel cables, plastic oil buckets, fuel drums, beer cans. Or trash: tires, kids' toys, rusted fridges. The forest could not ingest such things, but embraced them with lichens and creepers. Mice claimed an old mattress and wasps built their paper palace in a discarded pet crate.

Sometimes Ben brought a pack lunch and he'd find a quiet place away from the deer flies or the black flies. He might open a beer. Or two. Once, a young bear ambled out of the shade and began scratching her back against a maple. When she noticed Ben, she gave him an annoyed look, as if she knew the rules required her to give up her scratching and run away.

But the time always came, the task was always at hand, it had to be done, and Ben climbed into the cabin of the feller buncher. He put on his ear-protection and turned the ignition. The great machine trembled beneath him, all around him. The creatures of the forest had no reason to fear the noise; they could not know what it meant. The generation that might remember was gone, the memory collectively erased. People didn't understand this about logging. They didn't want to know the consequences. They thought the foxes and birds and snakes just moved somewhere else. But they died, every last one, a thousand small deaths of hunger or animal war, bodies that never accumulated but dissolved into the earth or into the bellies of others further up the food chain. Ben became their death and there was no accounting for the dead of the forest.

He turned the feller buncher northeast of the landing, attacking a copse of Ted and Evie's beautiful old birch. The machine's hydraulic arms grabbed the first birch in their steel embrace and the saw jutted out from the base and severed the tree from its roots. The spinning steel spines of the de-brancher ripped up the length of its pale white trunk, amputated its limbs, and then down again, rendering it smooth: 30 seconds from living tree to log.

Crystal Lake State Park, with its limpid water and long, sandy beach swarming with other children, had proven to be their favorite place to swim. Like dogs, Freya and Tom wanted most to be with others of their kind, making the same easy, momentary friendships.

While Kay set up a blanket on the grass, Freya and Tom ran immediately to the water. Tom, in particular, had marveled at the freshness, how he could open his eyes under the surface without burning his retinas. A London child, he'd only experienced chlorine or, once in Hastings, salt. "Mum, Mum!" he'd come running to tell her on their first outing here. "It doesn't have any taste. It's just water!"

She watched them swim out to the buoys marking the edge of the swimming zone. Freya, with her long arms like sculling oars, made sure, deft strokes. Tom, the product of multiple swim classes, had a workman-like skill, his feet out-boarding behind him. They were good swimmers, she noted; some of the local kids couldn't even doggy-paddle. Out beyond the buoys, the lake spilled placidly south, water-skiers and wake-boarders, kayaks and canoes.

Around her, other families dabbled infants on the lake edge or fired up the park's cement grills. Hamburgers, hot dogs, potato salad, cigarettes, sun-tan lotion, beer—the olfactory potpourri of mid-July.

Somewhere further along the beach, under the sugar maples, a man laughed, a loud, manly guffaw. Kay saw him, large, round-bellied, bare-chested, waving a pair of barbecue tongs about. He belched, and his son, a square-shaped boy of ten, laughed in the same blunt way, then mimicked the burp. Father and son cackled in joy.

Kay sat on her blanket, pulling her hat down to shade her eyes: out there, rounding the buoy and turning back toward the beach, Freya and Tom swam with their sleek wet heads. She could hear the burpers still laughing. Another man, tall and lean, entered her view and, for a moment she thought it was Ben Comeau. Instinctively, she touched her hand to her hair.

As he walked toward her, she could see more clearly now his lankiness, his hair dark because it was wet, he was only 17 or 18. The boy turned to a friend, laughing, and they pivoted toward a group of girls further down the beach. Kay watched them for a while, their new bodies and new voices, they laughed and flirted. Just beyond them: Tom and Freya now on the sand, intent on a sand castle. She closed her eyes against the sun's bright glare and she had the impression of Michael: he was there with her, beside her. They were lovers in a hotel room, clean cotton sheets, and her body was lean and brown. He marveled at her.

Then the light changed; the sun now surfed the tops of the surrounding hills. There was the slightest shifting down in temperature. Kay startled with the revelation that she'd fallen asleep. She sat up. Though the mass of children had begun to thin out, there were still a dozen or so splashing in the shallows on a flotilla of cheap plastic rafts. Her eye tuned to her children. She'd know them anywhere. But she did not see them. The water beyond the swimming buoys seemed heavy, oily in the evening light.

Standing up, she walked to the beach, scanning. Perhaps they had gone to the lagoon around the corner. Perhaps they were up at the swing set. She walked quickly, refusing to panic. But they were at neither place. She ran back to where she had last seen them, then waded into the water: "Freya! Tom!"

They were not there, she knew this. They were gone. But she shouted again, "Freya! Tom!" and then turned like a cornered animal, still calling their names. Freya Tom Freya Tom Freya Tom Tom Freya.

A man was there—the fat, burping man.

"Ma'am, ma'am, what do they look like?"

"Freya's eight, Tom's five. Blond, slim. Both. She's in a green swimsuit. His is red. They were just here, they were just here!"

"Don't worry. There's a ton of kids." His hand was on her arm, making the connection. "I'll go up to the ice cream stand and check the bathrooms, okay."

He peeled away. He must have told other people, check the lagoon, check the parking lot, check the playground—Kay had a sense of purposeful dispersal taking place around her. She kept running, shouting along the shore. Just 20 feet off shore, just beyond the benign sand, the lake got deep. They wouldn't swim out, she was thinking. Unless they thought they'd make for a far shore, a rocky outlet on the eastern edge, or the docks to the west. But Freya—surely—had a good sense of Tom's limits: he'd never make it that far.

She knows better, she knows better. Kay kept thinking this of Freya, even as a new idea formed, that, yes, she knows better, she's swimming him out, she's swimming him far out on purpose, a vengeful, siren sister, to where choices winnow in the glacial depths.

And Kay became certain, even as she lifted her gaze higher and further, out beyond the buoys, the glittering, slow water, the water skiers cutting the surface, they'd be unable to see two small heads, like otters, the spinning blade of the boat's propeller—

Freya, Freya, Tom, Tom. Kay waded further in, the water up

to her chest. Kay hadn't loved Freya enough as a baby. Kay had been gone, assignments in Yemen, Congo, Zimbabwe and when Kay came home to Nairobi Freya hesitated to leave the *ayah*, Kay kneeling down in the doorway, open armed until Freya conceded, trotting across the floor and Kay would bury her in, curl her in, but always, always Kay suspected her daughter's sense of obligation.

In the deeper water, she realized her mistake: the lower perspective gave her less visual scope.

"Freya! Tom!"

Her voice was drowned by the whining of outboards. One, in particular, headed in her direction. It was the fat man, a little dingy with a tiny motor on the back. He held out his hand, she stepped in. He leaned toward her, an intimate proximity, to speak over the sound of the engine: "Do you think they would be swimming out here?"

"I think so. I think they've got some crazy idea."

"Kids." He rolled his eyes and turned up the throttle, heading for open water.

"They can't be that far," he said. "How long've they been missing?"

"I don't know."

He looked at her.

"I was watching them, I was there, they were there, but I was, I don't—" Kay bit her lip. "But Freya knows, she *knows* not to go far."

"And you're sure they swam out. They didn't go with anyone."

Kay turned to him. Anyone, he was anyone. Of all the times Kay had told Freya and Tom not to go with strangers, and she'd done just that. Here she was with a stranger, in a boat, in the middle of a lake, losing sight of shore, a woman who knows better, who certainly knows worse. How easy it was to make a bad decision. Then a random thought, completely unhinged, entered her mind: Ammon. Ammon had taken her children. He had taken them into the dark woods.

A torrent of words—*hammer, squeal, duct tape, tarpaulin, earth, socket, bone, surgical, pig*. She forced her eyes open, gritted her teeth.

The fat man piloted the boat out, slowly, nosing toward the shore, then back again to the center of the lake. Twenty minutes, half an hour—how long had they been gone. Kay had no concept of time. An hour? Multiply minutes by Tom's doggy paddle—

"Is that them?" The man pointed to a rocky outcrop. Kay could just make out two small figures, two points of light.

"Yes. Oh God."

Closer in, Kay could see Tom's arms around himself. He was shivering, his face worried and uncertain. And Freya attempting to cover her fear with her casual jut of the hip.

Kay turned to the man. "How do I look?"

He squinted, confused.

"Do I look angry or worried?"

"You look scared shitless."

"I don't want to look scared, because I'll scare them." She tried out a smile.

"Now you look scary."

Kay tried again, without the smile.

"Better," he nodded. "Try adding some annoyed—they'll know it's all right if you're annoyed with them."

Her face felt tight with effort, a mask of skin obscuring the hundreds of muscles pulling on opposite directions, emotions that only had names in other languages like German or Japanese. If she knew those languages she could express all these feelings in dire conflict with each other.

"My son went missing in the woods," the man said. "It was hours. We were going nuts. Your mind makes up stories, always the worst. It turned out he'd fallen asleep in a pile of leaves."

Freya and Tom didn't move. Kay had the sense they were watching her carefully. The man decelerated, the dingy bumping gently against the rock.

Kay held out her hands, one to each child. "You want a lift back?"

Tom grabbed her fingers. His lip wobbled. His eyes were teary. Kay thought he would fall into her arms, but he moved past her and into the boat. The man put a towel around his shoulders. "Long swim, huh?"

As she took Kay's other hand, Freya lowered her eyes. "I didn't think it was so far." She was working hard to keep her voice steady, as if nothing was wrong. "I had to pull him most of the way in. He couldn't swim anymore." She stepped in the boat, Kay took another towel from the man—how grateful she was to him. He was looking at her and she could feel the tears burning in her eyes.

He gave her a quick answering smile. "Annoyed," he whispered. She blinked away the tears before Freya could see, pulled the towel tight around her daughter.

"Have a seat. This nice man will take us back to the beach."

"I've never been in a boat before." Tom held the gunwale.

"Thank you," Freya murmured, looking up at the man. "Sorry for the hassle."

On the way back to the beach, Kay regarded the back of her daughter's head. She wanted to kiss it; she wanted to smack it. She thought about herself in the basement with the hammer. She thought about her daughter out there in the deep water of the lake, the moment when her peevish wish became a terrifying possibility. The moment when she realized she would not always be good.

JAKE WAITED BY THE DOOR WITH HIS BACKPACK.

"He's been here for an hour," the daycare worker told Ben. "I tried to explain that you were going to be late today, and maybe we could do some more drawing. But he said he wanted to wait for you."

"He said that?"

"Well, you know, not *said*. But he shook his head. He wouldn't be moved."

Ben crouched down, touched Jake's cheek with his hand. His hand was filthy from work—the nails blacked from oil and grime—it seemed almost grotesque against the smooth, pale cheek of this boy. "I'm sorry. I had to finish up with work. You want to get an ice cream on the way back?"

Jake raised his dark eyes to Ben's. Still Ben saw nothing there; the boy's expression remained closed.

"What flavor? Chocolate cookie dough?"

Jake shook his head.

Ben thought hard. "Snails and spinach?"

Another head shake, a twitch at the corner of his lips as if trying to fight a smile.

"Frog leg pineapple?"

Jake wrinkled his nose.

"I know, I know!" Ben persisted. "Peppermint horse poop."

Now Jake covered his mouth with his hand. He leaned in, whispered into Ben's ear, "Strawberry."

Strawberry. The first word Jake had ever said to him. A ripe word, a summer word, sweet, plump and red, and he would never forget it.

"All right then," he said, as if nothing momentous had happened, the world carrying on diligently. "Let's go to Foxy's." So they went and sat by the river with other families and watched a pair of ducks on the far bank, drift and paddle, drift and paddle. Ben had come here a few times as a boy—the Baileys seemed to find the money to buy eight kids ice cream—and he'd watch ducks then, too. The ducks were soothing. They were comical and serious at the same time; they waddled, they quacked, they stuck their duck asses in the air; yet, they defended their babies against snapper turtles, they braved the coldest winters here, finding, by some mysterious sense, the only open water for miles. He loved their attention to task, and, he admired, like all wild things, their lack of self-pity.

At last, the ice cream was done. They got back into Ben's truck, sticky, sated, and started home on the interstate. But after only several miles, the truck began to shriek, and, within seconds, to lose power. The connecting rod had gone again. Ben managed to maneuver it to the emergency lane.

"Shit," he said, then glanced at Jake. But Jake stared straight ahead. He was gripping the seat.

"I don't think this truck's going to last us too much longer. And I don't know what we'll do then. Maybe just go to Australia. What do you reckon, Jake? You and me, we make a break for the outback."

Jake was gripping the seat so hard his knuckles were turning white, and Ben wondered if he was being triggered: Jake's mind, a pop-up book of horrors. He checked his phone. No reception, a dead zone between the hills. But they were only half a mile from the crest—a five-minute walk.

"Jake, we're going to walk up the road a little bit, okay?" Ben opened the passenger door, leaned in. "The truck is broken and I need to call Ed for help. The phone doesn't work right here."

Nothing from Jake.

"Is that okay? You come with me now. I'll hold your hand as we walk up the road."

When Jake still didn't move, Ben reached in and gently lifted him down from the cab. The boy was tense; there was a faint beading of sweat on his upper lip. Ben took his hand, began to walk up the highway, keeping himself between Jake and the road—as if his body may be sufficient buffer against the impact of one ton of steel traveling at 80 miles an hour. Cars and trucks roared past. He heard the occasional beep. Why? Did the drivers think he might not be aware of them—aware of two lanes of fast-moving vehicles about three feet away from his right hip? Jake trudged silently by his side.

At last, they reached the crest, and Ben let go of Jake's hand to dial Ed. Without warning, Jake veered, fled into the highway with the flawed instinct of a damaged animal. Ben lunged after him as a Dodge Ram blasted its horn. There was a squeal of tires just as Ben grabbed Jake's shirt and yanked him back. The Ram truck sped past, with a second, more forceful *WWWHHHHHHAAAAA* of the horn. But Jake's shirt began to rip, the boy pulling away, such surprising feral strength, and Ben shouting: "Jake, Jake! You gotta stop, stop, fuckin' stop!"

The boy pulled and writhed. There were other cars now, some slowing down. Ben was aware in the periphery of his vision, all his senses fine-tuned, collecting information. Now he grabbed Jake around the middle, the boy kicking him, thrashing against him.

"Cut it out, cut it out!" he implored.

A siren, a gathering of cars, and he was just holding the thrashing boy. "It's okay, it's okay," he was saying, shouting. "IT'S

OKAY, IT'S ALL RIGHT, IT'S ALL RIGHT FOR FUCK'S SAKE!"

"Let the boy go and put your hands on your head."

Ben heard this but it couldn't be right; he wasn't doing anything wrong. So he turned to the voice, the cop, who was pointing a gun at him, standing behind the door of his cop car, and the smell of Jake who had just released his bowels.

"He's my—"

"Sir, you need to listen to me. Let the child go. Put your hands on your head."

So Ben put Jake down, and Jake sagged, he collapsed, a boneless child, a pile of shitty rags. And Ben put his hands on his head. *He's my*— he heard himself say *he's my*—

In an instant, the cops swarmed, and Ben was spread-eagled on the ground. One of the cops was holding down his face with a boot. A tide of fear swept over him. What if this wasn't just because of Jake, but the DEA, this was a bust?

"This kid's crapped himself," one of the officers said.

"He does that," Ben began, "Because he's scared—"

"You, shut up," instructed the cop with the boot on his face.

There were more sirens now, more cops, the fire department, an ambulance—whatever for? Ben could hear the cops talking to Jake, talking at Jake: Do you know this man? Is he your dad? Is he your uncle? Do you know him? Is he trying to hurt you? It's okay now, son, it's okay now. Where is your mom? Where is your mom, son? The cops shoved Ben in the back of a squad car, making sure they bashed his head on the door on the way in.

"Is this man your daddy?" he heard. And then, "Don't worry, we'll find your mommy."

At the state police headquarters, Ben was allowed to call Lacey. The cops glared at him; he was scum and should have his balls cut off, stuffed down his throat.

An hour later, Lacey arrived, looking as if she'd come from gym class, or perhaps just a sofa, in sweatpants, no make-up, purple sneakers. She nodded at Ben, gave him a quick I'll-sort-it-out smile. Ten minutes later, she brought Jake, carrying him on her hip. He'd been cleaned up, dressed in a pair of My Little Pony pyjamas several sizes too big for him.

Ben feared the boy's rejection. How crushing it would be if Jake turned away from him, as if from a plate of distasteful food. What if Lacey tried to hand Jake over and Jake screamed? What then? All these cops watching, reluctant to dispense with their suspicions. Who could blame them, Ben thought, what they saw every day—men like him, suspects, dirtbags, abusers. And they were right, they had some deep cop sense that he was up to no good. But he knew, also, that they had nothing. If these assholes had the faintest whiff of his involvement in drug trafficking, they would have stripped the paint off his truck, they would have searched every one of his body cavities. He would not be sitting in the glare of the fluorescent lights and their bitchy stares. He could feel his luck like a single gold coin.

Lacey moved with particular grace for a large woman, gliding across the floor toward him. Her eyes fixed on his. She did not waiver. She came directly to him and handed him Jake.

Jake clung to him. And Ben wrapped his arms around the small trembling body. "Sorry, sorry I scared you. I did not mean to."

"One person," Lacey said. "You're his one person, Ben. Are you ready for that?"

S he'd left six messages for Michael—which he probably erased just as she erased his. But, at last, just as she was about to lose reception up the driveway, he texted back: *Facetime at 8*.

And so, obediently, after supper, the brushing of hair and teeth, Kay had the children crowded onto the toilet, shoving and arguing about space. At 8:10, Michael finally came through. He was in the back of a taxi.

Tom pushed in front of Freya, grinning *broadly*: "Dad! We nearly drownded in the lake!"

Freya shoved him back, hard, so he almost fell off. "You almost *drowned*, I was fine."

"What?" Michael frowned, "What happened?"

"No one nearly drowned," Kay interjected. "Freya, you explain. Without hysterics."

Michael regarded Freya through the portal. "Tell me, Frey."

"It was her idea to swim out to the rock. She said she'd heard there was treasure there!" Tom, again, thrusting his smiling face into the phone. "She told me there would be treasure."

"You said you wanted to play pirates," squawked Freya.

"You said not to tell anyone. You said Mum would be—"

"I did not!" Freya turned away with the phone so abruptly the connection jolted.

"One at a ti—" Michael froze. Then reappeared just as Tom made a grab for the phone: "Freya said Mummy was asleep so we could."

Kay pulled him off the toilet. "That's not helping."

"It was not my idea!" Freya scowled. "It was a game. We were playing. Why is it always my fault? He wanted to do it. I kept saying 'No,' I kept saying—" And now her voice broke and the stored tears flooded out. She flung herself at Kay, the phone tumbling to the floor. Kay held her, rocked her, and felt absurdly, appallingly grateful she was able to comfort her daughter.

Freya could not stop crying, her sobbing so intense that her body began to shake. Kay picked her up, nodding to Tom. "Tell Dad we'll call him back." She carried Freya—whom she had not carried for two years; it was an awkward shuffle—and tucked her into her own bed, stroking her forehead.

Tom burst into the room, jumped on the bed, shouting, "Freya, Freya cry baby."

"For God's sake, Tom, knock it off," Kay implored.

"Cry baby, boo hoo!"

In a flash, Freya leaped up and grabbed him, with the speed of a wild beast be-setting its prey. "You, shut up!" she shrieked. "I hate you. I wish you'd drowned!"

Kay broke up the fracas, but not before Tom had accidentally kicked her in the neck. "Stop! Both of you, goddammit!" She held them at bay. All Freya's sweet regret dissipated and Tom's dark look indicated he'd taken her words to heart.

"You don't mean that, Freya; you don't mean it, so say it to your brother."

Freya looked away. "Sorry."

Kay grabbed her arm, too roughly: "Say it to his face, Freya."

Freya's head drooped, and Kay felt a surge of pity—the enormity of Freya's mistake, the fear and guilt and shame of it was too much for the narrow shoulders of an eight-year-old. Freya turned at last to her brother. "I'm sorry, Tom. I don't wish that at all."

They went to bed, but the kisses she gave them, the reassurances, spattered uselessly on their wet faces. At last, they settled. She found the phone in the bathroom, five missed calls from Michael. Bracing herself, she Facetimed him back. He was walking, an airport somewhere—she could see the strip lights above him, the gate numbers, other passengers passing through the frame.

"It's okay," she began.

"Is it?"

"We were at Crystal Lake and they swam out of bounds. They ended up on some rocks on the other side of the lake."

"The other side of the lake, for Christ's sake, Kay, that's at least a mile."

"No, not the complete other side, just across from the beach. It wasn't that far."

"And Freya led the way in this exploit?"

"I think it was a game and they just got carried away."

"So they swam past the safety buoys and out to the rocks, and Tom did that, Tom was able to swim that far? He couldn't even get to the buoys that time we went. He was afraid."

"Yes, they swam, both of them, they were obviously exhausted."

Michael stopped. He looked away from her, as if he couldn't walk and think at the same time; the thought was so big and so important. Then he turned back to her.

"Where were you, Kay? Where were you?"

She now noticed the corner cupboard, the laundry basket askew, the door cracked open. She was certain she'd closed it, clicked the latch.

"What was that?" she said to Michael. "You dropped out."

"I said, 'Where were you when all this was going on?'"

"Asleep. I was asleep, fast asleep." Then she shifted the phone so the single bar disappeared, and Michael was gone.

Kay watched her children sleeping. Children grew in their sleep. They were growing now, bones lengthening like bamboo. If she could affix a time-lapse camera, she could see her babies growing. They would not be contained. They would make their way to adulthood. Freya's eyes were closed, her pupils shifting back and forth. Dreams were upon her. The dark lake moved beneath her. She looked back to shore and saw her mother was not watching but sleeping; her mother was not attending, she was never attending. She was in Djibouti or Mombasa, and she pushed on, she tried to blot out Tom's tedious whines: *I'm tired, Frey, I want to go back, I'm scared, Frey*, and how his voice looped into fear at the receding shore, how far out, how very far out she'd come.

Later, as Kay locked the door, she thought of herself with the hammer in her hand, all that pooling anger, and had she somehow transferred this to Freya? As if anger might be a black stone that you passed from person to person—impossible to destroy, you could only get rid of it by handing it on. And what of Michael? How reasonable, how moral the face he showed. Had he stood over her as she slept one night, a pillow in his tensed hands?

Our house in Nairobi was on the other side of a gate, manned by armed security guards. I hate to write "gated community" because that suggests a modern construction of cluster housing surrounded by a uniform wall; this, on the other hand, was a collection of old colonial houses connected by a rambling series of lanes. Once open bi-ways, these were now controlled by armed guards at sturdy gates. All the short-cuts and pathways working-class Kenyans once took to get to their jobs and their buses and their homes had been barricaded by high-voltage fencing.

Racism had given way to classism. A decade ago, as long as you were white, the guards would raise the gate. If you were black, you had to answer questions. If you were black—even if you were driving a late-model Mercedes, the guards would write down your license plate and name. By the time we had moved in, the guards stopped any car that didn't have tinted windows and government plates. Kenya had, at last, become a post post-colonial country.

I'm certain—now—that it was this equal-opportunity deterrence of the less well-off that allowed Michael and I to stomach living there. We excused ourselves because so many of our neighbors were wealthy black Kenyans, far wealthier than us. Others were Somalis, rich from piracy. Or bankers from Lagos, investors from Johannesburg. We excused ourselves because we wanted to sleep well at night—who doesn't? We wanted our child to play safely in our large manicured gardens. And in the very back of my mind, I had the idea that being a journalist was a civic duty, I was doing a service. These were the calibrations, the calculations I made, as a white person, living safely, warmly, sybaritically. They were my justifications.

Which isn't to say that reportage isn't important, that I was never brave: it is, I was. The world must know the truth, must be given the details, and I took the trouble to do my job with care. As for the civic impact of what I wrote, well, it's an individual choice—one of the few we genuinely have—whether or not you turn away, or if or how you incorporate the suffering and violence of others, often others who are far away, into your own life.

It's easy to conclude that mere awareness of suffering does absolutely nothing to change it. And therefore, what's the point of making anyone aware of it? Suffering is everywhere, every day; what is gained by knowing how people are dying in Palestine or the torment of starving zoo animals in Aleppo?

Michael and I were surely among the most aware in the world, and yet we were not prepared to surrender our comfort. We didn't encourage poor families, refugees, desperate single mothers, teenage prostitutes to live with us, to camp on our lawn. We kept them on the other side of an electric fence; in fact, further: on the other side of town. I argue now that our knowledge perhaps made us more complicit in suffering because we could switch it on and off; we knew, and we turned away when sushi was served, when a dusky French cabernet was opened. We were complicit because our professions had sheen, we weren't accountants or plumbers. We were journalist and filmmaker, we were glamorous. I liked that glamour, it was important to me.

Recently, in London, I met a young woman who had never given a thought to the life of a woman her age in South Sudan or rural Tanzania. She lacked the imagination—let alone the empathy—to not only see her cohorts' wretchedness, but their blamelessness. Surely, their own bad decisions had led to their living in a refugee camp, this young woman seemed to insist in her argument about free will: "It's all a choice." She couldn't comprehend being pregnant from rape at 14. Couldn't these women, these girls just go to the doctor for their STDs, their fistula, get some therapy, go to school? I exaggerate, but not much. Her ignorance was stunning, made insurmountable by the self-help jargon she'd stuffed in her head instead of actual knowledge. I told her stories, dealt out statistics, maternal mortality, infant mortality, she was unmoved. By the end of our conversation, she had not changed at all; but I—oh, I felt infinitely superior because I knew—I knew—the real world.

That night in Nairobi, we had friends over, cocktails on the veranda—this would have been daringly colonial if our guests hadn't been a mixture of races and sexual persuasions, a gay Nigerian couple, a Maasai businessman from Tanzania and his Venezuelan wife. Ice cubes clinked in our glasses. The evening light flashed on the bright feathers of the sunbirds feeding on hibiscus and lily. The Venezualan was an artist, she took found objects and turned them into masks, humorous and terrifying. She preferred to scour the slums for her materials.

And Freya was playing with their children, a posse of varying color. She was barefoot, as always, sun-browned, her hair a tangle of blond. Freya was a happy child. I am aware of that now. I took her happiness for granted with my coming and going—she loved her nanny, she went to daycare, she *was self-sufficient, a natural loner. I wonder what it was like for her to lose that, as suddenly as she did. A month later, you see, we moved to London.*

Unusually, both Michael and I were home from our wars. I was pregnant with Tom, my third trimester. The sun was slipping behind the Ngongs, our cook was serving around some canapés he was particularly proud of, and I noticed one of our night watchmen—Josiah—hovering on the edge of the scene like an uncertain stage hand. When he caught my eye, he beckoned.

"There is a man here for you."

"Let him in."

"No," Josiah said. "He is not a guest."

"What sort of a man?"

"From another country."

"What does he want?"

Josiah didn't know; but he was unsettled. The man was "not regular, not a regular man."

I excused myself from our guests and went to see this irregular man.

He was very dark, and I guessed immediately that he was from South Sudan. He stared at me through the gates, the whites of his eyes flaring in contrast to the dark of his face and the cloaking dark falling around us. He shifted into a deeper shadow and all I could see of him was those whites. I stepped through the gate, into the street.

"Can I help you?"

In Africa, you get used to people asking you for help—total strangers requesting that you send their children to school or buy them a cow or give them your shoes. And you become accustomed to stares—you are a minor celebrity merely because of your skin; in far-flung towns children gather to watch you walk across the street, you hear them narrating your every move. "Look, the whitey is taking out her phone, now she is dialing it."

But this man regarded me blankly. "I have a missive for Kay Ward."

"A missive?"

"Are you Kay Ward?"

"I am Kay Ward."

He removed a cheap pay-as-you-go phone from his shirt pocket, handed it to me. "The General requests you, Kay Ward."

"I know several generals." But I knew which one, there was really only one.

"Instructions will follow."

Then he turned, slipped into the darkness between the security lights. Only then did I wonder how he had gotten past guards at the gates.

General Christmas wanted an interview, an exclusive. If I got myself to Obo in the Central African Republic, he would make arrangements to get me to Gol, which was otherwise inaccessible. Even MSF couldn't get there.

"Who even cares?" Michael responded when I told him.

"This is a major scoop!" I retorted.

"You're just giving him what he wants."

"And you're certain you know where the line is between covering a story and creating one?"

"Jesus, babe, you're seven months pregnant. The airlines won't let you travel."

"The airlines? I'm going to take an airline?"

He looked at me. He rolled his eyes. "Forget it. You're not going."

I began to put some clothes into my travel bag.

"If anything happens," he said, "I'll never forgive you."

THE DAY BEGAN.

"Thanks for coming." Ed jerked his head toward the barn. "She's in there."

They crossed the muddy yard to the barn, ducked into the dim, looming interior. The radio played a country song, a man with a phony twang singing about beers and barbecues. Ben privately noted the irony of singing about hamburgers in a cow barn.

Ed kept it the best he could, only 30 head now, milking, mucking, feeding by himself since Border Patrol had rounded up all the Mexican illegals working the dairy farms. Pablo and Leandro, they had been hard workers. They were good with the cows, good to them.

"She went down last night," Ed sighed. "Been trying to treat her for mastitis, but I just couldn't get ahead of it."

The cow, a soft-eyed Jersey, lay half in the drain, half in her stall. Her head was low, she barely acknowledged them, even when Ed kicked her in the haunches. "She was one of my best. Three hundred goddamn dollars in antibiotics."

Ed had already maneuvered the tractor into place, the fork-lift resting six inches from the cow. Now, he got on board and started the engine. The cow looked startled, tried to stand with the last she had in her. Ben jerked a feed bag over her head, blocking her vision, calming her, and Ed moved quickly, sliding the forklift under her as Ben held her tail and her ear, pulling them both toward him. Within seconds, Ed had her hoisted into the air, faceless, her legs dangling, her swollen, wretched teats on display. Like a rabbit in the clutches of a bird of prey, she did not struggle, the loss of the tethering earth rendering her immobile. Ed backed up out of the barn, and Ben watched him drive out across the muddy yard, until a stand of beech trees obscured his view.

An empty wine bottle lay on the floor beside her. The broaching sun turned the low mist pink as the hued interior of a rose. The air was cool through the open door. For a moment, Kay thought she must have spilled the wine—she didn't remember drinking the bottle, didn't remember lying down on the sofa. But the tinny taste of tannin in her mouth was an unavoidable fact. Her tongue, dry as a lizard's, slipped out and scraped over her parched lips. Her skull seemed to have shrunk around her brain, pressing down mercilessly on the soft tissue. She acknowledged that it was dawn.

Slowly, deliberately, she levered herself upright, though this was no better. The wine in her stomach sloshed to a new position; the effort of putting her feet on the floor made her eyes ache.

She got up. Obediently, she laid the table, filled the water bottles, folded towels with the swimsuits. Tom's shoes gave off a powerful cheddar stink and she dowsed them with baking soda.

At breakfast, Tom wondered, "Mum, how many different types of caterpillars are there in the world?"

Kay put on the kettle. "Five hundred and sixty-seven thousand million."

"That is a lot!"

"She doesn't know," Freya declared. "She's just making it up."

Vaguely, Kay became aware of a burning smell, similar to the smell of fires in urban slums, the distinct tang of melting plastic.

"Mum!" Freya shouted and Kay was up, across the floor to the stove where the electric kettle was beginning to slump and bubble on the gas burner.

"Fuck fuck fuck shit," she yelped.

"Swear word, four swear words, four dollars!" Tom burbled.

"Nice one, Mum," Freya snorted.

Kay grabbed the kettle with her hand, her reaction time so numbed and slow from the hangover that it took her complete seconds to realize her hand was now melding into the kettle's handle. She let go. By now instinct kicked in, and she stepped back quickly as the melting kettle hit the floor, spewing near boiling water into the air.

Tom and Freya were howling with laughter. She saw them, hooting like monkeys, their mouths open, half-eaten cereal visible. Her hand sizzled and seared.

"Fuck you!" she screamed.

Tom kept laughing, mistaking this for another dollar. But Freya's mouth snapped shut, and with a swish of her pony tail, she turned her head away from her mother. Kay grabbed the back of her chair, jerked it around.

"You little bitch. You just sit there looking down your nose at me and everything I do is wrong or stupid."

She heard herself, she heard the word *bitch,* she could have chosen any other word—*brat, princess*—but *bitch* had risen to the surface first, *bitch* had the most buoyancy. *Bitch* had been waiting. Her daughter looked back at her. Kay watched her brows furrow. There could be no *sorry, I didn't mean it, honey. Bitch* was a hammer blow.

And Kay did not feel sorry. She was angry. These children—these interlopers—had colonized her life, infested it, altered its form so completely she had become someone else, a bloated, slow-moving host, who fed and watered and cleaned and tended and found lost shoes and endlessly, endlessly cut the crusts off the bread.

"Get in the car," she said. "We're late for camp."

"TIME TO GET UP." BEN STROKED THE BOY'S head.

Jake was a small, warm animal in its burrow. A child could sleep no matter what. Ben had slept in cars, in closets, on the bathroom floor. Sleep, like a metal shutter, came down between you and the world.

But waking to the bold light, the hard fact of a new day, Jake startled upright, staring at Ben without recognition. And then, Ben saw fear; the steadfast, trained-in fear flashing across the child's face, his pupils dilating, his eyes wide, mouth opening to increase his oxygen intake. Ben recognized the fizz in his blood, how he might even feel his muscles responding to endorphins, his body preparing to flee. Jake coiled and crumpled the blankets up to his chin.

Ben stepped back. "We've got to get going, bud. Breakfast is ready."

In the kitchen, he found Jake's lunchbox. It was empty, so he set about making a PBJ sandwich. Deep in the fridge was a bag of baby carrots he'd bought just for Jake, unopened. In the cupboard, he saw all the snacks he'd bought, Goldfish and granola bars, fruit roll-ups: all un-opened. What—exactly—had Shevaunne been putting in her son's lunch all these weeks as she handed it to him with a smile? Nothing, he realized. *Not a fucking thing.*

He glanced over at her asleep on the couch. Under her skin, buried inside, was some other Shevaunne, who she might have been, shiny and clean, and he should feel sorry for her. She'd been 11 when he'd met her at the Baileys'. Stories had already circulated—her abuse was legendary, even if only half of it was true. "How does a grown man even fit his dick inside?" Frank had wondered. Ben hadn't been able to look her in the eye; all he'd seen was a naked girl and some old man's rubbery penis looming into view. Her father, his brothers, cousins, the stories claimed, the postman, the road foreman, the mechanic. After a while she expected it. You can train a dog to think being kicked in the head is completely normal.

Jake rubbed his eyes and sat to eat his cereal and toast, and Ben drank his coffee. He could hear the clunking of machinery—Ed was cutting the hay after all that rain—and he opened the door. The smell of the sweet cut grass soared across the field and into the kitchen, this bright, hot Cheerio morning, and in the midst of such summer, winter could be forgotten, the sleet and snow, the wind punching down from Canada. Winter was six months, the dark drilling down and down into your skull. By March you were gasping for sun and heat, the thin jackets, thin cotton socks, the boots duct-taped against the wet snow, the cold like iron nails in your bones, and that was the one good thing about motels—they were warm, and you could press your body hard up against the radiator.

On the way to Little Feet, he and Jake listened to the radio. When Golden Earring's *Radar Love* came on, Ben admitted, "I like this song." Out of the corner of his eye, he noted Jake listening attentively, a recalcitrant pinkie tapping against the seat. At the door, he crouched down. He wanted to hug Jake. But instead, he simply straightened his t-shirt. "Have a great day. I love you."

Turning out of the daycare, he reached the main intersection in East Montrose. There were no other cars, though he could see a group of women coming out of the Congregational Church after morning yoga and on the other side of the street, a veteran-looking guy in fatigues gazed at floral fabrics through the window of the quilting shop. There was a Subaru with *Bernie for Prez* stickers and *Save our Ridgeline* stickers, and Ben wondered vaguely if it was the same car he'd seen on Diamond Hill. The same one that followed him that night. Had he been followed? There was chattering around him, too many things he didn't know but needed to know.

A horn beeped behind him. In the rear-view mirror another truck, another guy in a ball cap, a logger, a sugarer, a landscaper, a seller of firewood, carpenter, day jobber, builder, dairy farmer, snow plower, small-time dealer; one weary hand held the wheel, the other a cigarette, and like Ben he had no idea how he'd come to this point in time, the slide of years, the tide of bills, the relentless here and now, the person he was and did not want to be.

And then he saw Kay.

How silent they had been in the car. Tom had whispered, "Sad bunnies." Freya hadn't even mouthed "hello" to Adele. As they trudged away from the car, Freya had taken Tom's hand in solidarity—the suckiness of adults. Kay drove on to the drug store in East Montrose, her hand wrapped in a dish towel. The pain was sharper than the muffled ache in her head, but they worked in concert—loud, smashing cymbals in her hand to accompany the dry *brum-brum-brrrummmmm* drumming in her head. The physical pain still occluded the shame trying to feather the edge of her thoughts: *I called my daughter a bitch.* Squeezing her hand, she welcomed the fresh, clear clash of pain. She found the first aid aisle, scanned for antibiotic ointment and dressings, threw sufficient quantities in her shopping basket.

"Hey."

She knew the voice. She turned and he was right there. He saw the dish towel. "What happened to you?"

He followed her back to the house, led her into the kitchen, and held her hand under the cold running water, wincing himself. "You poor girl." He'd exchanged her ointment and dressings for silver sulfadiazine and plastic wrap, something he'd learned from a field-medic course in the Marines. Smearing the cream over the plastic, he then carefully wrapped the mitt of her hand. As the burn had affected several fingers, he cut smaller strips to individually dress. When this was done, he swaddled the whole hand in a bandage.

"Better now?"

She should have moved away from him. She should have stepped back—always the *shshshshush* of should should should. She should say "thank you" and offer him a cup of coffee. But instead hot, treacherous tears rolled down her face.

"Kay," he said, and she shut her eyes, the tears dripping off her chin. She wished he was not kind. She leaned in, did not intend to but it was unavoidable, gravity pulling her, the weight of her own pride leaning like Pisa against him. He put his arms around her, held her. She sobbed like a child. She could not remember when she had last been held by Michael.

Right then, right then was the moment for her to say, "You'd better leave. I'm sorry, this has been a mistake." And he'd leave, he'd go quietly, politely, cap in hand. She would never see him again. He would be just a man she never slept with, any man, any man at all.

Instead, she took his hand. She led him upstairs to her office with its single bed. She started to take off her clothes, but he stopped her.

"No, let me. I want to."

His fingers fumbled with the little buttons of her dress, and when they were undone, he peeled the fabric back off her shoulders, so it hung from her waist. His hands were on her skin, her breasts, up her back, the nape of her neck and he kissed her.

He kissed her like a boyfriend, tenderly, with a kind of wonder, the kisses she hadn't had for years and years, the kisses lost to vodka and war and marriage. Her body became liquid, permeable. He took her good hand and put it over the front of his jeans so she could feel how hard he was. She couldn't unbutton his jeans, so he did it for her.

There were things they could do, there were techniques, his fingers, her mouth. But Kay just needed him inside her. She wanted that uncomplicated proximity. She took him to the bed, they lay down, he did not stop kissing her. She could smell herself, her arousal, and they moved each other, articulated their limbs, so that he could be inside her, lodged deep, and with their mouths they were inside each other. They were disappearing.

Hours. Shadows wandered across the room. She'd forgotten that she'd called her daughter a bitch. Now, remembering, she let self-disgust wash over her. How odd to be undergoing such an intense emotion, and this man knew nothing, felt nothing of it—he could not judge her failure—and this relieved her. She was a lover, anonymous, functional. She lay with her head on Ben's shoulder. He did not move, and she half-wondered if he was asleep. Glancing up, she saw his eyes were open.

"Are you okay?" he said.

"Yes. Are you?"

"I was just going in to buy some Tylenol."

"You mean this doesn't happen every time you go to Kinney Drugs?"

He laughed softly. "Not every time."

She put her chin on his chest. "Are you married?"

"No. But you are."

"But he's gone. Left."

"Is this a revenge fuck then?"

"It's just a fuck."

Sliding his hand down her waist to her hip, he traced the vivid keloid scar across her belly. It traversed from hip to hip, as if she'd been torn in half. "Are you sure about that?"

His eyes were on hers. She turned her head away, and he moved down, kissing the scar.

When they were done with each other, he gathered his clothes and walked to the bathroom, turned on the shower. He had a certain ease in how he moved about the rooms. He knew the house, just as he knew Frank. She wondered if he also knew of Frank's cupboard, for she might reveal it to him and see surprise or familiarity. But she couldn't bring herself to leave the immediacy of him, their sex—to have him dismiss her again. She was still damp from him. She followed him, studying him: the lean structure of him, the fine, long muscles and tanned forearms. In his frame, he saw both her son and her husband—the otherness of men.

He caught her looking; this seemed to embarrass him, and he turned away as he washed himself.

"Where are your kids?"

"Camp."

"Which camp?"

"Are we chatting? Is this a chat?"

"Sure." He made a smile, his lovely, pretty actress smile. "Why not have a chat."

"They're at Kamp Wahoo."

"Takes you, what? About an hour, there and back?"

"About that."

"Do they like it?"

"They love it."

"I've heard great things about it. I might send my son next summer."

Kay thought of the boy outside the trailer. *Jake, get the fuck inside.* The woman in pink leggings—the sordid air about her. *My son.* So what was his relationship with the woman? Kay felt the greasy smear of jealousy. She picked up her phone; she wanted to put something between herself and Ben—the old habit, as

Marco and Sam did with their cameras, as she did with her notebooks.

And as Ben washed his face, eyes closed, Kay took his picture.

He got out of the shower. He dried himself.

"How's your hand?" he said as he dressed.

"It's okay, better. Thank you."

There was no kiss. He did not even look back.

BEN APPROACHED THE HOUSE FROM FURTHER down the road. He'd parked well out of sight, then cut up through the woods, pushed through the brambles and hobble-bush, clambered over the degraded logging debris, for a moment wondering if he'd gotten his direction right. Here in the deep woods, mid-summer afternoon, it was easy to miscalculate. Deer flies assailed him and when he caught one against his cheek, it was a pleasure to feel it pop between his fingers.

At last, he reached the pond, wildly ringed with reeds, and from here he could discern the old path, kept worn now by deer and moose. He wondered where Ammon had been putting his traps, and why. No one cared about coyotes up here, and the price for pelts was nickels on the dollar, so it was likely just spite. Spite. It would be on his gravestone: *May he rest in spite.*

Ten minutes along the trail and Ben glimpsed the house through the thick stand of trees. He felt his ears attune to the possibility of human voices. But it was quiet, only the tilting lilt of wood thrush and the insistent hammer of a downy wood-pecker. As the trail opened into the overgrown cow pasture, Ben became more discreet, hugging the edge of the open land, weaving in and out of the screening trees.

Her car was gone, as he'd calculated. He had an hour for her to get to Kamp Wahoo and back.

His key worked; there'd been no need to change the lock. Junkies from town would simply smash a window if they wanted to get in. Everyone else either came with a key and a reason, or stayed away. He stood for a while in the mud room, listening, but there was nothing to hear. The walls were mute, as they had always been.

In the deep silence of the still house, he moved swiftly from room to room. Kay's possessions and those of her children lay on the surfaces, a dense residue, while the obsessive order underneath remained undisturbed. The order was a symptom of Frank's madness. Or perhaps, Ben mused now, the opposite: his attempt at sanity—to control what he could control. The crazy tidiness was the tick-tock; for the broken bits were all the way inside Frank, the tiny springs and screws and levers, bent and smashed, deep down.

He went upstairs, moving efficiently through the bedrooms, and at last to the room Kay had claimed. There was a stack of books on the table beside her bed, thick novels, a copy of *Africa Today*.

Also: a bottle of skin lotion with a nice lemony scent which he rubbed into his worn hands. He wondered if she rubbed this onto her scar. What had happened to her? It looked as if she'd been sawn in half, a magic trick gone wrong. He was almost reassured by the scar. She was damaged. He sat on the bed, and despite himself, leaned over to smell the pillow.

He imagined her, head thrown back, lips parted, taking him into her. He imagined himself the man he might be for her. "Shit into one hand and wish into the other," Ammon liked to say. "See which fills up first."

Focusing on her desk, he considered turning on her computer. But he knew very little about them. He worried that she would know someone had trespassed. He flipped through a stack of notebooks, frayed and worn, certain pages stained with what looked like wine and maybe coffee. He couldn't read the writing, it was shorthand, only occasionally strange words: Owale Ndugu, Lira, Juba, Lokchoggio, Mwangi Micah, General Christmas, Gol. Were these names, places, codes? What was she doing with all these words, these pages and pages of notes? She was a journalist. Was she writing a story? About him, about Frank, their grubby drug dealing?

On the floor, under the desk, was a box containing more notepads. He realized they were dated—a start date, an end date—some reaching back into the mid-'90s.

He pulled the one with only a start date, two weeks ago, flipped through. And there, nestled among the impenetrable squiggly lines, were names:

- Frank, Maria Wilson
- Ben Comeau
- Paul Steiner
- Ammon

Was it possible she was a DEA agent? Not a journalist. All this was a ruse. Did she even have kids? *Undercover bitches.* His heart was pounding. There was roaring in his ears, and he had the idea that what he needed to do was go and get Jake and run, out West, maybe Canada. Right now, forget Slim, forget Shevaunne. But he knew in the next breath the impossibility. He needed money, they needed money, they needed a fresh start—a life, free and clear; not hiding under freeways, not the cash-only jobs even illegal Mexicans wouldn't take. He'd never wanted anything, and now he did, and what he wanted was simple and wildly complicated; he wanted to be safe, to be quiet, hollowed in, he and the boy, the days and years before them, Jake in a cap and gown graduating from high school, and when he threw the cap in the air it twirled in slow motion.

Ben regarded Kay's notebooks. He was like one of Ammon's coyotes: he could sense the trap, he knew it was there, underneath the leaves, the dead bracken. But he had to keep walking on the path, there was no other way.

Leaving the basement until last, he hesitated at the top of the stairs. There was nothing to fear. He opened the door and he hated this house and he turned on the light and he hated this house and he took a step downward and then another. The inventiveness of Ammon, he thought, so inventive, so creative, all that *effort*, and then he pressed his hands against his forehead, as if it might physically stop his thinking. It sort of worked, his mind spool merely spluttered with the squealing, the shapes moving. The rest was mercifully redacted.

At last he was in the basement, the solid floor beneath his feet. Frank and Maria had cleaned, painted, ordered it, in their Tyvek suits and masks, spraying first bleach then this sterile white. Ben swelled with respect for Frank, the courage it must have taken him to come down here, let alone attempt repossession.

Right away he saw the plastic tubs. One wasn't perfectly square on the shelf, so Ben knew someone other than Frank had touched it. He peeked inside: Frank's mother's prize-winning quilts, Maria's recipe books. He hadn't known she'd used books; she'd always struck him as improvising or remembering, her ingredients spread out on the counter, her mortar and pestle, her jars of spices, the bunches of herbs. The healing power of Maria, as if stews were magic potions. Maria, who had painted and scrubbed and bleached, who had hired a Mexican witch from Littleton to exorcise the house's bad spirits. If anyone could have mended Frank, it would have been that small, round woman who somehow managed to love Frank or some approximation of love, kindness, and loyalty, whatever the trade to bring her boys here.

Straightening the tubs, he thought about her *tamales*, something he'd never eaten before, the steamed cornmeal surrounding green chile and melting cheese and tender beef, all wrapped so delicately in corn wrappers.

"*Te gusta?*" she'd giggled, serving him three more. "Eat, eat, Ben, I find you a wife, like me, good Mexican lady."

Ben checked his watch, realized he'd been longer than he meant. He climbed the stairs, left through the kitchen. Outside, the shadows grew bolder. A flock of jays passed overhead, their sharp shrieks grating the late afternoon. Kay would be back soon. He could almost feel her. He almost thought he might stay, he could convince himself she was a lonely housewife here on vacation with her kids, that was all, and he was her lover; she was here because of the house, and it was a different house with her in it.

But the house was only one house. It had only one owner, no matter the occupants.

Ben turned and jogged back down through the overgrown cow pasture. Just before he entered the woods, he glanced back, upstairs, the bathroom window. Frank was hiding there, tucked into his cupboard, and Ammon was looking for him. The pigs were ready, the pigs were waiting.

Freya and Tom stood, forlorn, with their backpacks and wet towels and a fat, sad boy. Phoebe Figgs pressed her lips together as Kay pulled to a stop.

"I'm so sorry. Does he need a lift?" Kay looked to the other forgotten boy, as if she might absolve herself of sin piling upon sin.

"No, he doesn't." Phoebe was unmoved.

Freya huffed her backpack into the car. Tom kept his eyes down.

"Sorry," Kay mumbled to them. Sorry, sorry, sorry.

Freya frowned as she did up her seatbelt. "I want to speak to Dad."

Kay offered her the phone. "Hello, by the way. How was camp?"

"Mum, Mum," Tom began. "There's this boy who can bend his arms all the way behind his back. It's called double-joineded, and Mrs. Figgs told him he shouldn't do it because he could hurt himself but he kept doing it, and she said—"

"Hi, Dad, it's Freya." She was speaking loud and for effect into his voicemail. "I need to talk to you. Mum called me a bitch. That actual word. Can you please call back."

You deserve each other, Kay thought savagely, then took a

breath. *You're her mother, you're the mother, the mother.* "We need to talk, don't we, Freya."

"Well, uh, I'm not talking to you." Freya dropped the phone on the passenger seat. "I'm talking to Dad."

"Don't leave out the part about laughing at me when I burned my hand."

"Mum, Mum, is that your hand?" Tom stared at the bandage. "Is it broken? Does it hurt?"

"It's fine. It does hurt, but a nice man helped me dress it."

"Who?" Freya's instinct was sharp.

"A man, just a man."

"Can we get ice cream?" Tom wanted to know.

"Not today."

"The man at the lake?" Freya probed. "With the boat?"

Kay kept her eyes on Tom. "We can't get ice cream every day."

"Maybe just on the days you're late." Freya gazed out the window, her voice lazy and calm. "Oh, wait, that is *every* day."

Abruptly, Kay pulled into a gas station, braked a little too hard. "Listen up. I was late, 15 minutes. It's not as if I've abandoned you or hurt you or put you in danger. So get a grip and keep this in perspective."

"You called me a bitch."

"Yes, Freya, and I'm truly sorry for that. I can't take it back. I hope you can forgive me."

Tom began to cry, a soft weepy noise.

"Tom, honey."

"I thought you weren't coming. You were mad at us."

Kay bowed her head, she shut her eyes. She got out of the car, walked around to Tom's door, and she opened it. She kissed him, her son, her little boy: "I'll never leave you. I'll always be there. It's my job as your mum and because I love you. Do you understand?"

He nodded and threw his arms around her neck. "Where's Dad?" he mumbled. "When is he coming back?"

"He's working. You know that. He goes away, but he comes back."

Then Freya reached out and put her hand on Tom's head. "It's okay, he really does love us."

Kay was afraid to catch Freya's eye, to see the waiting sneer; she hoped so much the gesture was genuine. So she didn't look. She kept her gaze on Tom. "You remember how you wanted to explore the woods, try to find that path down to the pond? Let's do that."

"Can we collect tadpoles? Please, Mum?"

There was no hurry, the warm, soft air and the house hung among the round hills—what they had come for, with or without Michael. Tom and Freya slathered on insect repellent and danced ahead of Kay with nets and jars. "This way, Mum, this way!"

Into the woods, the damp scent, mud, earth, uncoiling green; the light flickering through the canopy obscuring the sky in an umbrella of green. They were held in green, the layers of it. They were wading through it, ferns and brambles, a carpet of lilies with tiny white flowers. So much was unseen, but Kay sensed it happening around her, earthworms, insects, small birds, and deeper in, the dark-eyed doe with her fawns moving neatly on mute hooves.

"Look, Mum!" Tom thrust a leaf toward her. She refocused to discern a tiny green caterpillar. "Can we keep it?"

"Yes, Mum, yes! Say, yes!" Freya took her mother's good hand and Kay felt a hard jolt of relief, and love. Why can't adults forgive like children?

"Yes," Kay said.

"We'll show Mrs. Figgs! Mrs. Figgs loves caterpillars and

butterflies. She knows all about them!" Tom could hardly stand still as Freya helped him put the leaf in one of his jars.

At last they reached the pond, the path petering out in the pliant mud and solid tufts of yellow marsh grass. Here was a small oval of water: one half held a perfect reflection of sky; the other half, shaded by tall pines, was dark, occluded. Closer in, Kay saw how the still surface in fact seethed with pond skimmers, dragonflies, all manner of tiny fluttering insects.

She stepped forward, and noticed her shoe fitting within another, larger print. Quickly, she pulled back, peered down to better see the boot print, but the mud sucked at it, and then she couldn't be sure of the shape. Or if it had been there at all. She leaned over, scrutinizing the mud. She could see where the marsh grass had been bent at several even intervals, she could see the remnant indents. Someone or something had passed this way not long ago. A moose, she thought, that's all, that's all.

"Here!" Tom yelled, and Freya ran to him. "Mum, Mum, tadpoles, hundreds of them."

SURPRISINGLY, SHEVAUNNE WASN'T ON THE
sofa, though the TV babbled on, alone, a mental patient on a
park bench. *You bitch never you always you don't you always you always
you bitch I hate—*

"Shevaunne? Jake?"

He heard only the *brrrrrr* of the fridge.

He listened hard. He could almost feel his ear canals opening,
the delicate aural hairs stiffen.

At last he heard the low breathing of a child.

"Jake?"

He turned into his bedroom. Jake was sprawled asleep on
his bed and Shevaunne sat in the chair by the window. She had
an unlit cigarette in her mouth. Ben studied the scene, there
was something wrong—not just her presence in his room—but
wrong in the subtext, as if a picture was suddenly hanging askew.

Shevaunne smiled. "Hello, Ben." She held up a manila
envelope.

He felt a sense of violation knowing she'd been through his
things, carefully turning over his socks, his underwear, the cutlery, the dishes and coffee filters. Diligently, she'd investigated
the underside of his bed, of every table and chair until she'd
arrived, at last, at the fridge. And she had done this instead of
making lunch for her child.

"Trucking manifests," she said, opening the envelope. "Forestry approvals."

He took off his cap, put it on top of the bureau. "I'm shipping logs to Canada."

Wetting her finger, she flipped through the paperwork. "Why'd you hide this, then?"

"I don't know what it is you think you have there."

"Ben," she sighed. "I'm a junkie whore."

All he could do was wait, regard her impassively.

"I'm looking at these forestry things, and they're completely blank except for the signature. You can fill in anything you want." She smiled. It was almost genuine, how happy she was. "You're shifting smack to Canada, aren't you, Benny."

Now Ben surveyed Jake. The child was fast asleep, yet it was early evening. He looked at Shevaunne. "What did you give him?"

"He was driving me nuts."

Ben stood quietly. He did not raise his voice. "What did you give him?"

"Some over-the-counter sleep shit."

"You drugged your child?"

"Oh, mister, it's just *sleep*." She pulled out her lighter, lit up, boldly. "So, you're gonna cut me into the next haul, right? I'd like to move back to town. I'd like a car. Me and Jake. We don't want to stay out here in the boonies."

"I'll think about it," he said as if he might think about it, might give it a moment's consideration, then walked back into the kitchen to clean the dishes in the sink. He did this calmly, plunging his hands into the warm, soapy water, carefully scrubbing the pan, the plates, between the tines of the forks. Shevaunne followed him out, puffing her smoke. She sat on her sofa like a duchess, for she possessed it now—it was her residence. He could feel her watching him, and she was imagining him thoughtfully thinking. But Ben did not need to think, he had arrived at the end of his thinking. He was 100 percent concluded.

The general showed me around his shop, the Alice Lakwena Good Buy. Alice Lakwena was the general's patron saint, a visionary who'd convinced her followers they were impervious to bullets. In the 1980s, thousands died believing her— and not just the first hundred who so obviously died from bullets, but those after, row upon row, year upon year, convinced that their fate would be different. Such is the human capacity for wishful thinking.

"And here are the washing powders." Christmas gestured to a surprisingly wide array, including imported French brands that must have come from Kinshasa. "And here, cocking oil."

I smiled to myself, the naughty joke at his expense. Cocking oil. It almost made him comic; I almost said, "And what do you cock with your cocking oil?" But he would recognize my sarcasm immediately. So I nodded, and he showed me the flip-flops he imported from India. "They are very nice colors and of superior manufacture."

Out of the corner of my eye, I noticed a girl, perhaps 15, diligently wiping down each can of tomatoes and replacing it with excruciating exactitude. She leaned into the shelves, so close I wondered if she had poor sight, and positioned the can, adjusting it several times. Her efforts were in vain, for Christmas tutted, pushed her aside, fine-tuned the placement by half a millimeter.

"A hair's breadth," he chuckled. "When I first heard the expression, I thought it was a hare's breath—you know, the distance of the breath of a rabbit. Poff." He blew. "Not far!"

"Yes," I replied. "That makes a certain sense."

"How about a refreshment?" He turned to me, his generous smile. "We can go to my guest house."

We walked together across the sunny, open courtyard to the Sleep EZ. It was, like the shop, fastidious. I wondered how he dealt with blood and excrement, the mess of slaughter. We sat in large, over-padded chairs upholstered in purple ripple velvet. Another girl, the same age as the last, silently placed a tray of tea and coffee on the table. Under the cups, jug of milk, sugar bowl, and thermoses, was an immaculate ironed linen cloth embroidered with primroses.

"Tea or coffee?"

"Tea," I said.

"I shall be mother," he tittered. Where had he learned this? The missionary school in Kitgum? A colonial memsahib, *perhaps, tucked into the mountains of South Sudan, like a Japanese soldier who didn't realize the war had ended long ago. Is that where he got the tea service?*

"You are not afraid?" He handed me the tea.

"Of what?"

He gestured to my belly.

Casually, I moved my hands to cover it, something we both knew to be instinctive and pointless. My belly, like a ripe peach for Christmas and his elves to split open and remove the pit. They had proved adept at this—I had read the Human Rights Watch reports, I had even seen the photograph of a woman who'd survived.

As a pregnant woman, I discovered I was paradoxically more inviolable and more vulnerable; I was large and slow-moving, my swollen belly almost a deformity, yet I was an object of atavistic respect. I was doing my part for the species.

I raised my eyebrow to General Christmas: "Should I be afraid?"

He laughed, his warm chuckle, as if we were two old friends sharing a joke. How many psychopaths does it take to change a lightbulb? It depends who the lightbulb is attached to. Oh, ho ho, ho, that is so funny. "Ah, Kay, are you referring to certain reports? These are mere propaganda."

"The incidents certainly happened, General. Maybe you don't accept that your men were involved."

He was still smiling and expansive. "You are trying to be clever with your words, 'you don't accept.' I do not accept because my men would never do such things. These are our people, all of them. Why don't you ask Foranga or SPLIF? They are interlopers, not from this region."

Foranga, SPLIF—part of the myriad of militias operating in the nasty triangle of death between northern Uganda, South Sudan and eastern Congo: Hutu, Tutsi, FNP, PPT, WTF. They all had acronyms, their clubhouses, their uniforms, their a la carte vengeance, their vague mission statements invoking "people" and/or "freedom."

Now I ran my hand over my belly, almost provocative. "I wonder what it feels like for a man to do such a thing. Does it make him less of a man or more of one, that you are not afraid of committing the worst crime." I looked at Christmas now: "It seems almost brave because it is such a terrible, terrible thing to do."

He held my gaze. He knew my trick. I watched his liquid dark pupils and thought about what they had recorded, how the neurons in his brains stored the images as memories.

Whatever he had done he may deny or excuse, but he wouldn't forget.

"Anyway, Kay." He liked to use my name. "I was speaking of your advanced state of pregnancy and you are here in this country where—thanks to Mr. Foranga and his greed—we have inadequate medical care. I am surprised your husband allows you to travel."

"Did you know at least one baby was full term, it—he—was born alive and your soldiers—"

"Foranga's soldiers, Kay."

"We disagree then."

He splayed his hands, a gesture of reason. "I am simply expressing concern. My own wife lost a child. If you should need my assistance, please do not hesitate. My resources are at your disposal."

"I will be returning to Juba tomorrow. Thank you for the offer, though." I gave him an obligatory smile, then took up my notebook. "You wanted to speak with me. What do you want to say?"

He lobbed back his own smile. We were smiling at each other. "I am very surprised, Kay. For years you have been trying to meet with me. I thought you had the questions."

So he wanted to be flattered; he had in his mind an interview not a monologue. He appreciated the difference between conversation and rhetoric. He wanted to appear reasonable. But why now—what was his motive?

I could ask him about his civic vision for peacetime, or about his past—had he tortured kittens as a child, had his mother shamed him while toilet-training? I could ask him about his influences—Marx, Castro, Donald Trump? What music he listened to, books he read, movies he watched; did he prefer Coke or Pepsi? But I had only one question—there was only one. I'd been asking it for years, drilling down into the African soil. I leaned forward, aware that he could glimpse my cleavage. "How did it begin for you?"

He frowned. "It?"

It has so many names. The names all have their roots, their reasons—their pathologies, physiologies, psychologies. But in the end, there's only the single, singular noun.

"Evil," I said.

"Evil." He mulled the word, rolled it around on his tongue like a boiled sweet. "Kay, we are fighting for freedom."

"Yes, yes, of course. But I'm not interested in that. I want to know when you first felt evil."

Leaning back, he began to drum his fingers on the arm rest. At last he gave me a grin. "You speak as if it is a feeling, like happiness or coldness. That you can define from one moment to the next."

"Is it?"

"And you speak as if you have never felt it."

"I've never killed anybody, General."

"And that is the defining act of evil—the, what do you call it, hallmark?"

"Is it?"

"Killing." He sighed: oh, the grating ennui of waging civil war. "Is easy, it is the easiest thing. We are designed to kill. Killing is our history, our design. It is our hands, our brains."

"So is art, so is medicine."

"Really? You think there is good and evil, salt and pepper?"

"Not so simply delineated, of course not. But at a certain point relativism becomes an excuse for atrocity. I'm interested in that point."

"So you're not here to write about me?"

"I'll write something, the usual thing."

"You are here to examine me, then, like an ape in a cage. The big black man all you whites fear."

"No. Not that."

"But it's a story you like to tell yourselves."

"It's passé."

"So you think there is a door that you open, you step through, and you are evil?" he pondered. "Or do you think it is a corridor, long or short, moving from light to dark?"

"I want to know what it is for you."

"Why, Kay?"

I shrugged. "I want to understand why terrible things happen."

"Understand? You sound like a dilettante. One of your white tribesman drinking martinis, shooting elephants. 'Bring me more ice, boy.'"

"Forget that I'm white and you're black."

"That's impossible."

"Then it's beside the point. Race has nothing to do with evil."

"To answer your question, I have to admit that I'm evil."

"But you are." I smiled.

"You think there's you and there's me, there's what you do and there's what I do."

"You want me to say there isn't? That given a set of circumstances I could round up a group of school children and burn them to death in a church. I don't believe I could ever do that."

"I'm disappointed in your lack of imagination, Kay. You want to understand? Then imagine. You are in a different world to my world, Kay, a gated community, a real passport. You don't know, you haven't the faintest idea what you would do in my situation. Your innocence is just a failure of imagination."

"Others in your exact same circumstances don't—"

He cut me off, his hand coming off the armrest like a knife. "Where I am, who I am. Here, now, the accumulation of what I have done and what has been done to me. I cannot be anyone else."

"You could meet with the opposition. You could sign a truce with Museveni. He'd give you amnesty."

"He'd give me amnesty with the crocodiles in Lake Victoria. You know that."

"You keep killing, then, to avoid dying yourself."

"Because we are in a war, Kay."

"That you perpetuate."

"That would perpetuate itself. As long as there are people, there will be war. This is basic." He shook his head. He was getting bored.

"What is it, then, that you want to tell me? Because you did bring me here. Not just to repay me for my efforts. Tell me, tell me."

We were back again to his expansive smile. "Okay. I admit. I heard you were pregnant. I wondered to myself, this white woman, how white people think they are special, will she come all this way to see a man who cuts babies out of the belly?"

I held his gaze, impassive. "I am a trophy?"

"Not yet."

Back at the Hotel Gol, I poured myself a small beer and reviewed the HRW files, the many eye witnesses that corroborated accusations against Christmas and his elves. Foranga was just as bad: a five-year-old girl raped so violently and repeatedly that her pelvis had been broken and she now walked like a dog.

I finished my beer and took a bath. I was almost too large for the tiny hotel tub, which anyway filled only halfway before the water ceased. I washed, I could barely reach my toes. I was much bigger with Tom than I'd been with Freya.

Rising from the tub in the Hotel Gol, my vast, heavy belly like a masthead, I thought about hell. I am an atheist, but allow for the infinite universe—possibilities quite beyond our simple sketch of God or time: some massing or conglomerating or dispersing of matter, the pliability of dimensions. Why not?

Explain evil. This is always the problem for theists. So they invent Satan, and Satan and God become puppet-masters. We humans, flippy, floppy, string-tied, we cannot help ourselves. General Christmas, therefore, cannot be blamed. But I don't believe that. Cannot believe it. And yet if you bring in free will, then what's the point of God—other than as an arbiter of culturally relative morality. He sends you to Heaven or Hell.

Once, in rural Nigeria, Michael and I had witnessed a traditional dance involving full body masks. The dancers came out, the central dancer wearing an eland mask made elaborately of grass. The dancer was completely encased in the mask—only his feet were visible, scuffing the dust. The eland strode and shied, bucked and turned, elusive, all power and elegance. I had mistakenly thought the point for the dancer was to become the eland, to take on its qualities—as with warriors who used to eat the heart and brains of their vanquished foes. But Michael told me it was more beautiful: wearing the mask, the dancer ceased to be a dancer—he shed his human skin—and leaving his human-ness was able to enter the plain of pure being where all living things existed as spirits. All were equal on this spirit plain: there was no rank and file, no leaders, no predators nor prey, no ego, no desire.

And what if we somehow might transcend to that other plain, stripped of our physical encasement, human or animal, some High Catholic idea of Holy Spirit—ego dispersed, and *all of us become all evil and all good, undifferentiated, the molecules blending. And in this way I might finally understand General Christmas, I might be him, and he me. Not nirvana, not some painted-up sop to the lonely and the bigoted and the suffering, but a complete neutrality of being, like the atoms in an acorn or a stone.*

The water was cold in the bath. I had not realized the passage of time. Time felt like a tunnel that I could look through and move through, from the first glimmer of human consciousness a million years ago to my own present—my own miraculous hand against the white porcelain of the bathtub. It was the same tunnel for all of us, the same way back, the way down, and we were running with fear, trying to escape ourselves, the cages that we build; sometimes we were putting on masks and dancing, sometimes we were raping and plunging ourselves into the bodies of others, all of this a frantic attempt to escape: to shed our wretched selves.

While I was convulsed with thought—so self-important, so proud of my existential adventures, my bravery, my steadfastness under Santa's scrutiny—my body, my mortal body, the manufacture of millions of years, was betraying me. I stood up and felt dizzy, saw myself briefly in the cracked mirror across from the bath, hideous and bloated, and I saw myself fall, heard a sound like firecrackers which I later understood to be my head smacking against the wall and the side of the tub on the way down. Because the tub was only half-full I did not drown.

YOU YOU ALWAYS YOU NEVER YOU NEVER YOU
never you you you don't love you don't love me me me—

Ben heard the voices through the wall, the voices slamming like bricks. All the loathing and self-pity. People dwelt on the wrongs done to them, attentive as dogs licking and licking wounds to keep them open. They became their wounds.

It was nearly 4:30. Dawn began its slow stalk across Ed's fields. A single chickadee, like an over-eager chorister, announced the day, then fell silent, and the humans resumed their complaining. *You you you always you you you never.* The shame, the blame, the bewilderment at life's mundanity. Hadn't love been promised? Roses, beauty, a prince on a white horse? *Ronaldo! Brianna!* Whatever the show, it had an exclamation mark, a host in a bright tie with a shaved head or a hostess, plump and comfy, your less-pretty best friend.

You always you always I hate you I wish you were dead you never I hate you don't love you never listen never we'll be right back—

The motels, no matter how wretched, always had TVs. Motels with their ceiling stains, their paper bathmats, their child-sized towels. He'd loved the soaps, the plastic cups in their wrapping, the white altar that was the bathroom sink. He'd had the impression these had been put there especially for him: gifts. He learned to bring a pillow and the bed cover into the bathroom with him before the grown-ups shut the door. *Don't open that fuckin' door.* He counted the tiles on the floor, he listened, he was like a blind boy interpreting sound. You can shut your eyes, you can shut the door but you can't un-hear. The TV, the delicate *pffff* of the lighter, low voices, his mother murmuring-laughing with Billy or Joey or Wheezie or Pete or Honey Baby, the stink of their unwashed jeans, their unwashed hair, their cigarettes, their farts. He hoped they'd ignore him. He prayed they did not see him, he was a pile of laundry, he was a floor tile.

Don't open that fuckin' door. As if the door was sound proof, fist proof, boot proof. Count the tiles, 98, 99, and hear the sound of a zipper, of sucking, *oh yeah baby.* They always wanted a piss afterward and he would hide in the shower, the smell of their urine, its confident fizz in the toilet water. They didn't care if they missed or splattered.

"And who do we have hiding in here?"

"That's just Ben. He's all right, aren't you, my Benben. You're cool with Momma partying."

Sometimes they did not see him, sometimes they did. Sometimes they smiled before they hit him. They spoke in soft, low voices. They gave him candy from the vending machines.

The twilight of drapes, brown as late fall, dead leaves; the world outside, bright sun, the humming interstate or banks of dirty snow. The light through slats, vertical, in small pieces only, as if there wasn't enough. Sometimes the men stayed, Nick, John, Moose, Goose. They strapped up, the magic needle, *oooohhhhm-mmm*, like a little kitty-cat walking up my spine his mother said. Sometimes they pissed and zipped up and left, his mother running into the bathroom to rinse out her mouth, turning her face this way and that in the mirror.

Ben sat up. He was sweating though the dawn was cool.

He will get rid of the TV. He and Jake will take it out to the woods and shoot it. He and Jake, he and Jake, me and Jake.

Jake was sitting six inches from the screen. A woman,

over-exercised as a freakish greyhound, her skin stretched across her face like vacuum-sealed jerky, spoke in rapid, un-connected exclamations. She was selling a miracle lotion of some kind—*my skin doesn't just look younger*—Jake watched passively.

Shevaunne lay on the sofa, fast asleep. Her t-shirt rode up her belly, revealing the striations of stretch marks. Her bare arms and ankles were pocked with needle scars, some blistered with knots of tissue where infections had set in. Her body was a road map of her life. He should pity her, the narrow class-4 road that ran directly from her shitty family to his shitty home. It was a straight line, the ink indelible and black. But she'd made no effort to veer off or double back, she'd taken the path of least resistance, and down it she was sliding still, down down the mire and mud, she was taking her son with her, holding him fast, simply, simply because she didn't want to be alone when she at last stopped sliding.

Ben sat beside Jake. At first, the boy did not acknowledge him, fixated on bodies that were now flying through the air, a soundtrack that resembled a circus calliope. What was this, re-runs of *Jackass*? No, it was the human condition, a messy splat upon the pavement.

Then Jake began to blend into Ben, to lean his arm on Ben's thigh, his palm open, his body tilting, so that Ben scooped him up and brought him fully onto his lap. He felt the weight of the boy and a fierce stabbing in his heart. He'd never understood why love should be felt by that organ, as if it had anything to do with the pumping of blood, the circulating of oxygen.

The feeling of love, this irrational, unreasonable love for a child, this sacred child, pinned him to the floor so that he could not move and could scarcely breathe and his eyes filled with tears. He rested his chin on the top of Jake's head. He held the boy.

Just this moment, this perfect, unstirred moment, before the inhale, before the exhale. But the time always came, the task was always at hand, it had to be done.

"Jake, I'm going to turn the TV down and we're going out for the day. You and me."

Ben could see the TV reflected in Jake's eyes, the images printed directly onto his retina. "Jake, I'm going to turn the TV down now. Are you listening? And we're going to be quiet so we don't wake your mom."

Jake nodded. Ben reached out his hand. All this was part of it, all this was meditated, his hand reaching through the air, a sequence. What if he stopped now and left on the TV and the boy in front of it? But he did not. His fingers reached for the remote. He felt as if this had already happened, a long time ago, maybe even before he was born—old-timers in frock coats and calico who believed that if you spare the rod you spoil the child. They made sure not to spoil the child.

He pressed mute. Jake blinked and looked up at Ben, almost surprised to see him there. Ben smiled, mouthed, "Let's go."

On his way out, Ben pulled a spindle from the back pocket of his jeans and left it there upon the counter, just where the dawn light caused the plastic wrapping to glow and luminate.

S ad bunnies."

The shed door cracked ajar, the white electrical cord trailing out. Why should the half-open door be more frightening than one that's fully open or closed? Kay turned up the radio, Adele still moaning on about the guy she'd known five years ago. Jesus Christ, just get *over* it, Kay thought. If there's one thing she could teach Freya it would be about moving on, not wasting *years* sobbing into a hankie about a guy.

"Did you know a blue whale is the largest animal that ever lived?" Tom chirped.

"Hellooo," sang Freya with all her heart.

"Did you know that many moths do not have mouths?"

At Kamp Wahoo, they fledged from the car, giving her the briefest of kisses, off toward the warm Pop-Tarts and dodgeball and Phoebe Figgs with her clipboard and her certainty.

In White's, Kay roamed the aisles, hunting and gathering, pasta, eggs, peaches, cheese, ice cream. At the checkout, she tossed in a copy of *The Caledonian-Record*. Then she took it out. It was just a newspaper. She held it, light in her hands, words and paper, the headline, "**BARNET WWII VETERAN CELEBRATES 100TH BIRTHDAY**."

"Ma'am?" the woman working the checkout was poised. "Do you want that?"

"Sure." And so the belt slowly conveyed the paper toward the bread, the butter, the corn-on-the-cob, and it occurred to Kay that the half-open door suggests the moment of just before the decision, the commitment, the this or that. Like a De Chirico painting: what is impending but has not yet arrived, threat or promise, salvation or annihilation, too soon to tell.

BEN GLANCED BACK AT JAKE IN HIS CAR SEAT,
unnerved by the precision of DNA: Shevaunne's eyes and forehead. But the jaw line of some unknown junkie fuckwit.

"I've got a surprise for us," he said.

Jake beamed. "Walmart?"

Walmart. Strawberry. The total of Jake's vocalizations. Ben
wondered if it meant anything—these two words held some
clue. They were positive, glimmers of light. "Better than
Walmart, way, way better."

Ben parked outside the museum in the cool, spreading shade
of a spreading maple. A bright banner read:

*What's Up Down Under! A roving exhibit of the unique flora and
fauna of Australia.*

Ben couldn't remember what he and Frank had seen at the
museum, only that there had been wonders, pink flamingos and
a polar bear, the world's biggest butterfly, a giant tapeworm in
a bottle: the first inkling they'd had of the world beyond the
Kingdom. They had raced from exhibit to exhibit, pressing their
greedy faces against the glass. There was somewhere else, they'd
finally understood. If you drove south on I-93, you didn't just
get to Boston, you could keep going to the Amazon or Tibet or
Alice Springs.

Their plan for Australia began there and then, aged 13, amid the colonial plunder of taxidermied animals and bats in form-aldehyde, it grew up around them, a wild, exotic plant fed in equal measure by their despair and their hope. Frank had found a book in the library, *A Pictorial History of Australia*. They'd sat on the cabin's porch and turned the pages, smudging the images with their sweaty adolescent fingers and beheld the opposite of everything, the opposite landscape, opposite colors, opposite side of the world. The people looked tanned and open and happy, the sea, the bleached and eternal outback, the red earth. There was a huge desert area called the Nullabor Plain, which sounded at first like a native name, like those on the map, Wagga Wagga, Wollongong, Ulladulla; but Frank read the caption, it was Latin for No Trees, *null arbor*. The Plain of No Trees. Imagine—they had imagined—driving for three days, straight, and not seeing a tree or a person, only the sky and the horizon, stars and earth and the sounds of the planet: wind, insects, your own breathing.

They worked out they'd need five grand each, a small fortune, but attainable if they worked two jobs over the summers. Visas, airfares, and they'd need to buy a car when they got there, have enough money to drive around until they found the right place. They'd burn their passports, blend in. "G'day! G'day, mate!"

"We could kidnap rich people," Frank had said. They'd laughed.

"Yeah, and bring them to the cabin." Ben added. Because, maybe.

"We wouldn't even ask for a million. Just, like 50 grand."

"And we'd be nice to them. We wouldn't hurt them." Frank's eyes had glowed. "Flatlanders pay serious money to stay in cab-ins like ours. They might even like us and just give us the money."

Ben felt Jake's hot hand buried in his. He always left it to Jake to give him his hand first, so that it felt like a choice—Jake seek-ing the physical connection. Thus, hand-in-hand, they toured the exhibits. Jake loved the interactive video on the outback. "Kangaroo," he said.

Kneeling down, Ben put his arm around Jake. "Would you like to go there?"

Jake nodded.

"We could see the kangaroos and the koalas."

"Kooka—"

"The kookaburra bird."

Ben looked at the boy; Jake was expecting him to pull it all back, to sneer, *Stupid, dumb kid.* The years it would take before Jake's first reaction was something other than a flinch.

So he cupped Jake's face with his large hands: "We're going to Australia, you and me, I promise."

K ay opened *The Caledonian-Record* on the kitchen table.

Fire Guts Concord Home, Cat Saved

Single-Payer Healthcare Back on the Cards

Bed Bugs Force Urgent Care Closure in Barnet

Perhaps she could convince Michael to move here. She could get a job, she could write about quilting competitions, the grand openings of feed stores. It wouldn't be so bad, the quiet Vermont life, a small school for the kids. There might even be Ben. From time to time. Or someone like him. She flipped through the pages, obituaries, the police log, a story about the refurbishment of the Veterans of Foreign Wars building, another about the director of a food assistance charity arrested for the theft of $42,000 worth of donations, a state symposium on the opiate crisis. There were right-wing columnists on the editorial page, and a smattering of national and foreign news toward the back. She almost tossed aside the sports section.

But: it's a strange thing how the eye works, identifying a

pattern, hurling a message to the brain, which lumbers on, still mulling Dear Abby's answer to 'Frustrated in Des Moines' several pages back.

Steiner.

Like an arrow in the backside. *Paul Steiner.* Kay leaned in:

Local Couple Peddle Donated Bikes for Youth

East Montrose—Paul and Trudi Steiner bought a weekend house in the Northeast Kingdom because they loved the mountain biking and the community. "But the more we biked and the more we got to know the community, we found there were many, many local kids who couldn't take to the trails because they didn't have bikes," Steiner said. "Trudi and I put out the word and within days collected more than 100 bikes from friends in the Boston area."

All the bikes are of good to excellent quality, and are available through the East Montrose Bikeway in East Montrose. Those seeking the donation of a bike must be between 8 and 17 years of age and have parental permission. They must also commit to volunteering eight hours of their time to work on the extensive Montrose Bikeway trail system.

Jim Maddox, head of Public Relations at the Bikeway, said: "We discussed this idea with Paul and Trudi, and agreed that rather than a free giveaway, we'd like to get the recipients involved in what we do, so that they not only value the gift but join the East Montrose biking community."

"We just started asking around," said Trudi Steiner. "So many people have great bikes that they never use or their kids have gone away to college and left their bikes; it doesn't make sense to throw them away. Not everyone needs to sell stuff on Craigslist. It feels good to give!"

Kay folded up the paper. The groceries were not yet unpacked, the ice cream just beginning to soften.

The lane made a dash toward the hills, past several small cabins, an open field, and into the woods. Kay measured the distance in her head, comparing it to the property map she'd photocopied in the town hall. In London it was almost impossible to find out where anyone lived, but here she simply went to the East Montrose town hall.

And there indeed was the driveway, graveled, ironed flat and straight under dark, heavy maples. It was a new house, a glorified cottage—over-designed, Kay thought. The windows were too big and sealed shut suggesting the use of air conditioning. An Audi TT with Massachusetts plates was parked in front. Kay pulled up behind it, slamming the door loudly as she got out. She walked to the front door, rang the bell. A thin blond woman in an athletic tank and hot pink biking shorts opened the door a few inches. In her arms was a small sharp-faced dog, yipping. "Ssshhhh, Lily, naughty dog," the woman murmured, then her voice hardened at Kay: "How can I help you?"

"I'm sorry to bother you like this." Kay summoned an apologetic smile. "Are you Trudi Steiner?"

Yip yip went Lily. *Yippity yip.*

"I'd like to know who you are." Trudi was appraising her, noting the bandaged hand.

"Oh, gosh, yes, of course. Hi. Kay. Ward. We have a place in Kirby."

Trudi nodded, stroked the dog. "Hello, Kay."

Kay extended her left hand for an awkward shake. "Do you, um, sorry, I don't know how to ask this, so I'm just going to come straight out with it. Do you know Ben Comeau?"

Trudi wasn't opening the door because of the AC. She was either going to have to come out or invite Kay in. Kay made a quick apologetic smile, then rambled as the warm air exchanged with the cool air of the Steiners' expensive interior: "I'm asking because my husband and I need to have some of our woods logged, and we want the best person and we wondered about Ben. He seems so nice but then we did some research online and saw something about a court case."

"I'm not sure I should discuss—" Trudi stepped outside, shutting the door firmly behind her. "This is just between you and me."

"Absolutely."

"Last year. About this time," Trudi began, the way people begin, in short bursts. "He just showed up. He was the nicest guy, polite. As you say, just so *nice*. Even Lily liked him, didn't you, little sourkins."

A brief hesitation as Trudi checked herself and scruffed Lily's ears and wondered, should she really be telling this story? But it felt good to let injustice slide off her tongue, the sweetness of outrage, and she gathered momentum. "Nice, nice, Mr. Nice, that's Ben. He started asking about our woods and who was logging them and Paul, my husband, said no one. So Ben said we should think about it, thinning out some of the less healthy trees. He went on about *curating* a healthy forest and that because there'd been so much bad logging over years—ironic, let me tell you!—so much clear-cutting, the trees all grow back in one big stand, so they crowd each other, trying to be the tallest, rather than the strongest. Such a nice guy, Ben, using the fancy word *curate*. He really gave the impression of being knowledgeable and all environmentally sensitive. He said he'd help us, his cousin was a forester, and they'd work up a plan to tag the best trees and weed out the weak. Ben offered us eight thousand."

Lily squirmed and Trudi put her down. *Yippity yip yip*, went the dog, wagging her fluffy tail, her bright eyes staring up at Trudi. "Mummy's busy," Trudi scolded, then continued to Kay: "Paul is a lawyer. He gets a contract for everything. Literally. You want to use the bathroom? You'll sign a liability contract. But somehow Ben, this nice local guy, gets my husband to verbally agree."

Kay looked attentive, nodding now and then.

"And then the forester came by with Ben. Quiet guy. But he knew about trees. He and Ben asked how often we were around because the logging can be noisy and they could see we come up here for the peace. So considerate, right? Paul tells them we're going to California for two weeks, to the wine country, he actually said that to them, *'We're going to the wine country'* and how that would be the perfect time. And Paul's all happy because now we've got eight grand for a bunch of junky trees."

Trudi gave Kay a rueful smile. "I mean, you've got to give them credit. We're looking at them like they're a couple of bumpkins as we gab on about *wine country*. So, they come when we're not here, when they know we're in *wine country* tasting a wide array of pinot grigios, because, *duh*, we told them. They strip it. It's literally stripped. Fifty-five acres, clear-cut, what they call—*apparently*—a 'high grade' cut. It looks napalmed. Paul freaks out, but then he really freaks out when he finds out there's nothing he can do. Lodge a complaint with the chamber of commerce. So that was it. Literally, *it*. Turns out there are no regulations, no oversight unless you have a contract and a contracted forester. Which we didn't have. We just had a conversation with the forester. Nothing was ever signed, and when Paul tracked him down, he just said he didn't know anything about it, he was so sorry, he thought we had decided not to log."

"Did you believe the forester?"

"It didn't matter by that point because there was no contract. What we believed, what we thought was bullshit. Because nothing was written down saying what Mister Comeau could or couldn't take, and we had invited Mister Comeau onto our land, we had *cashed* his check. Of course, Paul pushed it as a fraud case, but fraud it almost impossible to prove, and anyway he works in

Boston—he's already totally overloaded with major malpractice cases; he can't be coming up here to some *Deliverance*-country court for eight grand."

"Wow." Kay furrowed her eyebrows. "What a terrible story. I'm so sorry."

"He totally played us."

"The forester's name—do you remember?"

Trudi thought for a moment. "No. He was just a quiet guy, hung back, left the talking to Ben." *Yip yip yip*, Lily insisted, so Trudi bent down, picked her up.

Then, as Kay turned, Trudi added: "Just so you know, we'll get the last laugh. Paul kicked up a fuss. He has connections. Justice Department, high level. He's making all kinds of trouble for them."

Yip yip yip.

Even as Kay smiled and thanked Trudi, her mind was in the basement, opening the tub, flipping through Maria's cookbooks. She flipped *The Joy of Cooking* onto its side, shaking loose the notecards and clippings Maria had shoved into the pages including the fudge recipe from Candice to Maria. Kay was looking again at the notepaper, and there, across the bottom, Vermont Department of Forestry, and the logo for Parks, Recreation and Forestry.

The office of the Caledonia County Forester was in a square two-story brick and cement box on Route 2. Inside, there was no receptionist, just a high counter that separated off a large open area with several desks and computers where two men and a woman surfed a tide of paperwork. Kay waited, polite and patient, until the woman glanced up. She held a finger aloft, "Just a sec, hon."

After making a few definitive taps on her keyboard, the

woman got up. She was tall, big-boned—a strong woman used to working outdoors.

"Can I help you?"

"I'm looking for Candice."

"That'd be me." She made a jokey show of looking herself up and down. "Yep. That's me. What can I do you for?"

Kay leaned in, so that Candice had to follow suit. "Frank Wilson."

Candice pulled back. "I've already talked to you people."

"Have you?"

"Aren't you federal?"

"Federal what?"

"Let me get my supervisor."

"Candice—wait." Kay softened her voice, she knew this hide-and-seek, this stepping forward or back, peering, poking. It was always a kind of flirtation. "Frank is your friend."

The woman hesitated, her wide, strong back still blocking out Kay.

"You're worried about him, aren't you?"

Now Candice turned. "We should go outside."

They sat at a splintery picnic table under a spreading maple at the east end of the parking lot.

Candice's face was spare. "Start by telling me who you are."

"I'm renting his house for the summer."

Candice nodded, waiting for more.

So Kay obliged. She looked into the distance, as if trying to put her finger on the intangible—ghosts, God, the cold spot in a room: what Candice was also feeling. "No one will tell me where Frank is. I know I'm not from here, he's not a friend, I've never met him." Now she looked at Candice. "He's missing, isn't he?"

Candice scanned Kay's face with clear, perceptive eyes. "And you're not DEA or FBI or whatever? You're not wired. You have to tell me if you're wired, don't you?"

"I'm not anyone"—and this Kay could say with complete conviction—"I'm no one, no one at all."

For a long moment, Candice mulled, then she decided. "Frank was in trouble. His marriage. Maria and the boys left. He tried to put a good face on it, that it was just a temporary thing. But we all knew they weren't coming back."

"You asked if I was DEA."

"Yes."

"Because the DEA have already been here asking about him?"

"Some kind of task force. We have a huge opiate problem here."

"Frank was using, dealing?"

"I just can't imagine Frank—"

"Maria?"

"You must be joking."

"Imagine Frank, then. Imagine him doing something he shouldn't. Because people have reasons we don't know about."

Candice considered, then she nodded. "Okay. A couple of months ago—March, it must've been—these two DEA agents were here asking about problem loggers, dirty loggers, and they were really pushing Frank about a couple of his contacts."

The bad feeling, that cold spot in the room existed after all. "Loggers?" Kay said. "Why would loggers be involved with drugs?"

"It's a cut-throat business—it's the Wild West, and loggers are pretty scrappy people. They work hard, overheads on equipment are high, the markets fluctuate wildly, there's no safety net, no government subsidy. When prices tumble you're on your own to cover your ass. Mills are closing all over, the big ones in Maine and Canada. Mainly it's the damn Chinese bringing in cheap wood products. The big loggers are still doing okay. But the small outfits? They struggle. Our main job as foresters is basic oversight. Are they harvesting as they're supposed to, are they following the laws—not that there are many. To be honest, it's an almost completely unregulated business. And Frank, Frank—" she broke off again, and again looked behind her. "Frank is a bit of an oddball, a bit of a loner, we all are, tramping about in the woods all day long."

"What did the DEA want?"

Parading out on the edges of her mind, loyalty, fear, discretion, Candice took a long time to answer; but in the end, the human need to unburden won out. "Maria wasn't legal. Neither were her boys. They were hers, she'd brought them from Mexico when she and Frank got together. There was some problem with her birth certificate that made it difficult for her and Frank to get married; they couldn't enroll the boys in school. It was a mess, and the government has been cracking down on illegals. So they were afraid to even go out. The DEA somehow got wind of the situation. They said they'd either make it easy or hard for her, and they wanted Frank to wear a wire and set up some sort of sting with a couple of the loggers."

The question formed on Kay's tongue, a hard pebble. "Do you—do you know who?"

"Wilder Bundy, Ben Comeau."

Now Kay stepped forward, because it was important to give as well as receive: to share. "I met Ben. He helped me with a problem at the house. He seems like a nice guy."

"He is."

"You know him, then?"

Candice shrugged. "Here and there. Enough to know he's in deep, equipment overhead and such."

"How could logging and drugs be connected?"

"Maybe the cash. A lot of cash changes hands. And you got a bunch of guys who don't care too much for the law."

"Did Frank cooperate with the DEA?"

"He would never betray Ben. Never. They were like brothers."

Kay looked directly at Candice. "Where do you think Frank is?"

"Officially? He's still here."

"But surely someone's noticed?"

"His pay checks go straight to Maria. He set it up that way. So, we figure, until the cops actually decide he's missing or whatever, we'll screw the system right back. So far, no one's asked. Till you."

"But where is he?"

Candice raised her kids on a forester's salary. She was loyal and kind. She wanted to see the best in people. She took a long time to answer, appraising Kay one last time, still uncertain of her credentials. "I think," she said finally, "I think Ben knows."

BECAUSE AUSTRALIA HAD NO TREES, THE
Australia in his mind. No forests to plunder, no old growth to
diminish into pulp. Australia had no winter fist.

Jake tried to blow on the didgeridoo and made a noise like
a fart. They laughed. Ben tried and made a bigger fart, they
laughed and laughed, fart fart. But the spooky, beautiful sounds
the instrument could make played like a soundtrack over Ben's
imaginings: the lonely distance, the lightness of his body traveling on foot over red earth, Jake beside him, like ancient people,
the first people, father and son, upon a clean and wide land, they
could begin again, the whole human race, just start again.

Because Frank, because Frank could not.

Because he and Frank had kidnapped an overweight dachs-
hund named Otto who belonged to a couple from Braintree,
Massachusetts. It had been Frank's idea, after seeing the 'Lost
Dog' posters in White's. "Reward offered." How difficult could
it be to kidnap a dog? It made so much more sense than kidnap-
ping people, who were big and made a lot of noise and could
talk to cops.

They stole the aging Volvo from Old Lady MacDonough.
She was in for a hip replacement and had left the keys in the car,
an invitation—it could be considered—to the varmint foster
kids next door. He and Frank kept to the backroads. They were

outlaws, though they kept to the speed limit and ate M&M's, and Otto sat between them, bright and happy for the car ride. When they got to the cabin, Otto jumped out and raced toward the lake—he was enjoying his day out. He waded into the lake, which wasn't far given the shortness of his legs. "Good boy," Frank said, crouching down to give him a pat. Otto barked.

That night was the happiest Ben had ever been; he and Frank eating gummy bears and potato chips for supper, roasting a pack of hot dogs on the fire. They even drank two beers, lifted from their foster parents. They lay on the grass with Otto, looking up at the night sky, and Frank said there were kids in cities who didn't know the sky had stars. He told of this one kid at his school who was from New York City and he thought a cow was the size of a dog because he'd only ever seen a cow in a picture by itself. The kid'd had no way to reference the size. Ben and Frank laughed and laughed, imagining little cows the size of Otto and how you'd milk them by pinching your fingers, *squeet, squeet, squeet*. And Otto certainly appreciated his hot-dog supper.

By the light of the kerosene lamp, they wrote Otto's ransom note. "$1,000 to see Otto again! Do not call the cops! Put money in UN-MARKED $100 bills in a plain brown paper bag on the SE corner of Tunny Hill Road and Wiley View at 9:15am, August 4." They'd only have to do this nine more times and they'd have enough money for Australia. This suddenly seemed like a lot of dogs. They discussed and agreed they'd do it only five times. Five grand would be enough.

"Maybe we can just take Otto to Australia with us," Frank pondered. The dog was snoring softly, his velvet ears cast across Ben's lap.

In the morning, they shut Otto in the cabin and went for a swim. The water was cold and they gasped, striking out for the center of the lake with ferocity. They were all the way out when they saw a truck pull up to the cabin.

"Who's that?" Ben asked.

Frank didn't answer. His face didn't change. There was water in his hair dripping down into his eyes but he didn't blink or wipe it away. Frank didn't answer right away, and Ben had an animal sense of dread.

"My dad," Frank said.

"I didn't know you had a dad."

At the foster home no one discussed their parents. It would have been like playing Top Trumps: least able to provide food, biggest consumption of alcohol, most likely to pass out from a heroin overdose, most frequent sexual predator, most violent abuser.

It was a beautiful morning, the hills around them glimmering with green, the promise of a true, hot summer day. But Ben now felt heavy, as if his limbs were water-logged. The air was suddenly cold against his skin as he rose from the water and followed Frank. Frank walked up to the cabin, he didn't hesitate. There was no point in delay. Frank's dad was sitting inside, smiling, Otto on his lap. The ransom note was on the table. "Cute little fellow, ain't he."

Then this strange dad swiveled his head toward Ben. "Who's the circus freak?"

"Ben," Frank said.

"Hi," Ben offered his hand. "Nice to meet you."

Frank's dad laughed. The uninitiated, like Ben, might think the laugh jovial and embracing. He was petting Otto, stroking his long, soft ears, and Otto appeared to be enjoying the attention. This was how Ben learned that dogs have no instinct; they'll take affection from anyone. Evil isn't a smell, or a taste or a tone of voice, and it sure as shit isn't a pat on the head. Dogs are stupid that way.

"I like what ya've done with the place," father spoke to son.

"It's mine. So is the house."

"Yer mother." He smirked, rubbed his grizzled beard. Then he gestured to the ransom note on the table. "This yer idea?"

Frank nodded.

"I like it—very, ah, what's the word, *cunning*."

"We'll give you half."

"Half?" Frank's dad scratched Otto's chin and the dog closed his eyes. "I don't need the money. Why do ya need the money?"

"Ben's saving up to buy a car."

"He's 13. A little young. Mind, I can see yer already motorized."

Ben stepped forward. He wanted to help Frank. "Completely my idea, sir. My mother taught me to drive because sometimes she couldn't. I've been driving since I was nine, sir."

"Sir?" Both boys were standing in their wet underwear. Frank's dad scanned Ben from head to toe. It felt like an appraisal, the way judges looked at beef cattle at the county fair. He lingered on Ben's face, and Ben felt every pimple erupt and seep, his blackheads cluster like fungi. "I like 'sir,'" the man said. "Very respectful. Yer skin is giving ya some trouble."

"Dad, please."

His father shifted his gaze back to Frank, a thinner boy, smaller-boned, shivering in his wet underpants. "If this goes wrong, if the cops trace ya shitstains, this'll come down on me. I'm the adult, the parent. Ya think I want cops snooping around?"

"No. Sorry."

"We'll have to sort this out my way."

"Sorry. Dad. Please. Dad. Sorry."

Ben did not understand. The words were familiar, the conversation made sense, a parent to a son; but there was another level, below the soil. Ben had a sense of what was moving down there, toiling. But he could not see it.

"Come on, little doggie." Frank's dad shifted Otto so the dog was under his arm.

"Dad. We'll just take him back, we'll take him back right now." Frank's voice rose to an awkward adolescent squeak.

"Someone might see ya, son. They might have already seen ya."

"We were careful. No one was there. No one saw us."

"A coupla 13-year-olds driving a Volvo? One with poison ivy all over his face."

"It's acne," Ben corrected. "Sir."

Frank's dad examined Ben's face. "It's almost offensive."

Frank stepped forward. "Dad. Dad. I'll take the dog."

His father stood.

"Please. We'll leave him somewhere, outside the dog pound, outside the feed store. Someone'll find him and take him back."

But his father ignored him, moved deliberately toward the door. Otto now had a sense that all was not well. Perhaps he smelled Frank, for even Ben could scent his friend's fear sweat. Otto began to wriggle in the man's grasp.

Frank held out his hands. "Dad, Dad, I'll do it. Okay, I'll do it."

Ben merely watched, as if this was TV, he was seeing it through a screen, these were people he did not know. Frank took Otto and walked out, down the path to the lake. He held the dog against him, cradling him gently, speaking softly. And Frank's father watched, impassive as he waded out into the deep water with the dog.

A t three minutes to four, Kay pulled into the parking lot at Kamp Wahoo. She felt the old elation, her mind putting pieces together, her hand moving clearly across the pages of her notebook. Ben and Frank, running a scam, drugs and logging. How did that fit together? She recalled Ammon: "Ask yer boyfriend." She recalled Candice: "I think Ben knows."

Other parents waited in idling cars, windows sealed up against the heat. Kay put aside the notebooks; she was almost proud to join the line-up on time. Here I am: a good mother.

At last, children straggled out from the building, dragging towels and backpacks. Hitting open air, they began to run or skip or dance, it was impossible for them to walk. Tom and Freya always ran out from school as if they were late or in a hurry, and Kay sometimes wanted to stop them, slow them, tell them to be careful and remember *this*—this *weightless lightness* in the world, because you will have years and years to be a grown-up, heavy as lead.

The cars moved ahead of her, an orderly procession. She let several pass in front of her, their children lined up on the side walk. But not hers, Tom and Freya did not appear.

Like bags from the carousel at the airport, surely, the next round would bring Tom and Frey. Kay waited, children came, children went.

Until all the other cars were gone, all the other children being ferried home for supper.

Still hers did not appear.

Kay turned off the car, stepped out into the sun, seeking, searching. Again, again, straining to see them over the blue lake water, only here, instead, a building, a playground, today. She was continually losing her children as if they were car keys. The feeling of unease inside her again, a nut in its loose shell, rattling.

A final clot of children burst from the doors, one, two stragglers. She glanced at her watch: 4:30.

A boy went missing in the woods. His parents looked everywhere. Their friends and family joined in, they called the police who came with a dog, and they found the boy asleep in a pile of leaves.

A boy went missing in the woods and was never found. Or was found.

Phoebe Figgs exited, locking the doors behind her.

"Mrs. Figgs? Phoebe?"

She turned, and Kay felt as if she must perform, must present the right mother—not the mother who had nearly let them drown less than 48 hours ago.

"Freya and Tom…?"

Phoebe frowned. "They've left already."

"No, they haven't."

"Yes. Their father—"

"What father?"

"He came earlier to pick them up."

"But he's not here. He's in Côte d'Ivoire."

"I'm sure he—"

Kay was close to her. Kay wanted to grab her throat. She shouted: "Where are they? Where are my children?"

For a brief moment, panic flashed in Phoebe's eyes—doubt and headlines in national papers. Then she regrouped. "Michael.

Their father. They said he was their father and he said he was their father and he's on the list approved for pickup."

Kay's mouth, dry as ash. "What?"

"You put him on the list, don't you remember? In the application?"

"But he's not here!"

"Apparently he is."

"He can't be!"

Phoebe made a little shrug.

"What time did this happen?"

"Right after lunch."

"And they went with him?"

"Yes, they went with him."

"And you never thought to call me?"

Phoebe raised her hand, a stop sign between herself and Kay. "Look, Mrs. Ward, I don't know what's going on, if this is a custody issue or what. Your husband—their father's name is on the list. He came, the kids went with him, they were perfectly happy. That's the end of the story as far as I'm concerned."

Perfectly happy.

Phoebe very nearly let a delicate smile of victory touch her lips as she walked away from Kay, confirming her opinion. Not even opinion: the ruinous facts of Kay. Phoebe got into her Honda Pilot and drove off.

Kay's hands were trembling as she turned on her phone. One message, received earlier in the afternoon. While she was *interviewing* Candice for a story that didn't even exist.

"I've got the kids," Michael was saying. "They're fine, they're safe. We'll talk later." His tired, jet-lagged, man-of-the-world voice. His superior voice.

They're safe. And perfectly happy.

Despite the heat, goose bumps sprouted on her skin. She began to shiver. Freya. Of course, it would be Freya. Kay scrolled through her phone's call log. Four calls to Michael's phone between 4 and 5 a.m. So, Freya'd woken up, she'd taken Kay's phone, she'd crouched on the toilet. "Daddy," she'd have said, sobbed, her face illuminated by the slab of the screen. "I love you, please come and get me, I don't want to stay with Mum."

But it must have been further back, because Michael had to come from West Africa, not a spur-of-the-moment trip. He was in the airport yesterday—she recalled the gate numbers she'd seen during their Facetime. He'd already been coming back.

And there they were: a half-dozen calls at random times over the past few days—all made in the middle of the night. Freya, getting up in the dark house, an angry ghost, a disappointed ghost. "Daddy, Daddy, I miss you."

Kay's heart both broke and contracted like a fist. She let her forehead rest on the steering wheel and sobbed, ugly, heaving, snotty sobs of despair. Then the sobs ran out, and she was empty. All she contained was approximately 20 sobs, a few milliliters of tears. A dram of tears. She stared through her hands, over the rim of the steering wheel, out the windshield at the summer afternoon. Her hand was throbbing as if her pulse was a baseball bat. She started the car.

The Dirty Ditty was down near the railroad that bisected East Montrose. She'd passed it every day, she knew exactly where to go, the tiny Siri in her head giving perfect instructions: park the car, three steps down, open the door, and pass into the forgiving gloom.

She did not regard the other customers, that would have been impolite, but she ascertained there were three or four scattered along the bar. Private drinkers. She sat down. The barman, thin, long-haired, middle-aged, Black Sabbath t-shirt, his face incurious: "What kin I git you, hon?"

"Bourbon, straight, no ice. Wild Turkey is fine."

The glass came, the lovely amber glow catching what there was of sunlight. The bartender moved off, having done his part.

Kay drank, the warm liquid furring her throat, curling in her belly. She'd waited a long time for this moment, a simple drink in a bar, all by herself.

Because she could, she ordered another. There was no rush. The day was long and she had no supper to cook, no dishes to wash, no shoes AWOL, no child's turd abandoned on a fantastic floating lily of toilet paper. *Who forgot to flush the toilet?* It would never be claimed, not me, not me, pixies or Santa must have left it there.

She watched the barman wipe down the glasses, glide back and forth behind the bar, smoothly wheeled, ferrying drinks of regret or solace, depending. How much time there was, suddenly. She felt time stretch out and lie down, a cat in a sunny window. She had three drinks, that was enough. Her limbs felt looser in their sockets, her vertebrae soft and snakey.

AFTER PIZZA, THEY DECIDED TO GO INTO
Littleton for a movie. They didn't even know what was playing
and they ended up at Alvin and the Chipmunks' *The Road Chip*.
The noise of helium-filled chipmunks made Ben's head ache, but
Jake laughed and bounced in his seat. There were only a handful
of other kids in the audience: another dad who spent the whole
time surfing on his mobile phone and a mom wearing ear plugs,
taking a nap. This is what it's like, Ben kept thinking, this is the
other world outside the motel rooms and foster homes. Nothing
grand, no velvet drapes sweeping back to reveal mountain vistas.
Just a child laughing, the smell of buttered popcorn.

It was late coming up Jones Farm Road, fireflies swarming
above Ed's fields, the grass raked into neat concentric rows. Ben
stopped and turned the engine off so they could wonder at the
flickering magic lights, the feel of the cool, soft air on their skin.

"Dad."

Ben caught the word. It winded him.

"Yes?"

But it was a statement, Ben realized, not a question. An arrival.

They drove home. The door was open. Just for a moment,
Ben felt his mother's kiss, and the wild, blind lurching love he'd
had for her, regardless. Lying together on the motel bed when
the men had gone and her high was still soft, she'd kissed him.

"I'm sorry, Ben, I'm sorry, I'm sorry." But he hadn't known what for.

Ben got out of the truck, and he went around to take Jake's hand. They went in. Shevaunne was still asleep on the sofa. It was as if she had never woken from her morning slumber. But she had arisen at some point: the TV's sound was back on, the spindle was gone from the counter.

"Mom's still asleep." Ben gently maneuvered Jake toward the bathroom. "Go brush your teeth."

He looked down on Shevaunne, dribbling out of the corner of her open mouth. Her works were out on the table, the burnt spoon, the thick rubber strap, the clean needle, and the empty spindle with its special, secret spike of fentanyl. These were so normal to Jake he hadn't even noticed; the way other mothers fell asleep with their knitting or a book. She'd had time to put the syringe down after she'd dosed. He gazed at her placid face lost in nod. She looked so harmless. She was supposed to be dead.

The tap in the bathroom turned on, Jake was brushing his teeth. Ben leaned into Shevaunne, so close, the handsome prince to kiss the sleeping princess. She was still breathing, only just. He picked one of her pink socks up from the floor. With his right hand he shoved it in her open mouth as he took his left hand, finger and thumb, and pinched her nostrils shut. He felt her body buck weakly and he heard her gasp and gag. Her eyes opened. She looked out but not at him. It didn't take much, she was already dying, her heart maxed out, and within the count of one-two-three she receded. It was so simple. He felt a rush of fear and then joy and the smell of his mother's vomit. She'd looked surprised like a jack-o'-lantern when he'd found her, and he'd turned her over because he couldn't shut her eyes—they kept sliding back open like cheap blinds, those windows to her soul where none had been, only hollowed out, just like a pump-kin, and he'd calmly—then as now—picked up the phone and dialed 911.

The door to the bunny shed was wide open and dark inside. This was where night waited out the day, night stored itself away. Kay drove by, then stopped, turned around, parked. No one was about. She ambled over to the cages, eight of them, containing a dozen rabbits, and one with a mummy bunny and six fluffy babies. The rabbits barely acknowledged her, intent on cleaning themselves, nibbling their food, tidily excreting. Kay peered in.

"Hello, bunnies." Her voice sounded loud, so she whispered. "Hello, hello, hello, little bun-buns."

They were cute, they were adorable, snow white and clean, with pink eyes and white whiskers. Of course Freya and Tom wanted one to cuddle and pet; Kay herself felt the urge to reach in and take hold of one and press it against her, to feel that soft fur, that quick rabbit heart. While making a vain plea for one a few years ago, Freya had pointed out that rabbits made good house pets. They could be trained to a litter box and were fastidious. Would it really be such a big deal to have a house bunny, Kay wondered now.

"Do you know what you are here for, little bunnies?" she murmured. "Should I set you all free and you could bounce off into the woods?" They ignored her. "But, oh, no, Mr. Foxy-woxy would get you."

The mother rabbit carefully groomed one of her babies. Kay tried to remember the word for baby rabbit—kit, kid? What about "pip," wouldn't "pip" be a good word for baby bunnies? "Look at your little pips, Mama, aren't they beautiful?" She put her hand on the cage. The mother paused, eyed her suspiciously. Kay eyed back, noting the paler rose-colored iris around the deep vermillion pupil, the white fringe of lashes. The bunny sniffed, the triangle of her nose lifting above the cleft of her upper lip.

A woman's voice: "What the hell you doin'?"

The woman stood beside Kay's car, hands on her hips. She was hard-looking with bad teeth and a smoker's skin, crumpled like paper. Kay realized it was Alice.

"Hi, Alice, hi." Kay tried a smile.

Alice, however, did not return the smile. "This is private property."

"I was just looking at the rabbits."

"Why?" Alice had planted herself between Kay and her car. Kay realized she was holding her injured hand defensively across her body. Why, indeed, was she here talking to rabbits. "This is my business, Mrs. Ward, not a petting zoo."

Kay could still taste the Wild Turkey. "I'm sorry. I'll leave now."

"You should try rabbit meat. It's lean, tender, cheaper than chicken. I could bring some up there for you."

An image of roast rabbit brewed in Kay's mind, the little legs in the air, the stomach obscenely exposed, amid a garnish of roast parsnips. And Tom and Freya screaming.

"That's kind of you," Kay offered as she tried to edge around Alice. "But I think we're fine."

But Alice wasn't quite done. She shifted her bulk, blocking Kay's escape route. "Some do-gooder let them out last fall. It was all my money. That's what people like you don't think about, how hard life is."

People like you—but who was that, exactly? Kay herself had no idea, not a fucking clue. She stopped, turned hard to face Alice. They were uncomfortably close. "When did Frank ask you to take care of the house?"

Alice blinked. "What?" Kay could smell her nicotine breath and assumed Alice could smell her liquor. How intimate.

"Just tell me when."

"March. Early March."

"And you haven't seen him since then, have you?"

"Get off my property."

When she got home, Kay considered drinking more. Drinking was taking an eraser and smudging the outline of your brain until your thoughts were all soft, blurry. But it wasn't drink. She wanted out of this, away from this, to fold up and in, compact.

She climbed the stairs, into the bathroom, and crawled inside Frank's cupboard and shut the door. She cradled her burned hand and waited patiently in the dark, breathing in, breathing out, my children are gone, my children are gone, my children are gone, but she was anesthetized, she felt a glorious nothing, nothing at all.

BEN WATCHED THE MOTHS CAUGHT IN THE
vortex of light. They fluttered chaotically. It was the worst kind
of seduction, irresistible, self-destructive. And inescapable.
Once they were caught in the light's bright beam, they couldn't
leave. They wouldn't mate, they wouldn't lay eggs, they would
just dance themselves to death. He had the strange thought that
the moths were heroin fairies, or perhaps the spirits of dead
junkies. There was Shevaunne, fluttering pointlessly, hurling herself to the flame.

He held Jake in his lap. The red and blue lights whirled
against the side of his house, illuminating the mildew stains. The
ambulance doors were closing. Jake understood, but did not.
Ben stroked his hair. "We'll be all right."

A cop came over. She had a clear, intelligent face, Detective
Polito.

"You're not the boy's father, correct?"

"Correct."

"He'll need to come—"

Ben held his finger to his lips. "Let me explain it to him."

She nodded, stepped back.

There should have been another way, thought Ben, but that
other way would reach so far back, not just to Shevaunne and
her family, but to the very first man who abused a child, the very

first woman who abandoned her crying baby on the side of a grassy trail in Africa a million years ago. He propped Jake on the hood of his truck. He took the boy's hands in his. He could only do this, now.

"This nice lady is going to take you. You're going to stay with some other people for a little while."

"No." Jake shook his head.

"We have to do this. It's the law, and it's how we get to be together in the end."

"And Mom?"

"She's not going to be with us. She's not with us anymore." He found he could not say she was *dead*. He could not say she was *gone to heaven*. He remembered his own failure to grasp death, the confusing mixture of fear and sorrow and relief.

"Do you have a car seat for him?" Detective Polito stepped forward again. "And any clothes or comfort items he'll need. Nothing of value."

Jake didn't have a suitcase, so Ben put his clothes in a garbage bag.

"We'd like to search the house," she said. "We can get a warrant."

Ben shook his head. "You don't need one. Go ahead." And then, suddenly remembering, he led her to the trash and pulled out the Willow Bend Supplements wrapper. "I found this a couple of days ago. Do you know what it is?"

Detective Polito tutted. "A way to pass drug tests."

Ben looked confused. "I thought she was clean."

"Sorry for your loss," Polito offered as she stashed the wrapper in an evidence baggie.

I woke up in a hospital bed. It was not a clean bed—it was not a clean hospital—though I felt right away that this was not by choice. I could smell a harsh solvent. The room was neat, the beds aligned. Someone tried to keep order. But chaos prevailed: moaning, even screaming, from elsewhere; and in my room, a dozen women sharing eight beds, two women lying on the floor, which was filthy from mud. (The rains were beginning, those two distinct seasons of Africa, dust or mud.)

There were no sheets, there were no pillows, there were no curtains. There were, however, babies and children, suckling, sleeping, playing with odd bits of plastic and paper with quiet preoccupation. I had the bed to myself and a blanket that I noted came from the hotel.

As I stirred, the other occupants of the room turned their attention to me, grew silent, and stared. I regarded them back, the motley collection of women, some with patches of gauze on their faces or bandages haphazardly wound around limbs; they were grey-faced, pain-filled, anemic. They were waiting to get better or to die.

I felt my belly intact and waited to feel the baby move. When he did not I shut my eyes again, could not face the bright daylight. Please, I thought, Please, the pusillanimous pleading of an atheist. Please? Who? What? The indifferent universe would not even blink if my baby was dead. But then he squirmed, a little flutter kick. My child, my child, my son is okay. I exhaled.

"La Blanche." The word flitted from person to person, an incantation, the white woman. "La Blanche, La Blanche, La Blanche."

A girl ran out of the room, her flip-flops battering the cement floor. I heard her shout something about the "La Blanche." I was ashamed that anyone should notice me, the white queen in my bed with my blanket, and the doctor summoned. He never came in here for them.

The women continued to stare at me as if I had horns or blue polka dots. Then one—a granny with a small child on her hip—stepped forward with a bowl of rice.

"You."

I took it, suddenly hungry. As I moved myself to sit up, I felt dizzy and began to gasp for breath, as if I had just climbed several flights of stairs. The granny frowned and cooed, "oh oh oh oh." She put the palm of her hand against my cheek, it was smooth and cool, and her cooing gained the rhythm of a lullaby. I felt like a child. I realized I could only take small shallow breaths.

The doctor came and shooed the granny away, a fly or a stray dog. "She was helping," I rebuked him.

"She cannot help you, madam. You are very ill." He sounded weary. His thick glasses were taped together at the left edge, his coat was white but stained with sweat under the arms. Sitting on the side of the bed, he took my pulse, then shook his head. "Very fast, very, very fast."

He checked my reflexes, knocking my knee, tapping my foot. More head-shaking, tutting.

I had fallen in the bath, surely that was all. The baby was fine, he was kicking strongly now.

"Do you know what is preeclampsia?" The doctor regarded me.

Something that happened to other women, I vaguely recalled. An illness occurring only in the third trimester of unknown cause. "I know a little bit," I offered, though I was certain it must be a misdiagnosis, easily done in a place such as this without modern equipment. "But my pregnancy has been very good, very smooth, no problems."

"The problem, madam, is that the blood of your baby is becoming toxic to your blood. Your baby is poisoning you. I have given you some magnesium sulfate which gives temporary relief. But there is only one cure, and that is we must remove the baby."

"But he's too small," I replied.

"Then you will die. And the baby will die."

"There must be something."

"There is nothing."

He held my gaze now. "A caesarean. It is the only way."

I looked around, as if I might find this was a hallucination induced by the preeclampsia. Surely I was still in the bath—it would make sense when I woke up. I caught the eye of the granny, but she looked down. There was no one to help me. I wrapped my arms around my belly. "I can't do it."

"Let me show you." He pushed the hotel blanket up over my knee and tapped the reactive spot under the knee cap. My leg spasmed. "Hyperactive reflex because your body is already in toxic shock." He covered my leg. "Your blood pressure is too high; it will become higher. In a few hours you will begin to have fits as your organs shut down."

"But the baby."

He shrugged. "We can try. Keep the baby warm. It may be too weak to suckle but we try to feed it with a small syringe."

"I need to call my husband."

"Ah, sorry, there is no phone service. SPLIF, they blew up the cell tower."

"And General Christmas?"

The doctor—his name, his name, I cannot remember his name, and I will never find it because he's certainly dead now—the doctor regarded me sideways, "What about him?"

"He offered to help me if I need it."

Now he laughed—this was the funniest thing, I was such a comedian. He laughed and laughed, his laughing so contagious that the women in the room joined in, tittering, yelping, and giggling. They had waited days, weeks, months to laugh, and here was laughter like a 4th of July fireworks over the Hudson. At last the doctor calmed himself, the room subsiding with him, the odd snicker igniting in a corner like a recalcitrant sparkler.

"I will prepare the operating room." He stood, moved heavily toward the door. "I will do my best."

The grandmother—Tati—came with me. She held my hand as a nurse strapped me down. The doctor had padded the railings of the cot with towels. "With fits, a patient can hurt herself," he explained. And of course, with the insufficiency of anesthetic, I needed to be restrained. There was a glinting, and then my memory fractures. I can feel the splitting of my belly, I can feel tugging, I know I was gritting my teeth. Tati was holding my hand. Tati kept her eyes on mine. She did not waver or flinch, she hardly blinked. "We are mothers," she said. "This is what we do."

I remember the baby boy was wrapped tightly to my chest, skin to skin. He was silent, looking out with baby monkey eyes. Light came in the window, that particular powdery African light—I have never understood why it should be particular, perhaps the dust. I could hear voices out the window, two women chatting and laughing, and then Tati's old face, a rare smile moved into view.

Tati showed me how to feed the baby, who was too weak and small to suckle. She gently expressed the colostrum from my breasts onto a spoon, and with her pinkie, fed the baby. A few hours later, she produced a two-milliliter syringe; we filled this with my milk, then ejected it drop by drop into the baby's mouth. Tati had also brought a bright pink knitted hat, but it proved enormous, so she came back with a white cotton sock, and this was perfect. The baby, little skinned rabbit-baby, little pip, slept between my breasts. I slept with him, escorted from the pain of waking hours by miracle endorphins.

We floated through the days, tended by Tati, who took all care from me and provided all comfort. I learned her daughter was here because of a tumor in her womb. She and her two small children were awaiting ground transport to the refugee camp in Lokchoggio, but everything had stopped because of Christmas. A Christmas holiday. There was a small boy in the ward next to mine who had burned his esophagus. His moaning came from deep inside and vibrated up his ruined throat like a cello with one taut string: the pure articulation of pain. I grew to loathe the sound, in part because my loathing was so shamefully selfish. And then it ceased.

"They have taken him," Tati told me.

"Where?"

"Home."

We began to hear shelling, though it was still far away. I sensed an exodus, subtle, almost sneaky, beds emptying over-night, an increase in the sound of cars and bicycles—impres-sionistic, as I could not see, had no way to witness.

"People are leaving," I said to Tati.

She raised her eyebrows. "SPLIF may come this way, SPLIF may go the other. As God wills."

I had not considered the eventuality of the baby and myself. My world was this one room, the women in it, the occasional visit of the doctor, the sun and then, as there was no elec-tricity, the seamless and ecliptic darkness. Every nightfall, the women sang, and somewhere else in the clinic, men sang back. They echoed each other, a sonic connection traveling through the atoms of the air. I felt the singing enter me and the baby, I felt it bind him to my heart.

Because of the war, I had not been able to reach Michael; he was anyway in Tibesti or Khartoum. I lay with the baby, sus-pended in a hammock of time, until finally, the heavy cat-gut stitches like black spiders on my lower belly began to weep infection. I did not want to die, so I played the one card I had, the Christmas card.

Tati said she knew him, she knew his cousin's wife's mother. She waited outside his compound all day for three days to speak to him, to petition for a perfect stranger's life. He came that night. I heard shouting, running, doors opening, and in swept General Christmas. He strode over to my bed in full camo fatigues, his beret at a jaunty angle, ho ho ho. He smiled, spread his arms wide. "Kay, my friend, why didn't you tell me you were here?" He leaned in. "And this is your little fellow? Hello, hello!" He chucked my son's cheek. "I have arranged everything. Permissions, truces, my own personal helicopter to fly you and your little one to Lokchoggio."

"How much do you want?"

"Oh, Kay, this isn't a question of money! No, no." He wagged a finger, grinning. "I gave you my word."

Ah, yes, General Christmas, the man of honor.

Tati hovered on the periphery of my vision, standing in front of her daughter's bed. Her two grandchildren cowered under it. No one wanted to be seen by General Christmas. No one wanted to catch his eye.

"Thank you, General," I said—I said it softly, carefully. I said it with real gratitude. And maybe that was my mistake; he smelled the musk of my fear, his particular fetish. I said: "I would like another woman and her two children to come with me, please."

He opened his arms expansively. "But of course, Kay. If you think it necessary. Gol is in our hands; it will remain so. Your new friends have nothing to fear. But—" A warm smile "—but as you are asking, yes, there is room for them."

Now he tapped the end of my bed, a little drum roll with his fat fingers. "You will write about this. You will write about my kindness. I am a fair man. Not only evil."

In the morning, at first light, we heard the sound of the helicopter. Tati edged me into a wheelchair and wheeled me out, her daughter and two children drafting in behind us. Two of the general's soldiers lifted us into the chopper. I looked back and saw the doctor. He was leaning casually against the door frame of the clinic entrance. I could not read his eyes behind his glasses, but he twirled his stethoscope and turned back into the dark maw of the building.

We lifted up, the dream-sequence feeling of helicopters, that sudden blooming out of dimension. Above the clinic entrance, the scrappy compounds around it, roads, tracks, shacks, houses, huts, above the dirty war.

Tati's daughter grasped my hand, her children clinging to her dress, a boy, a girl. "Thank you," she said, the only words of English she knew.

Then the chopper tilted, moved away, away.

And it will happen, over the years, Kay dreams, the photographs of her will put themselves away. Gone from the mantle, gone from even Tom's room. And Freya's boyfriend, Sven, will be looking for a pen that actually works but instead he finds a photograph stuffed in the far back of her desk. A woman in her late 30s, she's on a rooftop, possibly of an African city—something about the light, the dusty air; she looks happy, but who's to say? We all smile for photographs. He asks Freya: "Who's this?"

Freya is on the bed reading *The Importance of Being Earnest.* She has a paper due tomorrow; she's just begun the book. Typical. She scratches a mosquito bite on her ankle. Her toe-nail polish is chipped and she should really shave her legs. She glances at the photo. "My mother."

Sven looks at her, he looks at the photo. There's a strong resemblance, same eyes, same hands, same slim build. "But I met your mother."

"You met Barbara, my step-mother. She's basically my mother."

Sven is well brought up. He has sensitive and intelligent parents. He tries to have some instinct about where to go next with this conversation. He loves Freya—what's not to love? She's smart and pretty and funny. She loves to fuck. But there are these blind corners in her—she'll be looking out the window and he can't reach her, can't follow her. She's a happy person, but remote. It's because he wants to know her better that he persists. "What happened to her? *This* mother?"

Freya doesn't look up; nothing in her voice changes. "She died."

"I'm sorry."

Freya shrugs. "It was a long time ago."

Sven looks again at the pretty woman in the photo. Death is so weird, he thinks. You keep thinking they'll come back or they've just gone on vacation. His dog was hit by a car a few years ago, when he was 15, and even though he knew that Sparky was dead—he'd seen the body, and they'd buried him in the back yard—he went out in the evenings calling for Sparky. *Spark, Sparky, Spaaarrrrkkky,* until he mother told him to stop it.

He sits on the bed, he puts his hand on Freya's impossibly soft thigh. "How?"

Freya shrugs. "We don't really know. We just assume."

"What do you mean?"

"She disappeared."

"Disappeared?"

"One summer. In America."

"So you don't know if she's dead or what?"

Freya puts the book down. "Look, I'm trying to read this, okay?"

Then Kay woke and she was buried alive and she hit out with her hands, her feet, screaming, floundering, attacking, her limbs on fire with cramp. She howled and raged at the blackness of her tiny coffin, unsure even of gravity.

At last she remembered where she was. The cupboard. Her breathing deepened, she began to calm. Her chin was damp. Christ, she'd dribbled in her sleep. The bandage on her hand had come unraveled, bits of plastic wrap slipping off, but she couldn't find them. It hurt, raw, pink fleshed pain. She grubbed along the walls, searching for the latch. In her panic she'd completely turned herself around. Finding it, she clicked it open. Cool air hit her face. She inhaled deep, and dragged herself out onto the linoleum. The bathroom was awash in moonlight.

She lay, face up, her arms and legs stretched out, wriggling her fingers and toes, the blood moving freely into her veins, gushing into the capillaries. Somewhere they'd kept prisoners in boxes, for years and years. A North African country? Or was it slaves in the Caribbean? Her mind always came to these horrors, a butterfly alighting on an oozing, dark flower.

Putting her injured hand on her chest, she felt her heart, insistent and indifferent to whether she was good or bad, mother or un-mother, indifferent as the stars to what she thought and felt and did. It would beat on if she never saw her children again, if Michael left her for Barbara, if school girls were raped, if boys were made to kill.

Now she got to her knees, stood, shook herself out like a dog. The house around her was still, moon-filled. How alone she was, a condition neither peaceful nor alarming; but particular. She hadn't been alone at night for a very long time. She saw her phone on top of the toilet's tank, the message light blinking.

THE ROOM SMELLED LIKE A NURSING HOME,
that piquant mélange of urine and cleaning solvent. The linoleum floor was tacky underfoot, his boots sticking, squeaking.
Easier to clean than carpet, though. The kids who came in here
had problems controlling their bladders and their bowels. They
ate with their hands. They probably had lice, worms, and possibly fleas. They had asthma and allergies. They had wet dreams.
They had nightmares. They had medical records and psychiatric
assessments, broken bones, lacerations, cigarette burns. They
had eczema, stammers and ADHD and prescriptions. They carried their belongings in garbage bags.

Jake was sitting on the floor with Lacey, staring at a pile of
interlocking plastic bricks. Lacey glanced up, acknowledging him
with a nod.

Ben squatted down beside Jake, his voice soft. "Hey."

Nothing. Jake did not move, not even his eyes.

So Ben sat down and began to pull out pieces and fashion
them together. Jake continued to ignore him but began to sneak
peeks at Ben's concoction, which was growing exponentially
with wheels and wings, a crazy heli-plane.

Sitting there, in the quiet room, the boy beside him, Ben
maintained his focus on his construction, carefully selecting
pieces, making adjustments, as a more extravagant vision took

hold of him. He was so intent, he hardly noticed Jake was mirroring him. When they went to grab the same piece, Ben caught the boy's eye.

"Go ahead."

"No."

Ben leaned in close. "I don't really want it. I need a shorter piece."

"No, you."

"Well, if you're sure?"

"Sure."

"I might use it here instead, as part of the missile launcher."

"Okay."

"Thanks. I like yours."

"Not as good as yours."

"I hope not. I'm 37. I'd be pretty lame if I couldn't make a toy spaceship better than a five-year-old."

Jake smiled, the tiniest crack. But Ben was careful not to see it as an invitation. He simply kept building.

"Boys?" Ben had forgotten Lacey. "The hour is up." She seemed to loom over them; Ben felt like a child.

"But I'm not finished yet," he said.

"Me not either," added Jake.

Ben made a face at Jake, who made one back.

"Why don't you go outside? I need to talk with Lacey."

Jake obeyed, joining the six other children who ran about in the long grass of what had been envisioned as a lawn. The screen door slapped shut behind him.

"How are you?" she said.

"Scared."

"Why?"

"That I'll lose Jake."

She put her hand on his arm. She had so much faith in him. "If there aren't any further complications, your guardianship should go through. It was Shevaunne's last wish, so to speak.

And there's no one else. You could even apply for adoption. Would you like to do that?"

"Yes."

"Good. I'll get the paperwork ready. DCF likes to get kids into permanent homes as fast as possible."

"Thank you." He put his hand over hers, his warm touch, his blue eyes. He saw her blush before turning away, and out the door.

From his truck, Ben watched Jake and the other children, bounding through the grass, bending down, then bounding up. He knew what they were doing because he had done the same thing when he was here, somewhere just like here.

The children were catching grasshoppers and pulling off their legs. Harmless enough. It was how he met Frank, little pale grub of a boy. Frank had found a mouse, trapped it against the side of the house with his foot. He was certainly very quick and surprisingly strong. A couple of the girls screamed, and one of the boys said they should tear its legs off like the grasshoppers, wouldn't that be funny. Ben had been certain that Frank would harm the mouse—this small, trembling creature in his grasp.

Frank saw him. "You just got here. What do you think we should do with it?"

Ben had studied the awkward squad encircling Frank, their eyes glittering with something more lurid than excitement, a certain cannibalistic hunger, perhaps.

"Dunno," mumbled Ben.

"Tear its legs off," said the hungriest boy.

"Just step on it," suggested a girl with eczema. "That's what my gramps does. Quick as."

"Gottave big boots," clarified another. "Nunuvushas."

They all stared at Ben, and most starey of all was Frank, and it chilled Ben, that intensity, to be so visible. He did not want to disappoint. He wanted to make the choice that would impress Frank. It was one thing or the other, there was no happy medium—no "let's put it in a cage and keep it as a pet." He took a deep breath. "Let it go." Frank's thin body turned, surprisingly supple, as he launched the mouse through the fence into the dense brush of freedom.

K ay sat on the toilet, turned on her phone. Michael was online. She Facetimed him.

"Finally," he said.

He sat at the table. She could glimpse her kitchen, the oven, the array of cereal boxes, Freya's Cheerios, Tom's Rice Crispies. They couldn't possibly eat the same cereal, could they? Michael adjusted the screen, adjusted his chair, getting comfy. "The kids are over with Mark and Gretchen."

"How are they?"

Michael had complete control of himself. "Okay, fine."

"So what did Freya say happened?"

"Tom did."

"Tom?" She kept a neutral tone.

"He phoned me. He can, you know."

"Yes, I do know." *Of course I know. I do know. I clean his foreskin.*

"He said you forgot to collect them at camp."

"I was late."

"A number of times."

"That's what this is about? My being late?"

"What do you think it's about, Kay?"

"For me, or for you?"

He sighed, he was a sighing mother-fucker. "If you're not going to be honest, there's no point in this conversation."

"Honest? And this coming from you?"

"Here we go."

"Okay, here's what this is about, Michael. It's about us getting a divorce, and you want to control custody."

"Freya said you called her a bitch, and you said 'fuck you' to her."

"So it *was* Freya."

"Did you?"

"I'd burnt my hand and they were laughing at me." Kay held up her hand in its dismantling wrapping. "I screwed up, absolutely. I apologized."

"Freya says you smelled of wine."

"Really?"

"She said there was an empty bottle on the floor."

"At no point have I put our children in danger. I would never do that."

"They nearly drowned."

"Oh my God, Michael. If you were around more, you might fail too from time to time. But you get to be the hero, swanning in, swanning out."

Suddenly, he held up his phone, a blurry image that took a moment to clarify. It was Ben in the shower.

Kay felt sick, heat rushing to her face that she hoped the early morning light might hide. Heat bloomed out from her face and down her neck. She could feel it prick her armpits. But she composed herself. "Freya had no right to snoop on my phone."

"Some... dude?" Michael raised his eyebrow. "Some plumber guy?"

"He's not a plumber."

"You're kidding me."

"You left, Michael. You were supposed to spend the summer with us, a family, that was the plan. And you left. So maybe this is either our kids being manipulative because they are hurt and confused by your abandonment, or—"

"Are you making an excuse for this?"

"Or—*or*—it's you feeling guilty because of your affair with Barbara."

"My affair? I'm having an affair with Barbara? You're crazy."

"I've known for ages."

"I was coming back, Kay—"

Coming back because he was summoned by his children. He'd ride in, heroically, to rescue them from their crazy, wanton mother.

Kay hung up, leaned back against the tank. She wished Michael dead, not a petulant, childish fairy wish, but the hammer-swinging kind. She wished he would spontaneously self-combust, the dry tinder of his hypocrisy igniting with a bang. She hated him, and in the sucking, delirious whirlpool of her hate she hated her children.

The hate felt good, to finally let it out, embrace it, smear it all over herself, roll around in it. Not pushing it back, not shaming it, not *pretending*. Oh, no, she was swinging the hammer, swing away, swing away. The hate was delicious. It smelled good. It was like baked goods or sex—it filled her up, filled all the empty corners, all the withered recesses. She was smooth and plump with hate.

She saw them, how they'd be sitting around the table—the table where she had laid meal after meal after meal and listened to *This chicken tastes weird* and *I don't like broccoli* and Michael working his phone like a masturbating teenager—they'd be sitting there contemplating their mother/wife's craziness, sad for her, worried, pitying, blaming.

And their warm puddle of self-satisfied, self-absolving blame would expand out from the kitchen, under the door, out to Mark and Gretchen, to Barb, to friends, neighbors, school parents, a contaminating slick. *Did you hear? Whisper, whisper! She was screwing the plumber with the kids in the next room! She had some kind of breakdown, if people still call it that these days. She was never very friendly.*

But then, like the insistent whine of a mosquito, she heard Michael—what he'd been saying, echoing back to her because she hadn't been listening: *I was coming back, Kay.*

For them, for them! She insisted, as she flipped through the days, how long it had taken him to get to Côte d'Ivoire, how long it would have taken him to get back to Vermont, and what airport he'd been in when he'd Facetimed her two days ago.

Of course, this was his plan, to lay full blame on her and exculpate himself. *I was coming back, Kay.* Exactly what he would say. He'd done the right thing. He'd been honorable. And then his daughter sent him a photo of her mother's lover, a naked man with a large semi-erect penis in the shower. You could see Tom's dinosaur soap on the edge of the bath.

ED MET BEN AT THE BACK DOOR, AND THEY
crossed through the dairy to the yard behind where Ben stored
his equipment and the logs. He and Ed did not discuss the process. They knew the routine. They pulled on their heavy gloves
and helmets. They set to work. Ben climbed onto the skidder.
The machine rumbled to life. Nimbly, he selected seven birch,
lifting these out of the pile with the grabber and placing them
down to the right. A hundred years ago this would have been
brutal labor. Ed was down there with the chainsaw, and he
began to make regular cuts at specific intervals along the middle
of the logs. Ben, meanwhile, maneuvered the grabber, picking
up a dozen logs and swinging them to the left and onto the logging truck.

When he was done, he jumped down and joined Ed. Taking a
small chainsaw, he cut horizontally and alternately between Ed's
vertical cuts, so that the logs had castellated grooves of a foot
each. Working together now, they took the ejected pieces and
carefully sawed out the cores. They made sure each chunk was
placed beside the space it had been cut from. This was time-con-
suming work, taking them about an hour. When they'd finished
all seven birches, Ben switched off his saw, lifted his visor, and
nodded at Ed. They took off their work gloves, pulled on latex
pairs, and Ed disappeared into the dairy.

Ben took a moment to study the chainsaw sculptures, in particular one of an Indian maiden. The papoose on her back looked like a spinal deformity, but her face was carved with surprising dexterity, almost tenderness. Possibly, Ed had real talent after all.

He reappeared pushing the wheelbarrow, the bricks of heroin neatly wrapped in waterproof plastic packaging. They counted out a hundred bricks, a kilo each. Carefully, they placed the bricks inside the concave space they'd cut out of the birches. From his pocket, Ben drew out a bottle of wood glue. He squirted the glue around the four edges of the chunks, then fitted these snuggly back onto the log. Up close, the cuts were visible, but from the casual distance the logs looked like any other. Ed tapped a nail into the end of each log, nodded to Ben when he'd done all seven.

With a surgeon's precision, he loaded the marked logs onto the truck with the grabber, interspersing them with untampered logs in the very center of the load.

By noon they were done and Ed invited Ben back into the house for a lemonade. They entered the kitchen. The trash was piled high with packaging for microwave meals and take-away pizza. Some time ago the Mr. Coffee machine had erupted. A lava-like seep of cheap coffee continued to ooze down the pot and over the counter. Ed's cat crouched under the table, eating a mouse. Ed gave it a kick as he went past. The cat skittered out of the way in time and hissed at him.

"I prefer to mix it myself," Ed said, popping the top of a Newman's tin, carefully measuring the scoops of yellow crystals into an unclean red plastic pitcher.

"That explains why it's so good," replied Ben, taking a seat.

"I can make it stronger or weaker." Ed stirred the mix. "Depending." He poured the result into a coffee mug, handed it to Ben. "I can combine pink and regular, sometimes half and half, sometimes one more than the other." He poured himself a mug, sat down. "I've tried other brands, but Newman's is the best."

Ben took a sip. His eyes began to water. He blinked rapidly.

"Hey, man." Ed was looking at him. "Don't you like it?"

"It's fantastic, Ed."

"Oh, man, am I stupid. Shevaunne, right?"

Ben was forced to wipe a tear away. He shook his head. "It's not Shevaunne."

But Ed leaned in, needed at last. "She was a nice gal."

"She was a lying junkie, Ed."

"You loved her. You did right by her and the boy."

The cat made a retching sound, then a long few minutes of silence followed. Ben finished his lemonade.

"You want another?" Ed was already up, reaching for the pitcher.

"Should we go through with this, Ed?"

"With what?"

"Canada."

Ed poured them each another glass. He sat back down. He drew a smiley face on the glass's condensation. "I'll lose my dairy without it, Ben."

The Dirty Ditty was quiet, empty in the hot mid-afternoon; Kay was the only drinker. The tall, skinny bartender slid over. His t-shirt read *Lemmy Lives!* "What kin I git you, hon?"

The bourbon came. She drank it slowly. She made it last half an hour. She ordered another, then got up to walk to the ladies' room. The light was dim. She squinted at the graffiti in the stall, the tepid obscenities. More intriguing was the sign by the sink:

If you are in here for more than 15 minutes, we will call the cops.

She washed her hands, peeling away what was left of Ben's dressing. The plastic wrap came off in soggy strips. Leprosy, she thought, and rinsed the pink flayed skin under cold water.

Back at the bar, she ordered another Wild Turkey while vaguely aware of a couple of drinkers positioning themselves south of her: men, anonymous in t-shirts and ball caps, one red, one blue. The Wild Turkey coated her mouth, bristly little burn on the way down. She felt marvellously free. She felt daring and in need of a cigarette and a dancing partner. She and Sam, that time in Juba at the Russian Club with the jukebox, Elvis songs in

Russian. She and Gina, she and Marco, those times in Kinshasa, in Kigali, in Khartoum.

When the bartender placed another drink in front of her, she was sure she hadn't ordered. Jägermeister. He gestured to the two men. So, these boys were not fooling around. Kay raised the glass to them, and tossed it back. Almost instantly, the gluey feeling in her skull thickened, so she finished drinking, it would sharpen her a bit.

"Hey, Slim," red hat hailed the bartender. "Another for the lady."

"Thanks, but I'm good," she said to Slim. *Slim.* What else would he be called? Why were fat people never called *Fat? Hey Fat, hey Big, another for the lady.*

Time slackened, time was already slack. Great pillowy hours to fill. And the memory of the tyrant it had been: the reduction of each day to a timeline, a schedule, the pettiness of minutes. The time it took Freya to eat her kale. The time it took Tom to brush his teeth. She was always counting or looking at the clock. Where are your shoes? Where is your coat? Have you made your bed? She was always late. Come on, hurry up, we're late. She used to feel—considering it now—that her children were eating her time, nibbling it like little rats, so there was never the time she'd thought. And they didn't understand; they had no concept of time. What is ten minutes to a five-year-old? How do you describe a minute? Kay had had to concoct reference points: as long as it takes to reach the corner, from here to school, from here to Pete's house and back again. She counted in days, never weeks or months, because a day could be comprehended—24 days until Daddy gets back, 61 days until your birthday, three days until the weekend.

What day is today?
Wednesday.
So when will it be the weekend?
You count the days, you know them now.

Everything had to be de-constructed. Everything had to be repeated.

What day is it today?

When will it be the weekend?

Why does water have no color?

Do octopuses pee?

Can we have a hamster?

Why do we have toes?

And she would be on her knees before the child, tying shoe-laces like an acolyte. *Please, please, Oh God come on, we're late, we're late.*

There was another glass in front of her, and she was very unclear whether she or the men up the bar had ordered it. Kay gave a good impression of a woman who could hold her liquor. She gave a good impression of a woman who could drink a man under the table. Before, before, before, in Addis, in Tabora, in Goma, before the nibbling, not just time nibbled, but her self, so that she was smaller than she was once, her edges marked by the many serrations of little white teeth, children's teeth.

"You wanna party?"

It was the one in the red hat.

"No." Kay didn't bother to look over.

Blue hat: "We got some nice weed, some E."

Red hat: "Where're you from, pretty lady?"

She kept her eyes straight ahead, drank. Slim cleaned the bar, dragging his cloth along the far end of the bar. He was aware of her, of the situation; she had the feeling he'd intervene if it got serious.

Sliding off her stool, she was walking elegantly across the room, she must not wobble or stumble. In the ladies' room, she knelt in front of the toilet and vomited. From this perspective, she could smell the cleaning solvent, and just below it, like layers in a stagnant pond, the urine, feces, and another layer down, the rusty stench of menstrual blood. She tried to stand, but slammed against the stall. Obviously, she could not drive. She would call a cab, but her phone was in her bag, where she left it, over the back of the bar stool, as if she trusted these people, red hat, blue hat.

Maneuvering herself carefully to the sink, she splashed her face with cold water. For an instant, she grasped clarity, but then saw her image in the mirror, greenish and unfocused, and the lines across her forehead, around her eyes, the end of beauty, the end of allure, what made men look, made men notice, shriveling. Who was she now, who the hell—

Ben, she thought. She would call Ben. She would be with Ben. They would talk. She could help him, whatever the problem, she was sure of it, and he would tell her, they would lie down together, talking, sharing, lying across his big brass bed, whatever colors she had in her mind, whatever scars, whatever he was doing with drugs, whatever she said to her children, she and Ben would absolve, and fuck tender, hard.

Her arms and legs moved as if directed by a drunken puppeteer. She opened the bathroom door and glanced out. Slim's back was to her as he conferred with the hats. It now occurred to Kay that he knew them, they were acquainted. She retreated to the bathroom, slumped on the floor, to wait until she sobered up.

At what point did she become foolish—the third Wild Turkey, the second Jäger? Or the moment she walked in the door, imagining she was someone else—the tough, independent, sexy woman journalist of before?

Oh, The Mighty Before.

The ladies' room door opened, one hat two hat, red hat blue hat.

"No," she said, mumbled, dribbled. "No, no, no, no."

Their arms around her, firm and possessive, they chatted to each other, "You got her?" "Yeah." And "It's okay, babydoll, we're just gonna have a party."

She swatted at them, they laughed. "Crazy ho is super tanked!"

"No, no, no, no, no." She was a basketball gradually losing its bounce. "No, no, no."

A door opened. Light blasted in so she shut her eyes, and she thought, Okay, whatever, really, I don't care, I deserve this, these men with their stupid penises, why does it always come down to this?

"My bag," she said.

"Your bag? You want your bag?"

"Money," she mumbled.

Blue hat chuckled. "We already got that."

They were somewhere in the middle of a parking lot. The sky was faded blue, denim blue, and around were tall red-brick buildings, the smell of hot tar, and a yellow butterfly dancing. Red hat kept his arm around her, familiar as a lover.

"Why do men wanna put their dicks in women all the time?"

"What? What?" Blue hat leaned in so Kay could see the hair in his ears, the patches on his neck he'd missed shaving.

"Why rape?"

"Rape? Honey, we're just going to party."

"I don't, no, please. I want to go home now."

"Whaddya say, honey? I can't hear you."

Kay was certain she was speaking, she was speaking clearly. "Leave me."

But they laughed, giggled. "Cat got your tongue?"

Kay could not find her feet, and very far away, a little thought on the most distant cloud, was the idea that it's not the booze, it's a roofie or whatever spike in her drink, and in some ways this was worse because they meant this to happen and so it will happen and she was beginning to become afraid. She was thinking about her body at the bottom of an embankment, on the railroad tracks somewhere. She wondered not about rape but how they would kill her.

"No," she said.

Red hat punched her in the ribs.

"Hel—" she started to say but the word stuck. Her mouth couldn't form the whole word, just heard: "Hel—" and then again "Hel hel hel hel."

Help will not come but hell.

She felt warmth on her inner thigh, wetness, something had been loosened.

"She's pissed herself. She's fuckin' pissed herself!"

Blue hat propelled Kay away from him and for a moment she was suspended in space before slamming into the pavement, the pavement slamming into her, Sam would say The Cosmic Frying Pan.

She started to crawl, inching toward the sound of the street, over there, she was certain, cars, people, children, her children. Her ribs exploded with pain again, then her back. She had this idea they were kicking her and she couldn't quite believe it as if there must be some other reason for the sharp electric stabs of pain. She couldn't quite breathe and yet she was aware of the grit in her knees as she kept crawling, the salty taste in her mouth.

BEN CHECKED HIS WATCH: 5:14. THE HOT, STILL
afternoon, this quiet backroad, grasshoppers sawing in the long
grass, purple vetch and Queen Anne's lace. A bee buried itself
in the bright yellow fronds of goldenrod. Ben leaned in to study
it and he was certain that the bee understood the beauty of the
yellow, felt not merely the utility of the yellow but the trembling,
neural charge of yellow.

Moses was on time, as always, his Ford Pinto grinding to a
stop. They hailed each other, then walked around the rig, Moses
touching the logs, tapping the chassis, taking possession. Ben
handed him the paperwork—the manifest, the forestry reports,
the shipping documents. Moses scooted his chew to the other
cheek with his tongue, checked the papers carefully, the signa-
tures, the pages. He tapped one page with his pen. "I've been
hearing things about Frank."

"What things?"

"Like, he's not around."

"He's around. That's his signature."

The trucker glanced at Ben, "Hey, man, it's my load."

"The signature is genuine. All the papers are 100 percent
clean."

"There was a big bust out of Lowell just last week," Moses
noted. "Wilder Bundy."

"This is not risk free, we are trafficking heroin," Ben said.

Moses answered with a wry smile, spat out a wad of chew, and climbed into the cab. "Thanks for the disclaimer." He tipped his hat and pulled out.

The truck had turned out of sight and Ben could no longer hear the gears shifting. He got into Moses's Pinto. It chugged and sputtered and stank and the clutch was badly in need of replacement. But it got Ben home. He waited on the sofa, checking his watch. 6:00. Moses would be at Derby Line. Customs and Border Patrol would be checking over the paperwork, checking the load. They'd be taking note of the forester's signature and it looked just fine. They might bring the dogs out to sniff around the cab or the wheels. The dogs would find nothing; they couldn't get close enough to the logs in the middle of the load. Everything was in order. They'd wave Moses through.

Ten grand. All this for ten grand. Plane tickets, Ben had calculated, a car, enough for gas and food. Sunscreen and hats with those corks hanging off, just for fun.

6:10 and Ben knew something was wrong. CPB had checked Frank's signature. They had a file. They had a memo. Frank Wilson is missing. Somehow that prick Paul Steiner with his shiny, tiny city shoes had made good on his threat. Hence: Wilder Bundy. And now Moses was in a small room with a large, short-haired man in a uniform. It was the DEA, maybe Kay after all. He'd never see Jake again.

He ran to the bathroom, fell to his knees in front of the toilet. His body heaved, the burning yellow bile spewing out. He listened for the sirens, a fleet of them stirring the dust of Jones Farm Road, four or five state troopers swarming into Ed's, the others were heading here, and who would milk Ed's cows, who would relieve them as they stood un-milked for days, their udders hot and hardening, and they could not understand their abandonment.

But there were no sirens, there were no cops.

From the living room, then, came the bright ping of a text.

"Thank you, General," I said—I said it softly, carefully. I said it with real gratitude. And maybe that was my mistake; he smelled the musk of my fear, his particular fetish. I said: "I would like another woman and her two children to come with me, please."

He opened his arms expansively. "But of course, Kay. If you think it necessary. Gol is in our hands, it will remain so. Your new friends have nothing to fear. But—" A warm smile "—but as you are asking, yes, there is room for them."

Now he tapped the end of my bed, a little drum roll with his fat fingers. "You will write about this. You will write about my kindness. I am a fair man. Not only evil."

In the morning, at first light, we heard the sound of the helicopter. Tati edged me into a wheelchair and wheeled me out, her daughter and two children drafting in behind us. Two of the general's soldiers lifted me into the chopper. I looked back and saw the doctor. He was leaning casually against the door frame of the clinic entrance. I could not read his eyes behind his glasses. He twirled his stethoscope, watching us.

Suddenly, from out of the dark maw of the building, came General Christmas. He walked toward the helicopter.

He had to shout above the sound of the blades. "Have a safe flight, Kay."

"They are also coming with me," I gestured to Tati's family.

"Ah," he said. "There has been a change of plan."

I held his gaze, saw the smile twitching at the corner of his lips like a restless fly.

"There is only room for you."

"There's plenty of room. We could fit ten people in here."

Christmas splayed his hands. "Is this your helicopter, Kay? Or mine?"

"I'll pay you, then, I'll pay you to let them come."

He looked at the chopper's captain, made a whirling gesture with his finger, the engine revved, the blades spun faster. Then he leaned in to speak to me over the din: "You asked me what it felt like."

He stepped back. The chopper began to lift.

I caught Tati's eye. I grabbed one of the soldier's arms.

"They are supposed to come," I shouted. "You said they could come!"

"You choose," the general said. "Leave your child and take hers."

Now there were other soldiers, other elves, grabbing Tati and her daughter, pulling them back, the chopper rising up. I was shouting, "No!" And Tati threw her hands up toward me, a pointless, hopeless gesture.

Then she screwed up her face and spat up at me, the gob of spittle hurtling uselessly through the air, it would never reach me.

The chopper lifted up, the dream-sequence feeling of helicopters, that sudden blooming out of dimension. Above the clinic entrance, above Tati, her daughter, the frightened children, above the scrappy compounds around it, roads, tracks, shacks, houses, huts, above the dirty war.

I held Tom close as the chopper tilted, moved up, up, and away, away from the town, as SPLIF slouched toward it. And while I was safely back in Nairobi, my private room at the best hospital on plush, clean pillows and Michael already making arrangements for us to travel to London, Great Ormond Street Children's Hospital, because there was a hole in Tom's heart, while heaven and earth were moving to save me and my son, the war surged and swallowed Gol whole, Tati, the doctor, the nurses, the women, the children.

The darkened room, though not pitch black, merely shadowed. Red hat blue hat. Red hat blue hat. Kay slowly slid her hand between her legs. No pain, surely she would know, there would be pain, there would be cum, men with their sticky, angry seed. She coiled onto her side, feeling the vulnerability of her body, soft-shelled, permeable. But not raped. Then she inhaled, an atavistic trigger, she breathed in, conscious that she was scenting the room.

The sheets were clean. A window was open, she felt a breeze. Someone was here, not red hat blue hat.

Ben.

He had fallen asleep in a chair in the corner.

Her mouth was furry, her tongue swollen as a dead animal left in the heat. She shut her eyes, but that was no better. She opened them again, slowly taking in the small room, the overall impression of masculine disinterest, pale light seeping through the blinds. His room, he had brought her here. She remembered only red hat blue hat.

His room, his house, the thin walls, the rickety window sashes, the blotches of mildew in the upper corners. She scanned over it now. He was poor. She felt sorry for him—pity, that most emasculating emotion.

He opened his eyes. She watched his pupils shrink, portals

closing. The blue of his irises symbiotically erupted, ocean depths radiating out from that dark center. They were beautiful eyes. But unreadable.

"You want a coffee?"

"What time is it?"

"Morning."

"What happened?"

He stood. "I'll get you coffee."

He did not touch her as he passed. He padded out of the room, and she could hear him in the kitchen, running water, scooping coffee grounds out of a can. No room service, as with her other lovers, no breakfast buffet of tropical fruit and soft white bread rolls with slabs of cold yellow butter, the waiter's slim black hands on the white china pot of coffee, the white starched napkins, everything a separation, a pretension, white, black, the extravagance of a napkin to someone paid less than a dollar a day. To be served breakfast by a black man in his ravaged country is complicated, too complicated to write about. So she wrote about what was easy, wars, refugees, General Christmas. To love was too complicated, so she fucked.

Ben came back, handed her a mug. He sat on the chair, not the bed, not close to her, and she knew he was choosing distance. From his pocket he retrieved her phone.

"The bartender looked on this to see if there was anyone who could help you out, any local numbers." He tossed the phone to her.

Her ribs, her head hurt. Red hat blue hat. "Thank you."

"Why were you there? At that bar?"

"I needed a drink."

He leaned in. For a moment, she thought he might hit her. But he splayed his hand on her chest. Kay looked up at him, his face was closed and she was far out, down a dirt road. No one knew she was here. *It may take me a few days to respond.* As if there was anyone she needed to respond to. She spoke, almost a whisper: "Can you give me a ride back to my car?"

But he did not relent, "Why were you in that bar?"

She shut her eyes. "I just needed a drink."

He withdrew his hand.

"Your clothes are over there," he nodded to the fake cherry wood bureau.

She saw them stacked neatly, freshly laundered, her handbag on top. She remembered pissing herself—he would have smelled this. He had bathed her while she was unconscious. He had taken off her urine-soaked panties and loaded her into the shower. He had held her naked in a way that was the opposite of passion. He had seen the bruises mottling her back and sides. She hunched her body away from him, drawing the sheets around her. He left the room.

For a brief, sharp moment, she wanted him to come back. She could call him, and he would return, there would be something other than this waxy sadness: touch, a smile. But she heard the sound of his truck starting.

The radio filled the gap between them on the way to East Montrose: *My Angel is the centerfold, na na na na na na.* What else might Ben listen to? Bach's cello concertos? Beniamino Gigli, songs of *L'Africain*? "Some dude," she heard Michael's condescension. "Some plumber guy."

Ben pulled into the parking lot behind the Dirty Ditty, stopped beside her car. She half-imagined she might see her own blood on the pavement, some residue—evidence—of the assault by the hats.

"I should go to the cops," she said.

"Don't do that."

"What they did to me, they'll do to other women."

"Other women don't go in there."

Kay sheltered her eyes from the sun's hard flare. An overweight woman with a child in a stroller was crossing the parking lot, smoking and talking on her phone. Kay put her hand on the door handle, but then she reached back for Ben, reached out for him, she wanted to retain something of value. She put her hand on his. He did not move.

At last, he exhaled. He removed her hand as if it were not her hand, not a hand that had caressed him and aroused him, but an object, neither cared for nor disdained, and put it back on the truck seat. "I didn't know you took a photo of me."

"I didn't know you'd looked through my phone."

"You sent it to your husband."

"No," Kay began, "that's not what happened."

But what did happen, she thought. My child sent it.

"Go back to Frank's, pack your things. Leave."

"Ben, please—"

Now he turned to face her. He was someone else now. "Leave. Just leave here. You have to."

She got out of the truck and he pulled away, before she'd even shut the door, tires screeching on the pavement. He made a sharp turn out of the parking lot and the door swung shut with the momentum, the truck and Ben gone in a loud burst of exhaust and burning rubber.

Kay stood, bewildered by the light, the light searing down her optical nerve like a laser right into her brain.

"You okay?"

The woman with the stroller. Only she was more of a girl, perhaps 18.

"Can I have one?" Kay gestured to the cigarette. The girl thought for a moment—the expense of cigarettes, to give one to a complete stranger; then extricated the pack from the pouch on the back of the stroller. She flicked on her lighter, and Kay lit her cigarette and inhaled, a diver going deep.

The baby was gazing up at her with bright eyes, his smooth, pale skin yet to be splattered by the brains of the world.

"He's gorgeous." Kay attempted a smile.

"Yeah, he's a good boy." The girl stroked her child's hair. "I know I shouldn't smoke."

"You're outside," Kay absolved her. "It's all right."

"My mom died of lung cancer. You'd think I'd know better."

So undefined, this girl, her shape all soft, her face without angles, a face you'd never remember, plain, functional. She had no barriers. She was open and guileless. She'd talk to strangers about her dead mother. "I'm sorry," Kay said. "That must have been really hard."

The girl stared at the cigarette in her hands, the fingernails chewed down, raw cuticles. "I've tried to quit a bunch of times."

"Was your mother a good mother?"

A considered sigh. "Good enough, I guess. I'm here, aren't I?"

Was survival the only criteria?

Kay took another long, grateful drag. "I'm not a good mother."

"Why do you say that?"

"I don't love my children."

"Love, oh yeah. Lots of people love their kids, still treat 'em like shit."

"But," and now Kay's face screwed up into an ugly knot. "I think I hate them."

The girl exhaled, regarded Kay. "They got a good dad?"

A man who flew back from Africa for his children. "Good, yes."

"They'll be okay."

"And you'll quit smoking?"

"Sure." The girl smiled, and this made her pretty, dimple-cheeked. She offered the pack to Kay. "You keep them."

"No, I—" but Kay took them. "I should pay you. These are, what? Twenty bucks now?"

The girl was already moving away, waving a plump hand. "The doctors said her lungs were like a clogged toilet. She died puking blood."

THE SUNLIGHT FLICKERED THROUGH THE

birches. Moses's Pinto was gone—though it had left a large oil stain on the bare ground. Moses had taken it, Moses was home safely. No CPB, no fleet of cops. Just the chickadees, the song sparrows. Ben stood for a moment, enjoying their songs. He felt a sense of tidiness—what Frank tried to achieve, as if life was at last in the correct order.

He entered Shevaunne's room, the bed unmade, adorned with pink clothing. A bra. He beheld this, the foam cups where she'd inserted her breasts. The bra was pink, with lace, a choice that was sexual, and this surprised him. She'd wanted to feel pretty, feminine, the bra meant for a man who might reach back with desire and tenderness and unhook the clasp.

He shoveled her things into garbage bags, clothes, the bra, towels, sheets. So much of it was pink and soft, even her shoes were the fake sheepskin slipper boots. Perhaps it was an attempt to buffer the hardness of the world. He thought about her slobbed out on the sofa in her pink fleece bottoms, and he decided, no, she just wanted to be as comfortable as possible, nothing to bind or chafe or constrain or provoke. She was so soft she'd actually begun to blur around the edges. If she hadn't died, she'd have eventually dissolved into lint.

But she had died, he'd killed her. He was a *murderer.* The word conjured up a perpetrator and a victim, like dealer, dealer and addict, clearly defined; only, he didn't feel that definition at all, just the gentle but firm closing of his forefinger and thumb and the fade out of someone who'd abdicated years ago. And wasn't she the murderer, relentlessly extinguishing hope and joy in her son? She might as well break his bones and twist them into crab-like deformity and set him on the corner to beg.

From under the bed, he pulled a stash of celebrity maga-zines, Jennifer Aniston was pregnant, Prince Harry and Meghan Markle. More pink socks, shed like skins, plus three empty Dunkin' Donuts cups. There were panties, dozens, that he quickly realized were dirty. He put a sock over his hand to handle them and closed his eyes; he felt both embarrassed and disgusted. She'd simply taken off her panties and stuffed them under the bed. She wasn't even able to wash her dirty underwear, how could she care for a child?

At the faint sound of car brakes locking, he sat up, cocked his ear.

A banging on the screen door. "Hello? Hey, Shevaunne? You there, Shev?"

Shev? Ben removed the sock from his hand.

"Hello?" the visitor said. Then chiming the syllables, "Hel-lo!?"

Ben did not hurry.

A small man with a scraggly beard threaded with grey peered at him through the screen door. "Oh, hey, man, sorry to bother you."

Ben, keeping the mesh between them: "No bother."

"Eh, I'm looking for Shevaunne." He held in his hand an extra-large Dunkin' Donuts pumpkin spice latte.

"You'd better come in." Ben opened the door.

"Dinko," the man said, awkwardly offering a dry hand.

"Dinko?"

"Duncan, but no one calls me that."

What sort of a man went around with a name like Dinko? This sort of man, Ben assessed, food-stamp thin with dirty fingernails and thrift-store shoes. He gestured to the sofa, now empty of Shevaunne. "How can I help you, Dinko."

Dinko looked around at the seating options, eschewing the sofa and stepping behind Ben to choose the grubby lounger. He sat with Victorian politeness. "Shevaunne, huh? She around?"

"What is it you want her for?" Ben kept his voice neutral.

"We go way back." Dinko smiled, revealing teeth like rusty nails. "A long time, but not, you know, romantically. Now." This added for Ben's benefit, in case Ben might be the jealous type.

Ben smiled back.

"I saw her a few weeks ago," Dinko continued. "In town. She said she was in a program. Said, to, ah, stop by."

"And you've stopped by a couple of times."

Dinko giggled coyly. "And, ah, she mentioned the boy. Jack."

Now Ben felt an electric spark at the base of his spine. But he kept his face closed, let Dinko talk on.

"She got him back from DCF. She said they gave him back."

Ben doled out the words. "Jake. His name is Jake."

Dinko rubbed his hands on his thighs. His hands were covered in tattoos, poorly done, even by prison standards. "Well, the thing is, I really need to talk to Shevaunne."

"She's not here."

"Ah. When might she be back?" Dinko shifted forward. "I can wait in the car."

Ben mirrored him, so that he was only inches from Dinko's face, and Dinko could not fail to realize that Ben was a healthy and strong man with a whiff of violence about him. "Why do you want to talk to Shevaunne about Jake"—and he tossed out the ridiculous name—"*Dinko?*"

Dinko stood up, quick as a rabbit. Prison had taught him to always keep one eye on the exit. Ben realized this was why he'd chosen the lounger. Nothing was between him and the door.

In response, Ben stayed put; he let his eyes pin Dinko. And he understood, quick and hard as a gut punch. "Is Jake your son?"

Hovering a few feet from the door, Dinko's eyes slid left to right; he nodded.

"Does Jake know that?"

Dinko shrugged. "I haven't exactly been around."

"And you want to be around now?"

"Shevaunne, it's really Shev—" he bleated. "She wanted me to, ah, get back with the boy."

"Shevaunne," Ben said slowly. "Shevaunne is dead."

"What?" Dinko leaned in as if he hadn't heard.

"Two nights ago, an overdose."

"But she was clean. She was staying clean for Jack—"

"Jake."

"For Jake, she was trying for Jake." Dinko's features collapsed together, and he let out a sob. "No, no, Shev, no."

"Sit down, Dinko," Ben murmured and Dinko shuffled back.

"She was going clean. She was doing it. She told me how really determined she was, and maybe she could get the baby back as well. She said it was tough but things were looking up. She said she was coming into money."

Ben nearly laughed, it was nearly funny.

Tears welled in Dinko's red-rimmed eyes. "I've known Shev for ages, years. The thing with Jake? We were friends, we got high one night, didn't even think about it, it was just a one-night thing. We were partying out at Willoughby, summer night, felt good, seemed an easy thing to do, and then three months later I see her and she's like, 'Remember that night?' And, I'm like, 'Oh yeah!' And she tapped her belly, 'Got us a little memento.' Then she went and got herself arrested so she could be off the streets and off the smack for the pregnancy. Bless her heart."

Down the road, Ed had the chainsaw out, preparing for the upcoming Caledonia County Fair. Ben focused on the bee-whine of the saw, rather than Dinko's shameless weeping. He felt he should soften, he should show respect: someone was grieving for Shevaunne, someone who believed she hadn't been so bad, she'd been trying, for her son. Dinko believed in another version of her, and, thus, another version of himself, a clean Dinko, a respected member of the community. And Ben might also have another version, someone with kind, compassionate thoughts, a twin who wore the same shirt in a slightly different way. However, Dinko was a junkie loser and Ben was not compassionate, and Shevaunne had been a treacherous junkie bitch and he'd killed her.

"Why are you asking about Jake?"

Dinko sniffed. "Sorry, man, I was just expecting to see her and she's dead, you know."

Ben quietly repeated himself.

"I dunno, man. I just thought I could meet him. We could start to know each other, hang out."

"And then what?"

Dinko shrugged. "I'm his dad. Dad stuff."

"Go fishing, do his homework with him?"

"Sure, why not."

Ben smiled pleasantly.

As Kay packed, she found the tadpoles her children had so carefully and proudly placed in jars. The jars were murky, torpid, and when she opened the lid, the stink reminded her of the rotting stalks of cut flowers. Nothing was alive, she could see, the tadpoles had congealed. She opened the window and hurled the jars far out into the long grass beyond the lawn.

Tom's t-shirts, Freya's panties, their books, colored pens, a paltry scattering of toys: everything fit into one suitcase. This had also been the point of coming here: to break from things, plastic, synthetic, technological. City children, they would commune instead with nature—leaves, earth, rain, sky. They'd learn the elements. They'd learn to track. They'd learn about different trees. They'd be barefoot, carefree. Not angry, scared, abandoned. Not finding their mother's porn. Not finding their mother, who she really was.

Children were under the impression that adults understood the world, were experts in its navigation. How frightening, then, to discover they were, in fact, lost, fallible, dull, and vain; that no one knew the way, after all.

Off her desk, she swept the notebooks, dozens of them, her former life. There would be no book, no ground-breaking memoir, no investigative piece about drugs and logging in not-so-quaint Vermont. She must burn these all or throw them out.

In the bathroom, she scooped up the shampoo, conditioner, toothbrushes and toothpaste, her single jar of night cream, a stray wand of mascara.

It was a whim, perhaps, but all she had left, because the mother person's skin did not fit, too tight, too loose, she was whittled down to the scurrying creature that rifled garbage bags on the side of the road. She went downstairs, to the kitchen sink and picked up the hammer. She grabbed the flashlight from the hook by the front door. She knew where everything was now, as if it were her own house. She returned to the bathroom.

She crawled into the cupboard on her hands and knees, then squatted.

The hammer swung back, then forward, the momentum of the heavy steal head. What tools are for, to improve on the human hand. The hammer's head split the wallboard. Kay swung again and again until she'd gouged out a hole big enough to climb through. She entered the crawl space under the roof.

Shuffling forward, she swung the flashlight around, scanning the eaves of the house, the floor covered only sparingly with wide, old boards; otherwise, pink insulation bristled up. She shuffled along, scraping her knees, squinting into corners, pulling up the odd bit of insulation.

There was nothing. She lifted the loose floorboards. Nothing. She pressed the flashlight into the corners. But there was nothing, nothing, only the house as it should be.

Kay sat, rubbing her knees in the dark. If Michael saw her like this, he wouldn't be surprised. Crazy, he'd called her, *you're crazy*. She was an unhinged person in a dark crawl space looking for something that wasn't there. She was a child stuck up a tree—a child who climbed there of her own volition—she could not see her way down. Or out. Or back. Or forward. She would put everything in the car and drive, any direction, until dark, and then find a motel. She would be a drifter, motels, inter-states, truck stops, it was almost romantic.

Switching off the flashlight, she grabbed the hammer and crawled back out. She shut the cupboard, and went back down to the cellar, to Frank's tool bench. She opened the drawers and mixed around the tools, tossing about the chisels, disorganiz-ing the screwdrivers. She took a box of screws and dumped them out on the floor. She thought to go on, but she'd made her point. She opened the drawer reserved for "Saws" and carelessly shoved the hammer all the way to the back. But it caught on a larger object lodged even further back. Pulling the drawer all the way to the end of its runners, she peered in and saw a white plastic handle, vaguely like an electric egg-beater.

She reached in, grasped it, retrieved it.

An electric carving knife. Smeared in a rusty substance.

The rust flaked off onto her fingers. She knew, of course, it wasn't rust.

BEN KEPT HIS EYES ON DINKO. HE KNEW DINKO saw the small muscles of his jaw twitch and then relax. Then Ben smiled at him, an unexpected smile. "Jake is a fine boy. I understand why you'd want to be there for him."

Dinko felt a flutter in his chest, as if a pretty girl had looked his way, for Ben aimed to flatter. The fineness of the child must reflect somehow on the father, the bloodlines after all. He'd done something good, at last, Dinko seemed to be thinking. Why not be a dad? He was so used to feeling either high or scratchy, but feeling like this—all happy-fluttery—well, he figured, actually, he would be a pretty decent dad. He had the right, being the father. His sperm was strong—his boys could swim!

"The thing is," Ben leaned forward, his hands making a little pyramid. "The thing is I'm planning on adopting him."

Things were suddenly happening, and Dinko was used to a slow, focused life. He slept a lot. He watched TV. He thought about scoring. He worried about scoring, he planned how and where to score, and when he scored, he didn't think much. He had a son, Shevaunne was dead, and now this random guy wanted to adopt her son—his son. And Dinko was realizing he had a possession of real value, something to keep or trade—this was Shevaunne's gift to him, like an inheritance in a will. Ben knew Dinko's brain was rattling down such a mental track. He knew Dinko because he'd known Dinko all this life—*And who do we have hiding in here? That's just Ben. He's all right, aren't you, my Benben. You're cool with Momma partying.*

"Adopt him how?" Dinko mused.

"A formal adoption," replied Ben. "He'd legally become my child."

"But what about me?"

"You would give up your right. You would terminate your parental right."

Termination was a polite way of saying abortion. Ben was, basically, asking Dinko to abort his child.

"Jake," Dinko said. "*Jake.* Is that short for Jacob? Or just Jake?"

"Just Jake."

"Sort of like naming your kid Bob instead of Robert."

"Is it?" Ben wondered.

"Termination." Dinko leaned back, the tough negotiator. "I don't know if I can do that."

Ben respectfully countered, "How might you know?"

"What do you mean?"

"I mean, what would it take for you to be able to know."

Dinko was on *The Apprentice*; he was tough, but fair. "Why do you want the boy?"

The question was so simple, delivered by a simpleton, but it hit Ben square in the chest. Why did he want Jake? Because he loved him. Because he wanted to help him. But there was something else, an unreasonable reason he couldn't articulate, could only feel his way around, as if in the dark, the way known objects became unfamiliar.

He kept his voice low, daring a secret. "How much smack for the boy?"

Dinko tilted his head. "He's not for sale."

"A kilo."

"You are sick, man."

"I'll give you a kilo of uncut heroin if you write a letter stating that you terminate your parental rights and you will never contact Jake again."

Now Dinko looked around. Were there cameras? Was this a sting? For a moment, Dinko stared at Ben. He would not take the deal. He would stand up and walk out into the afternoon light. He would go clean and raise his son right.

Dinko watched Ben and Ben watched Dinko back and saw the creature who squatted on the child Dinko had once been, picking at the fine brittle child bones. The creature scratched itself and opened its beak and smiled and said: "Two kilos and the kid is yours."

"Two kilos." Ben nodded. "We just have to go to my friend Ed's to get it."

And Dinko, who had survived jail and years of petty crime and badly cut smack, stepped in front of Ben, he stepped sprightly, leading the way to the two kilos of smack.

Having never strangled anyone before, Ben did not know if it would be easy. He simply took a pair of Shevaunne's panties and looped them over Dinko's head and pulled the ends in opposite directions. Dinko kicked and sputtered; his arms flailed, but he was a small man, 130 pounds, and his strength blunted by years of drug abuse. His eyes bulged, his tongue sprouted from his mouth, a final wind-milling of his limbs. And then he stopped. He went floppy so that Ben lost his balance and dropped him. Looking down at Dinko, he felt the same curious flatness as he had with Shevaunne. He nudged the body with his foot, no longer a man but more a ragged carpet, something to be removed. He looked down at his hands, his new killer's hands. They were not shaking—they were steady and strong, and he understood that this was who he had been becoming.

The pig blinked, its thick pale lashes sweeping down over the thumb-tack eyes. Standing, it was even bigger than Kay had first estimated—the width and breadth of a sofa, its snout the size of a dinner plate.

"Easy, pig," Ammon murmured unconvincingly, then leaned back to attend his beer. "Excellent noses, pigs."

Kay took the electric knife out of her bag, showed it to Ammon. He gave a little belch, his eyes never leaving hers, bold and amused. The pig edged closer, sniffing, snuffling. Kay could see below the nose, its tusks, its yellow teeth, its fat pink tongue. She stood dead-still, sweat pricking at her armpits, clamping her intestines, as the pig gazed up at her. She realized its principal interest was the knife. It grunted and began to drool.

"There's blood on it," she said.

The pig sniffed Kay's leg. She could feel its hot breath. Ammon drank his beer, considered her. "Where're yer kids?"

"What?"

"Ya heard me."

"They're safe."

"Every parent hopes so."

Kay held his gaze. "Did Ben do this?"

"Murdered Frank, ya reckon? Carved him up into little pieces?"

He seemed about to laugh, either because the idea was ridiculous or because killing was amusing. The pig licked her leg.

"Ya been askin' around about Frank," he said.

"Alice. Alice told you."

He shrugged. "So concerned 'bout Frank ya should go to tha
cops."

"Shouldn't you? He's your son."

Ammon took another long draft of his beer, then threw the
can at the pig. It hit him in the head, between the ears, and the
pig backed away from Kay. "Ya want me to take you to him?"

He didn't wait for her to open her mouth or nod her head.
"I'll just get my jacket. Back in a moment."

IT WAS AMMON'S VOICE. BEN DIDN'T REMEM-
ber the ring of the phone, did not remember lifting it to his
ear. For a moment, he felt as if Ammon was—at last—inside
his head.

"This gal," he was saying, "She's askin' questions about
Frank, Benny. I'm gonna take her ta tha cabin. Ya arrange for
her ta meet him."

Ben hung up.

He lifted Dinko over his shoulder—he was barely the weight
of a sack of grain—and, outside, flopped him into the back of
his truck, and drove to Ed's. He and Ed tossed the body into
the shit pit behind the barn. For a moment, Dinko floated in
the cow slurry. He looked small and vulnerable. He might have
gone away with his kilos and never come back. He might have
been no further trouble. The shit blubbed gently, enfolding him.

In East Montrose, Ben swung into Kamp Wahoo. The kids
were massed around the pool, they swarmed, interconnected by
hands, by laughter. Water arced into the air in silver drops, water
gleamed on their bodies, they were bejeweled with water. A boy
did a somersault off the diving board, a trio of girls jumped in
holding hands, screaming. Why had he never had this, why only
the bitter late autumn, the motel pools always empty?

Frank had given him summer.

He saw a woman with a whistle and a clipboard.

"Hello, ma'am." He tipped his hat.

"How can I help you?" She appraised him objectively, a good-looking guy, a man, a stranger among small children.

"I wanted to find out more about your program for my son," he said.

She softened, the clipboard lowered, she extended her hand. "Hi, I'm Phoebe. I run the camp. We'd love to have your son. How old is he?"

"Five."

"What's his name?"

"Jake."

"Five is a great age for Jake to start with us." She rattled off the activities, arts and crafts, field trips, all-inclusive lunch, the swimming lessons, the storytime, did he want to come this year—there were still a few places.

Ben nodded, attending. He took the flier she gave him that contained all the necessary information and an application form. "My friend's kids go here, and they just love it."

"Oh? I'm sure they do! Who are they?"

"Kay Ward's kids."

The woman looked back at him. "I'm sorry. We don't have them here."

Ben lightly tapped his open palm with the flier. He gave her his warm smile. "My mistake. But it looks like a great program. I'll definitely keep it in mind."

I'd prefer if ya didn't smoke in my truck." Ammon thrust his chin at her cigarette. She ignored him. She smoked on, the luxurious feeling of nicotine coating her throat, entering the delicate fronds of her pulmonary capillaries, her blood, her heart and brain. Maybe what she'd needed, all along, was just a cigarette.

Ammon drove her north, a road almost mindless in its calendar-photo prettiness, the farms, the cabins, the white houses, the patchwork fields, and rolling hills. The mild-mannered red barns.

Only the high-rise granite slab of the Willoughby Gap surprised her. With Nordic severity, the 1,000-foot cliff face plunged into an electric blue glacial lake. Here, summer continued, unperturbed: kayaks and canoes, flat-bottomed fishing boats, the scent of barbecue when they passed a nest of lakeside cabins.

After Willoughby, the land flattened, as if those bold, high thrusts of rock had taken all the seismic energy. The woods, now without geological relief, created a viewless channel, trees and more trees, the occasional cabin or trailer popping up roadside. At last, Ammon turned off the main road onto a graded dirt road, and then another, each road diminishing so that they were turn by turn siphoned onto a narrow track, the overgrown trees and brush slapping and scratching the side of the truck.

Kay continued to smoke, one cigarette after the other. Fear had quite gone; something heavier had taken its place, leaden and dense, as if her mind knew it was pointless to be afraid. She must not waste what was left on fear.

The track broke out into a clearing at the edge of a lake, a cabin hunkering to the right of the scene. It was a beautiful spot, the blue water, the emerald green grass under a clear summer sky.

Ammon turned off the engine. "Here we are."

There would be a trick, Kay knew. Ammon would pull a dead bird from the magic hat, instead of a white rabbit or a bright scarf. She got out, her ribs aching, her legs uncertain beneath her so she braced herself against the truck's sun-hot flank. Even if she wanted to run, she couldn't—not far, not far enough into the seamless flow of woods.

"In the cabin." Ammon flicked his hand toward the low wooden structure, slightly more than a shack with a porch and windows, forlorn and dilapidated. The grass had grown up around it. Rust smeared the tin roof like cancer. The light reflecting on the glass in the windows made it impossible to see in.

Regardless, Kay stepped toward the cabin. She'd been moving toward it for some time, since she'd seen it in the photo above the sink. She'd been moving toward its peace, its menace.

She climbed up the wooden steps, carefully, as they were loose, unpinned and rotting, details she hadn't seen in the photograph. Across the porch, until her hand was on the door. She was here, here we are, here we are. So she opened the door.

The shift from light to dark blinded her for a moment. She blinked as her pupils adjusted, seeing only outlines, a table, cabinets, a person. At that moment, she heard Ammon's truck start up, she turned to see him pull away, giving her a cheery wave. When she turned back, she could see Ben sitting at the table.

IT HAD BEEN MARCH BUT NOWHERE NEAR spring this far north. Impossible even to imagine earth and warmth. The snow rose into drifts six feet high; the trees were structures, frames. Ben loved their stark, dark lines against the white.

Out on the ice, a few locals had cleared trails out to their fishing holes. On weekends you could find them here, hunkered over the perfect circles they'd cut in the ice. They had thermoses of stew and battery-operated socks to keep warm. They came for the church-like solitude as much as for the thorny pike who lurked a dozen feet down.

Once, summers and summers ago, he and Frank had tried to reach the bottom, diving down, but the thick reeds frightened them—they seemed animate, reaching out for the boys with greedy tentacles, and they had twisted back to the surface, translucent and wavering, so clear they could see dragonflies on the other side, and laughing, broached the air, tossing the water from their hair. Summers ago. The summer of Otto.

The sun had not yet topped the encircling mountains, so the land lingered in inky shadow, reluctant as a sleepy child. Frank must have heard Ben coming. Sound traveled on such still winter mornings—the tapping of a woodpecker might seem close but was half a mile away.

Frank was standing on the lilac-colored ice.

Ben had stopped the truck. He got out and stood.

Frank smiled. "Helluva morning for fishing."

But Frank wasn't fishing. He was holding a large rock, so heavy he struggled to carry it. Heavier than Otto. The rock was tied to Frank's waist.

Ben had put his hands deep in his pockets. The air was crisp. He'd taken a step forward, then stopped as he saw that Frank had also taken a step forward. He could not run the distance between them, and he should not.

"It's all right," Frank said. "I've done my best."

"No." Ben shifted his gaze to the ice. To the fishing hole just past Frank, a black spot in the white. "Please."

Frank took another step out. The rock was heavy and awkward in his arms, he cradled it. "Maria isn't coming back." He shifted the weight of the rock. "I'm just tuckered out, Ben."

Ben had wished he could fix it, somehow. He'd closed his eyes. He was not so bold as to imagine he was dying with Frank, but he was afraid of living without him. Please don't leave me, he thought. Frank was his friend, his brother, all he had, and that was the reason he wanted to run across the ice and pull him back. It was also the reason why he did not. Frank had lived for all these years with what Ammon had done—he had borne the burden, he had done his best. Ben thought of the basement and how Frank had lived above it. He had sat at the kitchen table and eaten his *huevos* with Maria and the children, while right there, under his feet, below the floor boards and the rafters, was dark and remembering.

The beginning and the end was Ammon. Ammon had done this. Ammon's work upon a boy, the concerted application of that fucker's dark polluting spite for years and years. And the yield was a man who could not sustain himself.

"I've signed a couple of forestry reports for you, left the dates blank. They're in the cabin."

"Frank—"

The hole in the ice was like a mouth, rounded in surprise. O. It was a portal to another world, it was a socket, it was a fishing hole, it was the period at the end of a sentence.

"And I gave them Wilder. They said it wasn't enough. But I wouldn't give them you. I couldn't do that. They don't have you, Ben. You're clear, you're in the clear. So, you know, go clear."

Ben had neither stepped forward nor back. He had not been able to leave the spot on which he stood. He had been fearful. This moment ended some way of living and began another he did not yet know the shape of, could not imagine.

When Ben had opened his eyes Frank was gone. For a time he wondered if Frank had lost his nerve and cut the rope. Maybe he'd survived hypothermia and swum under the ice to the other side of the lake, to a warm getaway car, and was on his way to Juarez with Maria. Ben toyed with this particular fantasy, and how he may be called to corroborate the suicide—"Yes, I saw Frank Wilson drop through the ice and he did not come out"— and therefore collude in his friend's escape. Frank was going clear, not Australia, but a *hacienda* in a sleepy Mexican village, a rooster on the fence, a dog asleep in the dust, Maria and the boys eating ripe oranges from a red tin bowl.

Kay takes a step inside the cabin. She is an actor following a set of stage directions. Or, it is as if she's planned this herself months ago. She's been completely true to herself, and she's brought herself here. She wonders if Ben, too, has wheeled himself along the tracks he has laid with his own hands. It's as if they were supposed to be here, the Universe kept bumping them up against each other.

And here, right here, they collide.

"Why didn't you go? Why didn't you go, Kay?" Ben takes off his cap, smooths his dark hair, his voice is familiar but not quite his own. "I told ya to go, I gave ya the chance."

But she has nowhere to go, not the woods, not the lake. She sits down across from him. Her hands splay out on the table, she feels the rough grain. She wonders how Ben will kill her. She thinks he will either strangle her or drown her. There is a dog leash on the table between them. She thinks of the nape of Freya's neck, the way the fine pale hair curls in the deep dent of her atlas bone. She thinks of Tom's breath against her cheek, his kisses like butterflies. She remembers the rain on the tin roof, and the war coming closer to Gol, but Tom was sleeping, little naked rabbit, little pip, against her breast, and the wind and the rain, and the girl in the bed next to her bathing her own baby, a boy. He had hydrocephalus, his head like a melon wobbling on the vine of his neck. He would die within days, but his mother was smiling and cooing, pouring warm water over his smooth black body. Such tenderness in the broken world.

Ben can do anything he wants to her. He has become her death; he has become her life. She will simply disappear, she is already disappearing. Women disappear all the time—read the papers—no bodies are ever found in these woods, these lonely roads. "Nosey, hey," he says, he hears himself say in this other voice, this voice echoing back at him. "What ya wanta ask s'many questions for?"

I was on my way back. She hears Michael, only he is not angry, but anguished—she hears the difference in tone, and she lets him finish what he'd begun to say. *I was on my way back to you.* To you, Kay, to you. Those are the words, all of them. I was on my way back to you, he is saying to her, and she is listening. What if Michael isn't having an affair with Barbara? What if he has forgiven her for Gol because he knows her, the person who sees garbage bags on the side of the road and wants to look inside— she is still the vain, brave, curious woman he fell in love with. The kitchen is behind him, around him, where they live, the row of cereals—Cheerios, Rice Krispies waiting for her. What if she has forgiven him for the bucket, such careless cruelty, and the uncomprehending face of the child who owned it. But it's not enough to apologize, sorry-sorry; she and Michael need to sit at the kitchen table. They need to accommodate each other in some new way, not just the old lie of marriage. They must raise two fine children. It's not as simple as it looks. It's a life's work.

She begins to cry. She's no longer pretty, her face contorting into itself. She doesn't want to die. But what choice does Ben have? The vicious narrowing and winnowing to this point, this time and place, this table between them. He and Frank planned to steal the dogs of rich people. They were going to run away to Australia. And his mother's mouth agape, she's trying to explain or apologize—*I'm sorry, Benben*—but he didn't know what for.

Hunger was normal, fear was normal, what Richie-Dinko-Honeybaby-Bob did with their hands, boots, fingers, words was normal. There's a boy in the back seat of a Pajero who has never eaten a summer peach or been swimming in water sun-sparkling like champagne under a blue sky. He will not grow straight and tall but stooped and grey, a fungus child in the cellar. Every moment of Ben's life is happening concurrently, an unrelenting, crowded, shouting present, shouting so he can't hear himself, he hears Ammon, *Come on down, boy, come and join the fun.*

Her own death seems obscure, a date on a calendar that is suddenly at hand. There were many times she could have died. Life is not owed her. She has wasted, she has squandered. She doesn't want to die, of course not, but what she is realizing is that the not wanting to die is only part of it—not wanting; while there is this other pull, far stronger, this deep pulling riptide, this *wanting.* Her body fills with wanting—a howling deaf and blind wanting—*longing* for her children. Wanting, longing. She can see the street where they live, the steps to the front door. She goes up the steps, she peers through the window on the door, she presses her face against the glass. She would crawl through fire, she would cut off her own arms just for that last glimpse.

Here we are, right here. The past rushing toward us along steel cables, binding us to what has been done to us and what we have done, forcing us to this intersection, this particular nexus. Here, the future blooms outward, it frays or radiates.

Kay puts out her hand, her hand a fist that she opens, finger by finger, exposing the soft, vulnerable palm, the skin still raw and burned. Why is it so difficult to stop being selfish? Disappointed? How completely and wilfully we misunderstand each other.

"Ben," she says. "Let me."

Margot's clavicle. He had watched the bone move beneath her skin and she had turned and smiled and he fell into her, shining and clean.

He finds killing easy; this has surprised him, and he could keep on killing. Shevaunne, Dinko, this woman, they just disappear, he's tidying them away. He remembers Dinko's struggle, as if he really cherished his life after all. *Why do you want the boy?* Dinko asked. *Why do you want the boy?* The answer stirs in the corner of the room. Ben turns to see it, there, in the dark corner, the seam, the joist of the house. He keeps his eyes sharp, and after a moment, the shape emerges, trembling. He hadn't known that pigs tremble with fear. He'd come looking for Frank and heard noises he didn't understand. He opened the front door and heard noise in the basement, voices, and so he stepped down, and *Come on down and join the party*, Ammon said, and he slipped on the blood. He couldn't see, his eyes could not understand what he was seeing, the pigs, humpbacked, squealing, two or three other men and Frank on the far side holding up the electric knife, the kind used to carve the turkey.

Pig fights, Ammon said, Ammon grinned, teeth flashing. *The blood gets them all riled up.*

Frank turned on the blade. He looked at Ben and Ben said *Please* in his mind, he tried to send the message to Frank, he was thinking so hard. *Just come with me, we're faster than these men, let's just run away, up the stairs into the woods, we'll hotwire a car and drive up to the cabin, we'll cross the border, Canada then Australia*, but Frank plunged the whirring blade into the back of a pig.

Why do you want the boy? Dinko is looking up from his bed of slurry. *Why do you want the boy, Benny?*

Jake is standing with Lacey. She has brought him a suitcase. She hates how the kids have to use garbage bags to move their things, their second-hand clothes, their donated toys, greasy with the film of other children. She smiles at Ben, she walks toward him with Jake, "Are you ready?" There is kindness, there is grace. He wants to breathe it in and breathe it out; he wants to be this kindness. Ben kneels down, as if at an altar, to embrace this boy, this lost son, lost self.

This is what he wants.

Let me. Let me live. Let me love, Kay says, the words tumbling out from the mouth that kissed him. *Let me love, Ben, let us, let us love.*

Why didn't she go, he told her, warned her, who is she, a liar, a liar, yer nosey askin' after Frank and why why why what's it to do with ya? He moves his hands to the dog leash. She will not be found, nor will she be alone, down there.

"Do octopuses pee?"

He has misheard her; he tilts his head. Her nose is red, her face wet, misshapen, ugly.

"Do you know if they do?" she asks desperately.

The dog leash is smooth in his rough hands; he feels its texture, the manufactured strength of it. He lifts his hands up, up, as if offering a sacrament. Does she sense the shifting air or see his shadow? Can she hear the whispering spell of Ammon? Ammon is inside him. He is inside Ammon. He feels the hissing pleasure of spite: to hurt for hurting's sake.

But the lake glitters, he can see it through the cabin's door, the smooth absolving surface. Frank's grave, where he had been happiest, the water a blanket he pulled over himself to sleep soundly at last.

A dozen small birds flock across the water—he can't be sure from here, perhaps they are cedar waxwings. They move the air with their wings, and he feels the current all the way here. He feels who he wants to be, not hewn by the past, the lumbering damaged past but the unweighted possibility of the future. What may be, what may be despite, despite the past. He took this from

Shevaunne—this possibility; perhaps she wanted him to take it, why she came with him, surrendering the boy. With her junkie's intuition she saw in him Jake's only chance. And why he turned around, turned around and went back to Littleton. And why he wants the boy. Jake is his only chance.

There is a great turning inside his chest. The turning is difficult. The machinery is deeply grooved by habit; to ask it to rotate in the other direction, against the heavy gravity of the past, against the crushing weight of Ammon, the weight of his mother and her lovers, their careless, terrible cruelty. It takes all his strength. But he turns, he turns around, turns his heart, and the rusty hinges of his heart slowly open, the red, plush chambers, and his blood begins to flow the other way.

And he lowers his hands back down to the table. He looks at Kay, she looks at him.

"About the octopuses," he says. "I don't know, I just don't know."

HE AND JAKE ARE ON A PLANE TO AUSTRALIA,
to Sydney. The plane is already taxiing on the runway. Jake is on
the seat next to him, even now, and they are descending. He can
see the edge of the continent below them, land after so many
hours of ocean. Ben puts his arm around his son, pulls him
close, "We're nearly there."

Sydney is hot and bright and shining. They can see the ocean
from the car rental place at the airport. "G'day," people say and
smile. Everyone is smiling and tanned and wearing hats with
corks. Jake wants to sit in the front of the car but Ben insists on
the back because it's safer. They drive north of the city, a road
along the coast. They stop and run down to the beach—the feeling of the sand on their bare feet, the feeling of the cold water
sucking at their toes. The Pacific Ocean! Jake tastes the water
and makes a face, "Salty!"

After a few days of driving, they cut inland and the landscape
opens and flattens; it dries to red desert. They drive on a dirt
track, so deeply red it's like cranberry, and Ben lets Jake sit in
the front seat. They can do whatever they want out here. They
are safe and far, far away. The blue sky is a perfect dome above
them, and the earth races out, untethered, in every direction, red
sand, polka-dotted with spinifex. At night, there are stars, a mad
splurge of stars, so many there is real starlight, no moon, just

the light of the stars and the red earth turns dark purple, deep purple, maybe the color of a late-summer aubergine.

Meanwhile, meanwhile, Kay is walking along a street in London, she turns up three stone steps, through the open front door. The hall light is on, Michael cooking sausages because it's all he can cook. Her children look up from their homework, they rush to her, throwing their weight around her hips where she once bore them. "Mummy, Mummy, Mummy."

Let us love.

Acknowledgments

My life is now rooted in the Northeast Kingdom of Vermont. Opioid addiction is widespread, and its consequences fill the local paper, *The Caledonian-Record*, with crime, child abuse, overdoses, and sometimes, also, hope and redemption. The "*Cal Rec*" does a great job covering the epidemic, and I'd like to thank the Managing Editor Dana Gray for allowing me to use the paper's name. My particular thanks go to reporter Robert Blechl, who gave me some crucial steers. All the news stories in *The Underneath* are my own creation, though several are based on tragic fact. Hope Bentley gave me vital feedback on an early draft and my mother, Rosalind Finn, gave insight on a later one. Thank you both. Kate Shaw, my agent, continues to correct my course when I veer into self-pity or blind panic. I'm so proud to be published in the US again by Two Dollar Radio. Eric Obenauf and Eliza Wood-Obenauf are passionate about their books, and I love their sensibility, style and humanity. In the UK, Helen Francis at Head of Zeus swam upstream for me: thank you. Thank you to my daughters, Molly and Pearl, for all the times they helped me stack wood, feed the horses, and clean the house; mostly, for all their fierce, reminding love.

Two Dollar Radio
Books too loud to Ignore

ALSO AVAILABLE Here are some other titles you might want to dig into.

THE GLOAMING NOVEL BY **MELANIE FINN**

→ **New York Times Notable Book of 2016**

← "Deeply satisfying." —*New York Times Book Review*

AFTER AN ACCIDENT LEAVES her estranged in a Swiss town, Pilgrim Jones absconds to east Africa, settling in a Tanzanian outpost where she can't shake the unsettling feeling that she's being followed.

PALACES NOVEL BY **SIMON JACOBS**

← "Palaces is robust, both current and clairvoyant… With a pitch-perfect portrayal of the punk scene and idiosyncratic, meaty characters, this is a wonderful novel that takes no prisoners." —*Foreword Reviews*, starred review

WITH INCISIVE PRECISION and a cool detachment, Simon Jacobs has crafted a surreal and spellbinding first novel of horror and intrigue.

THEY CAN'T KILL US UNTIL THEY KILL US ESSAYS BY **HANIF ABDURRAQIB**

← "Funny, painful, precise, desperate, and loving throughout. Not a day has sounded the same since I read him."
—Greil Marcus, *Village Voice*

IN THESE ESSAYS Abdurraqib uses music and culture as a lens through which to view our world, so that we might better understand ourselves, and in so doing proves himself a bellwether for our times.

BINARY STAR NOVEL BY **SARAH GERARD**

→ *Los Angeles Times* Book Prize Finalist

→ **Best Books 2015:** *BuzzFeed*, *Vanity Fair*, NPR

← "Rhythmic, hallucinatory, yet vivid as crystal." —NPR

AN ELEGIAC, INTENSE PORTRAIT of two young lovers as they battle their personal afflictions while on a road trip across the U.S.

Thank you for supporting independent culture!
Feel good about yourself.

Books to read

Now available at **TWODOLLARRADIO.com** or your favorite bookseller.

WHITE DIALOGUES STORIES **BENNETT SIMS**

← "Anyone who admires such pyrotechnics of language will find 21st-century echoes of Edgar Allan Poe in Sims' portraits of paranoia and delusion, with their zodiacal narrowing and the maddening tungsten spin of their narratives."
—*New York Times Book Review*

IN THESE ELEVEN STORIES, Sims moves from slow-burn psychological horror to playful comedy, bringing us into the minds of people who are haunted by their environments, obsessions, and doubts.

SEEING PEOPLE OFF NOVEL BY **JANA BEŇOVÁ**

⇢ **Winner of the European Union Prize for Literature**

← "A fascinating novel. Fans of inward-looking post-modernists like Clarice Lispector will find much to admire."
—NPR

A KALEIDOSCOPIC, POETIC, AND DARKLY FUNNY portrait of a young couple navigating post-socialist Slovakia.

THE VINE THAT ATE THE SOUTH
NOVEL BY **J.D. WILKES**

← "Undeniably one of the smartest, most original Southern Gothic novels to come along in years." —NPR

WITH THE ENERGY AND UNIQUE VISION that established him as a celebrated musician, Wilkes here is an accomplished storyteller on a Homeric voyage that strikes at the heart of American mythology.

THE DROP EDGE OF YONDER
NOVEL BY **RUDOLPH WURLITZER**

← "One of the most interesting voices in American fiction."
—*Rolling Stone*

WURLITZER'S FIRST NOVEL in nearly 25 years is an epic adventure that explores the truth and temptations of the American myth, revealing one of America's most transcendant writers at the top of his form.

Did high school English ruin you? Do you like movies that make you cry? Are you looking for a strong female voice? Zombies? We've got you covered with the Two Dollar Radio Flowchart. By answering a series of questions, find your new favorite book today! ⇢ TWODOLLARRADIO.COM/PAGES/FLOWCHART

THE ORANGE EATS CREEPS
NOVEL BY **GRACE KRILANOVICH**

→ **National Book Foundation '5 Under 35' Award**

← "Breathless, scary, and like nothing I've ever read." —NPR

A RUNAWAY SEARCHES FOR her disappeared foster sister along the "Highway That Eats People" haunted by a serial killer named Dactyl.

FOUND AUDIO NOVEL BY **N.J. CAMPBELL**

← "[A] mysterious work of metafiction… dizzying, arresting and defiantly bold." —*Chicago Tribune*

← "This strange little book, full of momentum, intrigue, and weighty ideas to mull over, is a bona fide literary page-turner." —*Publishers Weekly*, "Best Summer Books, 2017"

NOT DARK YET NOVEL BY **BERIT ELLINGSEN**

← "Fascinating, surreal, gorgeously written."
—*BuzzFeed*

ON THE VERGE OF a self-inflicted apocalypse, a former military sniper is enlisted by a former lover for an eco-terrorist action that threatens the quiet life he built for himself in the mountains.

THE ABSOLUTION OF ROBERTO ACESTES LAING NOVEL BY **NICHOLAS ROMBES**
← **One of the Best Books of 2014:** *Flavorwire*

"Kafka directed by David Lynch doesn't even come close. It is the most hauntingly original book I've read in a very long time. [This book] is a strong contender for novel of the year." —*3:AM Magazine*

BABY GEISHA STORIES BY **TRINIE DALTON**

← "[The stories] feel like brilliant sexual fairy tales on drugs. Dalton writes of self-discovery and sex with a knowing humility and humor." —*Interview Magazine*

BABY GEISHA IS A collection of thirteen sexually-charged stories that roam from the Coney Island Ferris wheel to the Greek Isles.

Books to read

THE ONLY ONES NOVEL BY **CAROLA DIBBELL**

→ **Best Books 2015:** *Washington Post*; *O, The Oprah Magazine*; NPR

← "Breathtaking." —NPR

INEZ WANDERS A POST-PANDEMIC world immune to disease. Her life is altered when a grief-stricken mother that hired her to provide genetic material backs out, leaving Inez with the product: a baby girl.

THE INCANTATIONS OF DANIEL JOHNSTON
GRAPHIC NOVEL BY **RICARDO CAVOLO**
WRITTEN BY **SCOTT MCCLANAHAN**

← "Wholly unexpected, grotesque, and poignant." —*The FADER*

RENOWNED ARTIST RICARDO CAVOLO and Scott McClanahan combine talents in this dazzling, eye-popping graphic biography of artist and musician Daniel Johnston.

THE REACTIVE NOVEL BY **MASANDE NTSHANGA**

← "Often teems with a beauty that seems to carry on in front of its glue-huffing wasters despite themselves." —*Slate*

A CLEAR-EYED, COMPASSIONATE ACCOUNT of a young HIV+ man grappling with the sudden death of his brother in South Africa.

HOW TO GET INTO THE TWIN PALMS
NOVEL BY **KAROLINA WACLAWIAK**

← "Reinvents the immigration story." —*New York Times Book Review*

ANYA IS A YOUNG WOMAN living in a Russian neighborhood in L.A., torn between her parents' Polish heritage and trying to assimilate in the U.S. She decides instead to try and assimilate in her Russian community, embodied by the nightclub, the Twin Palms.

SOME RECOMMENDED LOCATIONS FOR READING TWO DOLLAR RADIO BOOKS:
On a beach, in the dark, using a lighter's flame; While getting a tattoo of an ex-lover's name removed; While painting the toe nails of someone you love; Or, pretty much anywhere because books are portable and the perfect technology!

THE GLACIER NOVEL BY **JEFF WOOD**

← "Gorgeously and urgently written."
—*Library Journal*, starred review

FOLLOWING A CATERER AT a convention center, a surveyor residing in a storage unit, and the masses lining up for an Event on the horizon, *The Glacier* is a poetic rendering of the pre-apocalypse.

RADIO IRIS NOVEL BY **ANNE-MARIE KINNEY**

← "[*Radio Iris*] has a dramatic otherworldly payoff that is unexpected and triumphant."
—*New York Times Book Review*, Editors' Choice

RADIO IRIS IS THE STORY OF Iris Finch, a socially awkward daydreamer with a job as the receptionist/personal assistant to an eccentric and increasingly absent businessman.

SQUARE WAVE NOVEL BY **MARK DE SILVA**

← "Compelling and horrifying." —*Chicago Tribune*

A GRAND NOVEL OF ideas and compelling crime mystery, about security states past and present, weather modification science, micro-tonal music, and imperial influences.

ANCIENT OCEANS OF CENTRAL KENTUCKY
NOVEL BY **DAVID CONNERLEY NAHM**

→ **Best Books 2014**: NPR, *Flavorwire*
← "Wonderful. Deeply suspenseful." —NPR

LEAH IS HAUNTED BY the disappearance of her brother Jacob, when they were children in rural Kentucky. When a mysterious man shows up, claiming to be Jacob, Leah is wrenched back to childhood.

MIRA CORPORA NOVEL BY **JEFF JACKSON**

→ *Los Angeles Times* **Book Prize Finalist**
← "A piercing howl of a book." —*Slate*

A COMING OF AGE story for people who hate coming of age stories, featuring a colony of outcast children, teenage oracles, amusement parks haunted by gibbons, and mysterious cassette tapes.

Books to read

HAINTS STAY NOVEL BY **COLIN WINNETTE**

← "In his astonishing portrait of American violence, Colin Winnette makes use of the Western genre to stunning effect." —*Los Angeles Times*

HAINTS STAY IS A NEW Acid Western in the tradition of Rudolph Wurlitzer, *Meek's Cutoff*, and Jim Jarmusch's *Dead Man*: meaning it is brutal, surreal, and possesses an unsettling humor.

SOME THINGS THAT MEANT THE WORLD TO ME NOVEL BY **JOSHUA MOHR**

→ **One of the Best Books of 2009:** *O, The Oprah Magazine*; The Nervous Breakdown

← "Mohr's prose roams with chimerical liquidity." —Boston's *Weekly Dig*

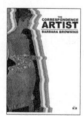

THE CORRESPONDENCE ARTIST
NOVEL BY **BARBARA BROWNING**

→ **Lambda Literary Award Winner**

← "*The Correspondence Artist* applies stylistic juxtapositions in welcome and unexpected ways." —*Vol. 1 Brooklyn*

CRYSTAL EATERS NOVEL BY **SHANE JONES**

← "[Jones is] something of a millennial Richard Brautigan." —*Nylon*

REMY IS A YOUNG GIRL living in a town that believes in crystal count. When her mother becomes sick, she sets out to accomplish what no one else has, and increase her mother's crystal count.